Paul was born in his grandmother's house on the High Street in West Ayton in 1958. Much has changed since then and with artistic license added to the mix, the fictional characters in the novel live in a village which resembles but does not accurately reflect the real place. The author has lived and worked in the UK, East Africa and now Western Australia, sharing life with his partner and soulmate Kerryn, who invariably is 'right' in all matters. His four offspring range from mid-thirties to mid-teens and he is proud of all of them.

Paul Coates

STRANGE GOINGS ON

First Edition.

© 2023 Paul Coates.

This is a work of fiction. Names, characters, places, and incidents either are the products of the author's imagination or are used fictitiously. Any resemblance to actual persons, living or dead, businesses, companies, events, or locales is entirely coincidental.

Special thanks to Corinne Hawke for reviewing and editing.

Cover design, illustrations, editing and typesetting by Karren 'Wren' Payne

ISBN 978 0 6455637 1 9

"I BELIEVE ALIEN LIFE IS QUITE COMMON, ALTHOUGH INTELLIGENT LIFE LESS SO. SOME SAY IT HAS YET TO APPEAR ON PLANET EARTH."

-Stephen Hawking

THE PROLOGUE

IN 1390, SIR Ralph Eure built a tower in a small Yorkshire village, which was known locally as Ayton Castle. Three hundred years later, it had been gradually dismantled with villagers using the stone to rebuild a bridge over the nearby river. Most of the current inhabitants maintained that not much of any note had happened since, until the soporific bubble of village life was burst following the unforeseen death of an upstanding member of the local community.

Fifteen months had passed since the murderer of the parish vicar had been brought to justice[*]. The village was in turmoil, and the dark cloud of suspicion floated over several residents with hushed accusations and innuendo raining down indiscriminately. Matters were made worse by the two assigned detectives, Hardy and Stanley, who stumbled down blind alley after blind alley until they found themselves in the inevitable cul de sac. Dogged determination, or perhaps blind luck, prevailed and the boys in blue were victorious, finally allowing the village to rest easy. Or could they?

Some villagers were unconvinced those responsible had been brought to justice, pointing fingers at others. Most felt that the situation was unresolved, and the question remained as to why the vicar was the target of a professional killing?

More sinister perhaps, who had paid for the job to be done? But normality and routine gradually prevailed.

---

[*]   An Unforeseen Murder

Gossip and innuendo died down and the world continued to turn slowly, uneventfully, on its diurnal rhythm. With a comforting inevitability, it had only taken a few weeks for village life to return to its banal indolence which had endured for centuries before this tragic event. Locals stroll lackadaisically along the high street, cows yawn in Farmer Higginbottom's field whilst others chew their cud with imperceptible movements of their ponderous jaws.

Overhead, a cloud reluctantly drifts across the afternoon sun, temporarily bathing the village in a cloak of grey. Sunlight beaming through the front window of the Old Plough is snuffed out causing the landlady, Dolly Wilkes, to look up from her half-completed crossword, allowing her only customer to catch her eye. Raising a pint glass above his head for a refill, she smiles in acknowledgement and walks over to him, wiping her pudgy hands on the apron stretched across her midriff.

At the grocery store, Betty is sitting behind her counter, she has barely had a handful of customers all day and is half listening to a play on Radio 4 with a diminishing level of interest. The shop bell tinkles playfully, heralding the entry of two residents who are well versed in doing the minimum and totally attuned to the inert lifestyle of the village. Phil Hayes is greeted by Betty using his nickname, Purple, which was given to him by a local wag who connected his name to the Jimi Hendrix classic, Purple Haze. His ever-present companion Colin Hendricks hangs back, leaning on the front door scratching his head through his bushy Afro. Swiping his credit card, Hayes pockets cigarette papers and tobacco, which would shortly be mixed with another substance wrapped in cling film in his back pocket. With a cheery goodbye they leave the shop, heading straight for their favourite copse near Higginbottom's south field. For them, a slow day would shortly become even slower.

Further along the High Street the weekly arts and craft class draws to a close. "Okay people, that will be all for today." Chris Ashton smiles apologetically at the four women who respond with a chorus of disappointed groans. Potting wheels come to a halt prompting the ladies to chatter amongst themselves each admiring the other's work. He circulates amongst them, congratulating each on their creations.

"Oh, well done the Addinalls, both lovely pieces of work and startlingly similar, just like you two." They both simper in appreciation and adjust their cardigans self-consciously.

"And Julia, that piece is as elegant as you." The local accountant's wife gives a playfully dismissive but secretly pleased wave of her slender clay covered hand.

"And last but not least Jenny, a mystic piece if ever I have seen one, with a very interesting magical design." The local white witch nods appreciatively at Ashton's insightful assessment wondering how he could possibly know about Hecate's Wheel.

Further up the high street a white van marked 'Neaves Construction' is parked outside the church. Inside the driver's cabin, the owner, Ronald Neaves, occupies two thirds of the bench seat. His friend and local councillor, Jeffery Mandelson, squeezes his slight body into the remaining space. Discussions on the church renovation and proposals for a hotel in the adjacent land are ongoing.

"So, Jeff, what do you think of it?"

Sneering, Mandelson snaps his response. "Well, at least this time it looks as though the West wall is going to stay put which in itself is a minor miracle."

"Take it easy Jeff, that was over a year ago and it wasn't my fault."

An uneasy silence ensues as the two men stare at the scaffolding surrounding the building works.

Out of sight, on the wall behind church, sit the Messruther twins. It has been a long school summer holiday with little to occupy them until today. For once, their auntie's annual visit had paid dividends in the form of an unexpected gift which is now placed on the wall between them. At their feet is the discarded box, torn enthusiastically apart by the excited and impatient boys.

Auntie Norene comes from the educated, wealthy side of the family and graces them with her presence once a year to check in on their welfare. Or, in her brother's quietly held opinion, lecture him and the boys. Arthur Messruther sits with supreme indifference as his sister describes how he should organise his life, how the boys should be brought up and, generally, how things should be done properly. Her way. She feels sorry for the twins who she is sure could turn out to be fine young men if only her brother would take heed of her sound advice. No wonder the boys' mother had left home two years ago was a thought she kept, almost, to herself. When the visit mercifully ends, Arthur sees her to the door, gives a half-hearted wave whilst muttering an unheard expletive of relief. Once the car turns the corner out of sight he heads straight for the beer in his fridge.

The twins pour over the operating instructions which may as well have been written in Mandarin or Latin. At school they were equal bottom in most subjects, though they had the all-time school record for the greatest number of visits to the headmistress in one term. Scratching their blond heads in deep thought, the eureka moment hits them both at the same time. Consulting with each other and agreeing the resolution, they high five in celebration at their joint discovery. With the missing component

4

identified, they jump off the wall and head directly to Betty's Store to get some batteries.

And so … life in the rural idyll goes on with aching normality, lethargy, and tedium.

That is, until all hell broke loose.

1

ARTICLE IN THE SCARBOROUGH EVENING NEWS 5TH JULY 2023

Local village an epicentre of a supernatural vortex.

Readers will no doubt have heard of Area 51, the highly secretive classified United States Air Force facility in Nevada. Experimental testing of state-of-the-art aircraft has made it the epicentre of UFOs, aliens, and a whole host of conspiracy theories. Some may be familiar with Willow Creek, the site of the most famous footage of the legendary Bigfoot or, as it is known to native Americans, the Sasquatch. Our investigations reveal that we appear to have a combination of the two on our own doorstep. Eighteen months ago, the normally sleepy hamlet of West Ayton, just five miles from Scarborough, was the centre of a murder mystery following the shooting of the parish vicar, Peter Dibley. According to residents the village is once more the centre of controversy but this time it is other worldly.

As wild as the claims are, there seems to be no shortage of witnesses to the bizarre events that are terrorising the local populace. Twin sisters who live on the High Street claim they have seen strange blue lights hovering in the fields behind their home. The Addinalls (aged 53) say that the appearance of the mysterious lights is becoming a frequent occurrence. When asked if the lights could be explained by an aeroplane or helicopter, they dismissed this possibility, confirming there was no engine noise accompanying the lights. Another villager who had also seen the lights, local artist and sculptor Chris Ashton, believes that the complex movements could not have been performed by any piloted aircraft of human design. Some theorise that the lights are alien spacecraft, and this appears to have some credibility according to two other local boys, the Messruthers.

These boys (aged 16) claim to have seen aliens near local farmland. Whilst they admit it was dark and visibility was poor, they describe an encounter when they were walking home along a road adjacent to a local farmer's field. They claim that two figures crashed through the bushes straight into their path a mere ten yards away. According to the boys, the 'aliens' raised their arms aggressively and, fearing for their lives, the twins turned and ran in the opposite direction. Despite the poor light and brevity of their sighting they believe the beings were of a similar height, the bodies seemed dark and smooth (no evidence of hair and clothing), and their heads also seemed hairless. Stranger still, according to the boys, both figures appeared to have large dark oval eyes but with no pupil or sclera (the white of the eyes) visible. Their description accords with many sightings around the world of extraterrestrial beings known as 'Greys.' For a village as small and quiet as West Ayton, one could be forgiven for thinking that this was excitement enough for the poor residents. It seems this is not the case. Two other locals have also reported the sighting of a large bipedal figure roaming the woods behind the village. Mr Phil Hayes and Mr Colin Hendricks were relaxing one evening in a nearby copse, enjoying a beer and the summer evening warmth, when they spotted a large figure bounding towards them. Feeling threatened and fearful for their lives they fled from the scene. From the distance they could make out a large head, no discernible neck and a bulky torso which appeared to be covered in stringy, lank hair.

In an interview with two local detectives (DS Hardy and DC Stanley) who have been assigned to investigate these disturbances, doubts were cast on the veracity of the sightings.

DS Hardy said, "From what I know of the activities of Mr Hayes and Mr Hendricks, what they saw could well be attributed to the amount of alcohol they had drunk rather than some sort of Yeti." When asked to comment on the reported sightings of UFO lights and aliens, DS Hardy did not want to offer an initial opinion as they were still at the very early stages of the investigation. He was, however, confident that there would be a rational explanation.

The Evening News will continue to monitor the activities in the local village and keep readers informed of any developments.

Lois Proudfoot - Junior reporter.

•¦••¦•

EVENING - 6TH JULY 2022

After a bit of a struggle, the Addinalls climb onto the high stools and the producer points to the headphones on the desk which they both carefully place over their greying ginger curls. They fidget excitedly as they stare, through the bank of laptop screens, at the host of the evening show. Norman Riders has a reputation as a shock jock on his regular weekday slot, 'Riders Brings A Storm.'

"And time for a short commercial break, listeners, then we will be back with tales of aliens and furry monsters." Riders gives a mock sinister laugh before he switches over to a pre-recording of a Scarborough businessman espousing the virtues of his carpets. The DJ winks and smiles at the sisters who look at each other and giggle nervously.

Leaning forward, he re-assures them. "Nothing to be worried about ladies. Have you been on radio before?"

"No," replies Mary.

"No," confirms Freda.

"Just going to ask you about what you saw, nothing difficult, deep breath now, we are about to go back on air." Riders flicks a switch. "Welcome back to *Riders Brings A Storm,* folks – it's the man of cool bringing you the hippest vibe on the local waves. The time is nine-o-five on a balmy evening and tonight we have a few guests who have witnessed, firsthand, supernatural happenings in the little quiet village of West Ayton. Some of you may have read of strange tales in the local rag, but you can now hear it firsthand from the horses' mouth. Tonight, in the studio, I have with me Mary and Freda Addinall, who live in West Ayton where all sorts of …. well … I am not sure what to say … let them tell you what has been happening." He gives Mary the thumbs up.

Quivering voice, Mary tries to respond. "W… w… well Mr Riders …"

"Call me Norman."

"Thank you … er … Norman. It all happened a few nights ago." Mary hesitates so Freda, brimming with confidence, takes over. She leans precariously on the stool to get near to the microphone.

"Yes, we were walking along Forge Valley Lane when Mary gasps and I look up at where she was looking and then, well, when I could see what she could see, I also gasped."

"Gasped?" clarifies Riders.

"Yes gasped," the sisters respond simultaneously.

"Ok ladies. So, what did you see?"

10

"Lights," says Mary.

"Blue lights," adds Freda.

"Four of them," says Mary.

"Four blue lights in a row," adds Freda, determined not to be outdone by her sister.

"Like a police car?" ventures Riders, seeking clarification.

"Not unless police cars can fly," giggles Mary, pleased with her little joke. Gently, Freda elbows Mary on her shoulder before giving her a supportive chuckle.

"So, the lights were in the air? How high?" asks Riders.

"Hard to say, I am not good at judging distance, but Mary thinks it must have been at least fifty feet," answers Freda.

"So, you don't think it could have been an aircraft then. No engine noise or anything like that?"

"No noise, although there could have been a low hum." confirms Mary. "It just hung there for a few minutes then shot straight up another thirty feet before retreating into the distance quite fast until it disappeared.

"What do you think it was ladies?"

"Mary thinks it was one of those flying saucers you see on TV programs. You know, the old shows like 'Lost in Space,' but to be honest we could not clearly make out any shape."

Riders smirks. "So did you see any aliens?"

"Oh no, all we can tell you is that we saw blue lights" the twins reply together.

"Well, ladies, thank you for your time. But please feel free to stay for our next guests waiting on the line who, with the permission of their father, can recount their experience with, what they claim, were aliens. Welcome to the show the Messruther brothers. Geez listeners it is a bit like the Twilight Zone, two sets of twins in one village and both witnessing the extra-terrestrials. Can you hear me boys?"

"Yes, Mr Riders."

"And which one of you am I talking to?"

"It's Billy, my brother Ben couldn't make it, he has his boxing class tonight."

"All good, Billy. Tell me what happened to you."

"Wow– not sure where to start Mister. Well ... it was *lit*, but *gucci*."

A look of puzzlement masks the face of Riders who, whilst trying to decipher the teenager's language, leans backwards in his chair. Reaching behind his head, he unconsciously tightens the band on his ponytail whilst he concentrates. Leaning still further, he pushes his chair into a gravity defying angle causing it to balance on two legs. His well-worn Led Zeppelin tee-shirt gradually hitches up and strains across his torso exposing a hairy beer gut. With the DJ's silence causing the cardinal radio sin, dead air, the producer waves frantically through the window.

"Are you still there Mr Riders?" enquires Billy concerned that he had been cut-off.

"Yeah, sorry Billy, just trying to work out what you are telling me. For our older listeners can you explain what you mean by 'Gucci' and 'Lit'? Are you saying that whatever you saw was wearing a leading fashion label and carrying a torch?"

Laughing, Billy responds. "No, don't be silly Mister. They weren't *snatched*, but it was *sick*."

Frustration begins to well inside Riders. "Billy, my listeners are going to need google translate if you go on like this. 'Lit', 'Gucci', 'Snatched', 'Sick' ... You are going to have to explain what you saw in old people's language like, maybe, your dad would use."

"Okay Mr Riders, it was ... err ... lit ... which means –

I don't know what old people would say, maybe you would say 'amazing'? And gucci means it was sort of good, or cool … not that they were wearing expensive clothes. They weren't snatched, in fact they looked weird."

Fearful that he is losing his audience, Riders tries, once more to regain control.

"Okay Billy, thank you. I want you to describe exactly what you and your brother saw. And … if possible … in the Queen's English."

"King's," replies Billy.

"Sorry?"

It is 'King's,' Mr Riders. The Queen died, didn't she? We now have the King."

Growing irritation was evident in Riders' voice. "Listen Billy, I just need you to tell me in straightforward language what it was you saw."

"Okay Mr Riders, no need to get *salty*."

"SALTY???" bellows Riders.

Fortunately for the radio station management, Billy continues his story which prevents the DJ inadvertently voicing, on air, the expletives bursting to escape from inside his head.

"It was like this, Mister. We were walking home through Forge Valley and, suddenly, two aliens came running through the bushes in front of us. It was mental and we were really scared at first but then, to be honest, we thought it was quite *dope*. That is, until they saw us and started to shake their fists at us."

Resisting the temptation to ask for a translation of 'dope' in the interest of story flow, Riders encourages more detail. "So, what made you think these were aliens as opposed to just two men or two other boys?"

"I know what you mean, and I admit it was dark and they were quite far away, but it looked as though they weren't wearing any clothes. I know it sounds silly, but they just had smooth bodies. Their heads were the same strange shape. They had no hair on their heads which just looked smooth. And another thing, we could see very large oval eyes as big as my hand. Their eyes were totally black. They looked like those aliens you see in films and TV. I am telling the truth Mr Riders, *no cap*."

"No cap?"

"Yeah, Mr Riders, *no cap,* y'know, honest. I'm telling you the truth."

"Okay Billy, did you see anything else such as blue lights?"

"No, Mr Riders. We got scared. We were dead worried and just scarpered."

"Okay, Well thank you for calling in Billy and pass on our thanks to your father."

"Before I go Mr Riders, do I get any *cheddar* for doing this?"

"What?"

"*Cheddar,* y'know, *dosh,* money. My dad said I might get an appearance fee."

Riders cuts off the teenager and moves on with the show. "Finally, we have another witness, Mr Phil Hayes. Are you on the line Phil?"

"Yeah Norman, it's cool, call me Purple, everyone else does."

A brief silence ensues so Hayes decides to elucidate.

"I'm called Purple 'cause of my surname and love of the rock god guitarist."

It clicked with Riders, "Oh yeah, a man after my own heart. Purple Haze and Jimi Hendrix for the benefit of those listeners not following us. Anyway, your story is even stranger than those of our previous guests. Tell us all what you saw."

"No worries. Basically, I was sitting in the middle of a small patch of trees having a quiet can of beer with my mate, Colin. It was night-time but nice and warm. It was getting dark, so we decided to get up and go to the Old Plough for a final beer before closing.

"Old Plough?"

"Yeah Norman, it's the local village pub. Anyway, it all kicked off. I don't mind telling you I almost crapped myself when Colin pointed out what he had seen. Oops sorry for the language, forgot I was on the radio."

"Don't worry, Purple. Go on with your story."

"Cheers Norman. As I was saying, Colin saw this figure in the distance coming towards us and then I saw it after he pointed it out. It was big and hairy and didn't look like it was in a good mood, if you know what I mean? So, we decided to make ourselves scarce and nipped off sharpish in the opposite direction."

"Thanks Purple. Can you describe what you saw in a bit more detail?"

"Not a great deal, man, it was all a bit trippy. As I told the local reporter, we didn't hang around to get a closer look. All I can say is that it had a large head, but not much of a neck, and covered in hair … but it was night-time, and it was dark. It was also some distance away so we couldn't make out any eyes. But its body looked bulky, y'know massive. It looked like it was covered in long hair. I could just make out long strands, of what Colin reckons was hair, moving around the arms and body as it ran. I'm not so sure. It was sort of hair but looked thicker."

"Anything else Purple? Did it make a sound, a growl or something?"

"I'm not sure man, can't honestly say. It did seem to give the odd grunt as it moved, but to be honest we were

Gonski pretty damn quick, and I only looked back for a few moments."

Riders thanks Hayes for calling and introduces an advert break to the listeners who hear the benefits of installing central heating before the winter months descend. A small, disembodied voice addresses him as he looks down to check on the next item in his program schedule.

"Is it okay if we go now?" asks Freda.

Slightly startled, the DJ had forgotten they were still sitting opposite him. "Oh, yeah, sorry ladies. Thanks for your time and don't forget to get in touch if you see any more lights, aliens, or hairy monsters."

"Oh, don't you worry Mr Riders, we will … " responds Freda as she struggles off the high stool.

Momentarily transfixed by the vision of the two sisters hurriedly leaving the studio whilst giggling with excitement at each other, Riders is caught off guard as the advertisements end. The producer waves through the window indicating there is, yet more, dead air and gets the thumbs up from Riders. "Welcome back listeners to the hippest show on the east coast. It's time for this evening's *Riders Retro Rock* spot. So, my friends, let's see what we have. Yep, it could only be one song by the maestro, Mr David Bowie. What do you cool cats out there think it is I wonder. I know what you are all thinking. You are saying to yourselves 'oh yes, yes, yes, I do know what the legendary Riders is about to play.'

Pausing briefly to check his emails, Riders references a contributor. "One of our regular listeners, Shawn from Snainton, has emailed into the show with his suggestion of a Bowie classic that fits the bill after hearing all the amazing stories from our guests this evening. Well, sorry Shawn … and to the rest of you I suspect, you would all be wrong.

I know we have talked about UFOs, but it is not '*Space Oddity*.' It's not even '*Starman*'."

Distinctive synthesized percussion plays over the DJs monologue. After the first verse finishes, Riders joins in with the only part he can remember, the chorus.

> *"She began to wail jealousy's scream*
> *Waiting at the light, know what I mean*
> *Scary monsters, super creeps*
> *Keep me running, running scared*
> *Scary monsters, super creeps*
> *Keep me running, running scared."*

2

During summer, the Addinall sisters love to go for a mid-evening tipple at the Old Plough and then straight back home to watch one of their favourite TV series. They like the old ones, such as Poirot or Midsomer Murders. *'Cannot beat a good whodunnit'* they would tell each other. *'Nothing like a good murder mystery that they can solve before the big reveal at the end.'* Weeks after the strange goings on in the village ended, they often reflected on the evening of the 29th of June as the start of it all, when they had just finished their white wine spritzers at the Old Plough.

Polishing the glasses behind the bar, Dolly calls over to the sisters who sit in their usual spot near the window next to the pub mascot, Kenneth the (stuffed) Koala. "Would you like a refill ladies?"

Freda looks to her sister for guidance and Mary takes charge. "Oooh, no thanks Dolly love, a third spritzer would be a spritzer too far for us two."

"Yes, I've already got a bit of a buzz," confirms Freda. "It is such a lovely evening we thought we'd take a stroll up Forge Valley Lane before going home to settle in."

"Well, I agree it is a lovely evening, but take care 'cause it's getting dark you know, and Councillor Mandelson still hasn't made good his promise to increase the street lighting up there."

"We are not going too far Dolly. Maybe just up to Jenny's cottage and then we'll turn back," says Mary.

Buttoning up their sage coloured cardigans and adjusting their floral dresses as they rise from their seats, they appraise each other's appearance. Once satisfied that they are presentable, they give Dolly a wave goodbye. Leaving the pub, they turn right up Forge Valley Lane instead of their usual left onto the High Street when they make their way home. A few yards up the Lane, Mary starts to feel uneasy.

"It's darker than I thought."

"I know," agrees Freda, "But it's a lovely night and I adore the sound of the river and the birds warbling and singing in the trees, so let's keep walking for a while longer."

In comfortable silence, they make their way into the valley bathed in the ambient evening summer warmth. As they walk, they are serenaded by the melodic sound of the birds, hidden by the cloak of night, high in the trees above them. After passing the Henson's house they continue towards the Castle ruins further up the Lane. Darkness deepens and the trees lining the lane seem to close in on them. This prompts Mary to consider suggesting that they turn back but, before she voices her idea, she is distracted. Staring up into the starry sky, she lets out a genteel gasp and then a less genteel surprised yelp. Freda, whose heart had begun to pound at her sister's reaction, looks to where Mary is staring and, also, gasps in surprise. Transfixed, they stare at a straight horizontal line of four blue lights dancing in the sky. A series of vertical, horizontal, and diagonal movements are performed above the sisters who stand in awe, wide eyed and open mouthed. Maintaining perfect formation, the lights continue with an array of acrobatic movements which become less extreme as they slow down and, almost apologetically, retreat into the distance across the fields of Higginbottom's Farm. The hypnotic trance of the two sisters is finally broken when the lights disappear into the woods at the eastern side of the field behind the vicarage.

"Oh, my goodness, tell me you just saw what I just saw!" exclaims Mary.

"Four blue lights, they were beautiful," replies Freda still wide eyed in wonderment.

"They were other worldly."

"I know Mary," says Freda who then realises the implication of her sister's description. "Wait a minute, what do you mean by other worldly?"

"I think they could be extra-terrestrial, like in the film we watched the other night. You know. That Spielberg film. You must remember. It was called '*Close Encounters*'."

"I know what you mean but the one in the film was enormous and made those trumpet noises, didn't it? This one's much smaller and I couldn't hear any sound at all."

"Maybe because it was further away," suggests Mary.

"I think we'd better get home in case they come back, or we might get abducted like those in the film," says Freda, only half-jokingly.

Mary nods in agreement and they make their way down Forge Valley Lane at a slightly quicker pace than that at which they came. On occasion they look back over their shoulder and then to their left across the field where the lights had appeared then vanished. A frisson of excitement grasps the sisters, created by the cocktail of fear and joy. Fear of the unknown tempered by the feeling that the lights were more beautiful than threatening. After all, the aliens in *Close Encounters* were friendly.

Turning into the High Street they pass the Old Plough and the convivial chatter and laughing of the villagers flows through the open door into the warmth of the summer night. Mary grabs Freda by the shoulder and explains her idea. Freda nods in agreement.

Approaching their cottage, they stop a few yards short of their own front entrance to stand at the door of their neighbour, Chris Ashton, who runs the village pottery classes. Their knock is answered almost immediately by Ashton who appears at the door, his black hair ruffled, a few beads of sweat on his forehead and his wiry athletic build framed by a Nike running kit. Barry, his Beagle, appears between his legs to greet the sisters with a friendly 'woof.'

"Evening ladies, you'll have to excuse me but just got back from our jog," he pats Barry in acknowledgement of his running partner. "So, I am a bit sweaty, but what can I do for you?"

"Oh, don't mind us, because we don't mind," replies Freda, who, actually, did not mind the vision in front of her at all. Mary glances at her sister in mild retribution and addresses Ashton.

"We wondered, Chris, if you had seen any lights from your back garden. We went on our usual evening stroll and saw the strangest thing. It was four blue lights flying over Higginbottom's south field."

"Sorry ladies, I've only just got back from my run and haven't seen anything like that. Maybe it was an aircraft or something. Could it have been one of those small planes from the Sherburn Aero Club?"

"We're sure it wasn't a plane," says Freda.

"Absolutely sure," replies Mary, "We would have heard the noise of the engine and it was too low for a plane."

"Or a helicopter," adds Freda.

Assessing the sisters with his grey blue eyes, Ashton jokes with them. "How many drinks did you two have in the Old Plough this evening?" They giggle confirming they stuck to their two-spritzer limit and that they cannot both have imagined the same thing. Grabbing the dog lead on the side table near the front door, he clips it onto Barry's collar and announces that they all should go together to investigate. The sisters clap in excitement and ten minutes later they are standing on Forge Valley Lane at the point where they saw the lights hovering and darting over the field. Dark bovine shadows in the distance are the only sign of life.

Ashton peers intently across the field and into the far woods which were now just a large dark blanket in the fading evening light. Guiltily the sisters protest that they did see lights, afraid that their neighbour might be thinking they were wasting his time with a hoax or just their silly imagination. They chatter nervously, but Ashton ignores them concentrating intently to see if he can see any movement in the night sky. Suddenly he raises his hand to silence them and points to the northeast section of the wood. Four blue lights lift in a perfect vertical trajectory and then hover, momentarily, before dipping below the treetops. The lights could still be seen flickering in the gaps as they pass behind the tree branches and leaves. Then, as quickly as they appeared, they are gone. Scratching his temple, Ashton tries to process what he has seen and gives voice to his thoughts.

"Well, that was definitely not a plane, but given the distance from us it was hard to get any feel for the size. I couldn't hear any engine noise either. I'm sure it wasn't a helicopter. The movements were not like any craft I've seen. Very strange."

"We told you Chris. We weren't playing a joke on you," announces Mary with a smug smile.

"I never doubted you ladies. But I honestly cannot tell you what it is."

"Should we report it to the police?" asks Freda.

"Not sure we have anything to report Freda, it doesn't look like any obvious law has been broken, no damage has been done and no one is hurt. Anyway, what do we tell them? That we saw a spacecraft or something?" jokes Ashton.

"We could," says Mary, taking the suggestion seriously.

Barry woofs in reply, prompting an affectionate pat from Ashton. "Well Barry, I think we'll leave this one to the Addinalls. What do you think?" Barry woofs in agreement.

Vindicated, the two sisters accompany Ashton back to the High Street whilst keeping an eye out for the mysterious lights. Nothing appears. They thank Ashton, wish him goodnight, and watch him, and Barry, disappear behind his front door. Unlocking their own door in the neighbouring house, they agree to investigate further and resolve to go for another walk tomorrow evening. Next time, they will take their phones to try to capture the lights with their cameras.

⁘

Having thought about the events of the previous night, Ashton resolves to take some action. Settling down on his sofa after his early morning run, he places a steaming cup of tea on the side table and makes a call to arrange an appointment with an old friend. Finishing his call, he finds Barry sat directly in front of him looking up expectantly.

"I'll be gone for a couple of hours Barry, you are gonna have to amuse yourself." The beagle tilts his head to the side trying to understand what he is being told. When the front door closes, he lays down in the hallway and stares, hopeful that he will be invited on his master's journey. The door remains stubbornly shut so he retreats to his basket for his morning nap.

Shortly after leaving the village boundaries on the road towards Scarborough, Ashton turns onto the A171 passing the woods, fields, and farmland adjacent to the Moor Road. In less than half an hour, the familiar sight of RAF Fylingdales comes into view. Thirty years earlier the famous radar base was known for its three dome structures, each with a forty-metre diameter, which resembled giant golf balls. Bizarrely, despite the secrecy of its work, the golf balls gave the centre unwelcome attention and made it a local tourist attraction.

Ashton could now clearly see the pyramid structure that replaced the balls in the early 1990s. Gradually he makes his way into the facility, firstly through the roadside checkpoint and then through the outer 8000-volt electrified fence and two further checkpoints at each of its interior fences. For the fourth time, he repeats his details to the final guard, who is stationed at the main gate and allows him into the facility. He parks his car in the designated space outside the main building. Greeted by two armed soldiers and an officious looking man behind the reception desk, he confirms the name of the person he has arranged to meet.

Behind the receptionist, a plaque with the motto of the facility adorns the wall of an otherwise soulless décor. It reads '*Vigilamus*' which translates to "*We are watching.*" Fylingdales is a Royal Air Force station in the North York Moors functioning as a radar base and is part of the Ballistic Missile Early Warning system. Sharing intelligence with the United States, the base houses British and American military and scientific personnel. It also functions as a spy satellite tracking system as well as detecting and tracking orbiting objects. During his military career, Ashton had cause to visit the facility on a couple of occasions.

Escorting Ashton through a labyrinth of narrow functionally decorated corridors, the guard opens a beige, nondescript door, and ushers him into an office to be greeted by a familiar smiling face. After the guard closes the door, his old friend gestures for him to take a seat.

"Can I get you a drink, Chris?"

"No thanks Steve. So how are you? Looks like you are seeing out your time running security here in the middle of nowhere. All hail, Rambo has retired. Looking for a quiet life?"

"You could say that," replies Steve, patting his hip. "Getting on a bit and needed to slow down after the latest operations. In fact, beside the plastic hip, I have now got enough metal inside me to set off the security screening at Heathrow Airport. And what about you, I thought you'd left the Intelligence Corps years ago? You sounded very mysterious, hush hush, not wanting to discuss it on the phone and all that spy bullshit. What brings you here, besides an ardent desire for the company of an old friend?"

They both laugh.

"Other than it's nice to catch up, I just wanted to run something by you."

Steve gestures for Ashton to continue.

"Well, you know I now live in West Ayton," says Ashton.

"Yep, I'm not the only one looking for the quiet life, am I?"

"Fair comment, though you probably heard that I had a bit of trouble in London. I was doing some personal security as a favour for a mate."

"What! You were a bodyguard?"

25

"Yep. Anyway, it turned out to be a very costly favour. The client he assigned to me is a local gangster who wanted a babysitter for his girlfriend. A Mister Edward Fraser. Long story short, the job went pear shaped when his girlfriend was murdered by a person or persons unknown. And before you comment, no, I wasn't on duty, but he seemed to want to blame everyone, including me."

"No, I hadn't heard about that. Is that what this is about?"

"What? Edward Fraser? No, but that's why I left. Or rather that's what finally pushed me to get out of smoky, bustling London and settle in an idyllic rural retreat. As for Fraser, I assume he is still breaking people's heads, and the law, down in the big smoke."

"Okay. So, if it's not this bloke Fraser, what is it? What can I do for you?"

Ashton eyes Steve warily. "Now, it's a bit weird and off centre, so spare me your sarcasm."

"Have you ever known me to take the piss?" laughs Steve.

"Why am I even asking you, of course you will. Well, here goes. I am here because my neighbours have witnessed mysterious lights. Lights, blue ones, flying around in a tight formation and then disappearing off. And before you ask, they don't look like they're from any aircraft I have ever seen. What is more, there is no engine noise."

"Are you effing serious Chris? What do you think I am doing here? Working on the X Files?" says Steve with a smirk.

"Yeah, yeah, yeah, here we go. Look I just wondered if there was stuff you lot were doing. You know experimental stuff. Spy craft or the like."

"We're not bloody Area 51 either. No mate, you must know we don't do that sort of stuff here. We are geared up for surveillance and warning systems."

Ashton scratches his brow. "Yeah, look. Joking aside, I know one thing you do here is tracking orbiting objects. I just wondered if you knew of anything or picked anything up. Or even wanted to know and would be interested in what we have seen for that matter."

Rubbing a scar above his left eyebrow and then scratching his bald pate, Steve responds. "Well, tell me a bit more. Were these lights high up in the sky or low down?"

"Not sure. They were at some distance when I saw them, but I guess they were very low, they didn't look as though they were much higher than the tree canopy of the local woods. Having said that, I was some distance away so the visual perspective could be misleading."

"It could be Chris, but by the sound of it they were relatively low, and no military craft would be doing what you describe, especially in that location or at that height. Regarding other possibilities, our radar hasn't picked up anything unusual for months now, as far as I am aware."

"Looks like I've drawn a blank then," replies Ashton.

"Sorry Chris, no unidentified flying objects we know of. Besides all that, we tend to only monitor objects flying much higher unless you think they have come down from space."

A smile of realisation grows on Steve's face. "Hang on. You don't think they're aliens in spacecraft, do you?" He laughs, wiggling his fingers whilst making an eerie noise.

"Just wondered mate if you could be any help or even if it is something you need to know about," responds Ashton with a tinge of irritation.

"Now, now mate, don't get arsey. Just having a bit of a joke. But seriously, thanks for coming to see me. I am sorry to say that nothing of what you told me rings any bells. I will, however, ask a few questions. Not everything that goes on here gets run by me. If something minor was spotted it may not have been brought to my attention. If I hear anything then perhaps we can catch up for a beer to discuss it. Other than that, I am not sure I can be any help, but thanks again for coming."

"Cheers Steve, if you do, give me a call."

"And if you see any green men give me a call," responds Steve whilst holding out his hands in a placating gesture.

"Very funny, Mulder," says Ashton as he rises and walks toward the door. He opens it and is immediately confronted by a surly looking armed guard.

"Private Hopkins will see you safely out," calls Steve and Ashton waves his acknowledgement in response.

3

EVENTS LEADING UP TO THE NEWSPAPER ARTICLE
8.45 P.M. 30TH JUNE 2022

Forge valley radiates the heat of the summer's day, but now the woods gradually cool as the evening wears on. Moonlight begins to replace twilight and the sound of birds chirruping defer to the low wavering hoot of the owl accompanied by the babble of the nearby River Derwent. Sat in their favourite spot, a small copse on the edge of Higginbottom's southern field, Phil Hayes and Colin Hendricks have spent the last two hours basking in the early evening warmth. In their minds, they claim this small, secluded corner of the farm as their own. Since they had discovered its special harvest of psilocybin mushrooms they frequent and guard the area as if nurturing a newborn baby. This gift of nature had supplemented their meagre income from casual labouring and provided a much-welcomed personal supply.

Both men peel their last remaining beers from the plastic yokes of their six packs. Scattered around them is an untidy array of crushed, empty cans. Two clicks of the ring pulls mark the beginning of the end of their evening supply of alcohol. Hayes slurps from the can, swallows noisily then draws a large pull of his reefer. His actions are mirrored by Hendricks. Physically the two friends almost present an opposite image of each other as if the negative of a camera film had been brought to life. Hayes' spectral complexion, sharp features and shoulder length blond hair contrasts with his friend's nut-brown skin and pleasantly featured rounded face skin framed by an afro haircut.

"Was watching the telly the other night and it made me wonder about the human race," announces Hayes, breaking the comfortable silence enjoyed by the pair.

Taking a small drag of his reefer then holding the smoke in his lungs for a couple of seconds before exhaling, Hendricks considers the statement and decides to pursue his friend's line of thinking. "Er, specifically what? What about it?"

"Well, I often wonder who the first idiot was to try all that weird dangerous stuff. Stuff that's life threatening and idiotic. What makes 'em do it when they have no idea of what'll happen to them?"

"Dunno, why, what did you see on the telly?" asks Hendricks with mild interest. Politeness victorious over ambivalence.

"It was about Eddie the Eagle."

"What are you on about? Was it one of those Attenborough wildlife programmes?" asks Hendricks with diminishing interest.

"Nah, stupid. Eddie the Eagle Edwards. Y'know that bloke who represented us in ski jumping in the Olympics thirty or forty years ago."

"Not following your point my man," says Hendricks, furrowing his brow.

Exhaling with minor frustration at his friend's lack of concentration or interest, Hayes explains. "What I mean is, who was the first idiot to think it would be a good idea to go down a vertical icy hundred metre slope at fifty miles an hour on nothing but a couple of flat bits of plastic. Then, at the end of the slope, launch themselves thirty metres in the air?

"Dunno, don't follow ski-jumping."

"I know, but my point is what possesses someone to do stupid stuff that has never been done before."

Stroking his moustache, the light bulb clicks. "Oh, I get you now. Like who decides to jump out of a plane strapped to a bit of cloth for the first time?"

"Exactly. Good example. Who decided to test the first parachute?"

"Yeah and who decides it's a good idea to eat that fish?" suggests Hendricks, deciding to run with the theme.

Stumped by his friend's train of thought, eyes screwed, Hayes seeks clarification. "Eh!. Eating fish? No, I don't think you're getting it mate."

"Yeah man, I do. I saw this programme about the Japanese who eat this deadly fish. If you eat it, you get poisoned. You get paralysed, choke, and then die. So, my point is … who thought it would be a good idea to cook up that thing for dinner? But they do it all the time in the Japanese restaurants. Do you see what I mean? Who was the first person to say to the chef, 'okay my man, cook me this poisonous fish and I'll eat it risking the possibility of a horrible death'?"

"Fair point," concedes Hayes scratching his head through lank strands of hair.

Black moustache widening with a triumphant grin, Hendricks offers another example. "Indeed, it is and, what's more, how about this one. What makes …"

The next point would forever rest in the recesses of Hendricks' mind. His sentence dies in the ether as he turns to his left at the sound of heavy footfalls tramping across the field. Pointing in the direction of the noise, Hendricks guides his friend to its source. Quizzically, they exchange glances then strain to penetrate the darkness as they peer out through the trees. Unable to pin down the exact direction of the footfalls, their concern grows as it draws closer with menacing rhythmic thumps. Then, momentary silence. The footsteps appear to have stopped. Distressed mooing, followed by new footfalls and the clumping of cow hooves, echoes around the dark field.

They shuffle toward the trees at the edge of the copse to get a clearer view of the open field. Simultaneously, they howl in surprise at the vision of a large shadowy mass running straight towards them. Taking shape as it nears, the friends see that whatever is approaching is large, bipedal, with a head that seems to blend into its body. It does not appear to have a neck, just a large head resting on its shoulders. Strands of what appear to be thick hair dance around the movement of its body and limbs. The dark, ominous mass draws still closer until Hayes, nerve broken, turns and sprints out of the opposite side of the copse, with Hendricks in hot pursuit.

Two minutes later, as the two friend's reach the comparative real or imagined safety of Forge Valley Lane, the figure enters the copse. Examining the area, it grunts, as it surveys the detritus of the nights drinking session. Two cans are squashed flat under its right foot.

Tripping over each other, the two panic-stricken men clamber through the gap in the hedge onto the Lane in a tangle of limbs and instantly sit up to stare back at the opening. No sound, no sign of the 'thing.' Tentatively they crawl back to the hedge and squint through the gap. Nothing moves in the darkness. There is no sign of their pursuer. They wait in silence, scanning back and forth for tell-tale movement or noise but the woods and the field both remain silent. Once they are confident that whatever was after them has given up the chase, they cross the

Lane and sit on the pavement opposite the gap still half expecting the 'thing' to come crashing through. Catching their breath, they try to make sense of what happened.

"What the hell was that?"

"Dunno mate, but I wasn't going to hang around to find out," responds Hayes.

"It was humongous, man, it was … huge. Those big arms and no neck."

"Never seen anything like it," replies Hayes, still breathing heavily.

Eyeing Hayes nervously, Hendricks looks hopefully for some sort of explanation. "What do you think it was?"

Hayes just shakes his head, devoid of any rational explanation. Hendricks offers some ideas.

"A gorilla or a bear maybe. Or, or … a bloke in a gorilla or bear suit."

"No, and no, and unlikely," responds Hayes. "I mean why would a bloke be wandering around in a blooming gorilla suit for god's sake?"

Undeterred by the rejection of his initial ideas, Hendricks takes a new tack. "Y'know what it does remind me of?"

"Do tell," says Hayes oozing doubt and scepticism.

"A Bigfoot or Sasquatch."

"Bigfoot? Sasquatch?"

Hendricks nods with increasing enthusiasm for his theory. "Yeah, a Bigfoot. Like off that show where they go looking for them, y'know, 'Finding Bigfoot.'"

"How do you know that looks like a Bigfoot? Do they appear on the show?" asks Hayes, totally unconvinced.

"No mate, but they have computer generated graphics when locals are recounting their stories of when they saw one. You might laugh but there are all sorts of evidence such as casts of footprints, recorded howling noises, videos, and photos." Hendricks looks at this friend expectantly.

Hayes sniggers and sneers at his friend. "You're joking I take it. Finding Bigfoot my arse. So, do they ever?

"Ever what? asks Hendricks.

"Find Bigfoot," laughs Hendricks. "Do … they … ever … find … Bigfoot? Have they ever caught one physically or on camera?"

Deflated, Hendricks responds sheepishly. "Well, I've not seen every episode of every series, but I have to admit that I have not really seen one where they actually caught footage on camera."

"So perhaps they should call the show 'Not Finding Bigfoot', with a tagline 'Because they don't exist'."

Sulkily Hendricks retorts. "Well, what's your bloody theory smart-arse?"

"Don't have one and frankly I am too wasted to think about it. But I do know two things," replies Hayes.

"What's that?"

"I ain't going back tonight to find out."

"And the second thing?" asks Hendricks.

"We do need to go back tomorrow, when it's light to clear up the mess we left. If we don't, old Higginbottom will be pissed off and stop us hanging around in our little mushroom garden."

Motioning for them to get moving, Hayes starts to walk down the lane. Each gives a surreptitious backward glance every few metres to ensure they are alone. Their self-confidence only fully returns once they reach the brightly lit High Street. Ironically, the comforting safety of civilisation comes in the form of a growl, that of an engine as a solitary car passes through the village centre.

Back in the copse their nemesis remains tramping around in the dark accidentally kicking empty beer cans as it circles the area. Seemingly satisfied there is no animal or human in the vicinity, it exits the copse and strides across the field causing the herd of cows laying together to quickly rise, disperse, then regroup after it has passed. Once it has disappeared into the woods at the other end of the field, the cows, satisfied the intruder has gone, lay back down on the ground to rest for the night. A nearby owl hoots as if to warn the other woodland creatures of the interloper.

.¡..¡.

Sat on the bench outside Betty's store, the two friends recount the events of the night whilst tucking into her homemade pasties. A rogue globule of tomato sauce has attached itself to Hendricks' tee-shirt as he goes through the process of smothering his pastie with the single serve ketchup container. With a mouthful of pastry, mince, chopped potatoes and carrots, Hayes attempts to make sense of their experience and vocalise his thoughts. The volume of food being chewed renders his attempt at conversation incomprehensible. His friend, who employs a steely concentration consuming his own pastie, just nods in agreement even though he had not understood a word. An interruption from young woman, prompts a fuller, more articulate, discussion of the nights' events.

"Hello, my name is Lois, may I join you?" she asks. Without waiting for the invitation, she lowers herself onto the seat next to Hayes. Hendricks, who is sat opposite, ogles her whilst Hayes nods obediently. They stare in silence as she eases a black jacket from her slim frame causing her white blouse to tighten round her chest. Hendricks' eyes widen. Placing her jacket between herself and Hayes, she cheerfully continues.

"My uncle is Mr Proudfoot the local butcher," she points to the shop next door. "He told me that there have been some strange things happening around the village, specifically mysterious lights seen above the fields of the farmland at the back of his shop."

Undeterred by the lack of response, she perseveres. "Uncle Stan put me in touch with Mary and Freda Addinall, the ladies who live just up this street. They have seen the lights. They told my uncle about it when they got their weekly joint of beef for their Sunday roast. Anyway, they have some very interesting things to say. And for that matter, so does Mr Ashton, their neighbour."

Ever cautious, Hayes seeks an understanding of the woman's motives. "Sorry Miss, I know you said you're Stan's niece, but why are you talking to us? Are you police?"

Chuckling at the suggestion, Lois explains. "No, oh no, not at all. I'm a journalist. Well, actually I'm an intern with the Scarborough Evening News to be precise. I've just finished my degree. They sent me here to do a local interest piece. You know, something that breaks up the usual stories of hospital closures, motor accidents, births, deaths, and the weather."

"I see," says Hayes. "Do we get any money if we give you information?"

"Goodness no, Mr … ?"

"Hayes, it's Phil Hayes and my compadre here is Colin Hendricks." Hendricks nods in affirmation trying to avoid looking at Lois' breasts, which sit prominent through her blouse.

"Well Phil, I don't even get paid myself as an intern, let alone have money to pay people for stories. The only thing in it for me is the chance to get a piece published in the short term and possibly a paid job in the long term." Lois laughs disarmingly.

"Will we get our name in the papers?" asks Hendricks, sensing the opportunity for fame.

"Possibly Colin, if you agree to be quoted and the

editor deems the story publishable. But that is not under my direct control. So, tell me, have either of you seen these mysterious lights?"

They shake their heads which elicits a disappointed frown from Lois. "Oh! That's a shame I thought with all your questions you sounded as though you have a story to tell."

"But we have something even better, even stranger than lights," announces Hendricks gleefully.

Narrowing her green eyes doubtfully Lois asks him to explain but Hayes takes up the reins leaving Hendricks pursing his lips sulkily.

"We were in the woods last night and we saw something that we can't explain. It was quite late and dark so we cannot be certain what we saw but, believe me, we saw something odd."

"Why were you in the woods at night?" asked Lois. The question throws Hayes off guard giving Hendricks a chance to intervene which he takes with relish.

"Just chilling Lois, just chilling with a few beers on a warm summer night, y'know, communing with nature and all that. Sinking a few cold ones. That is until it appeared."

"What appeared?"

"My good friend here," says Hayes, regaining the initiative whilst sneering at Hendricks "thinks we saw Bigfoot."

"Bigfoot, you mean like a Sasquatch or a Yeti!" exclaims Lois with no small degree of scepticism, immediately wondering if she had made an error of judgement in wasting her time with these two.

"I am not saying we did, but Colin here thinks it might be one. The truth is we're not sure but whatever we did see it's hard to explain."

Lois spends the next few minutes probing the pair to elicit a description of the large, dark, hairy apparition that appeared before them. Having exhausted her lines of enquiry she is as equally perplexed at what they had seen. Surprising herself, she begins to give their story some credence.

Maybe they did see something they cannot explain, she ponders.

She thanks them, offering her business card with an open invitation to call if they see anything else in the coming days.

Excited, she drives back to Scarborough to her allocated desk in the corner of a small cramped open plan office in the town centre - the hub of local journalism. With commendable endeavour, Lois spends several hours researching, following leads and making enquiries. By the end of the day, she is certain of one thing. Whatever the men had seen, it was not a gorilla or bear or any other escaped animal. All the calls to local wildlife centres drew a blank. Even the Yorkshire Wildlife Park near Doncaster does not have animals the size of the beast reported by Hayes and Hendricks. The park is home to apes and baboons, such as Roloway and Red Howler Monkeys, which are much smaller than the description she had been given. Nearest in size and shape to the animal that Hayes described are polar bears. A quick call to a senior park keeper confirmed that no animals had ever escaped from the sanctuary. That line of enquiry reaches a dead end.

Undeterred, she starts to google keywords such as 'Bigfoot' and 'Yeti' to see what evidence there is regarding sightings in England. To her surprise there are reports all over England in recent years. One famous sighting is in woodlands, similar to Forge Valley, adjacent to a village in Cornwall called St Mawgan. Like Ayton, this village is also near a seaside resort, Newquay.

Quite a coincidence, theorises Lois.

Nearer to home she finds a report, online, of a sighting near Cleveland, less than an hour's drive from Ayton. A blurry photo, taken by a local carpenter, accompanies the article. Biting her lip in concentration, she examines the picture which reveals a dark figure some hundred metres in the distance standing in the middle of a woodland grassy path between two lines of trees. She is not convinced that the foggy image provides any definitive evidence other than what seems to be a large, tall, and wide biped. It could just as easily be a man dressed in bulky padded winter clothes, than a gorilla or the much sought after Sasquatch.

Her draft article is completed with ease. Snapping her laptop shut, she is happy with her work and confident that she has seen and researched enough to complete the task to the Editor's satisfaction. With a self-congratulatory clap of her hands, adorned by bright red nail polish, a shade which matches her lipstick, she smiles at the prospect of getting her first article published in the Evening News. As it transpires, the Editor agrees with her assessment after reading her piece with interest and he promises, to her delight, that publication would be imminent.

4

A LOUD PIERCING siren rips apart the early morning silence of the main pedestrian shopping precinct in Scarborough. Two men, both holding black velvet bags, scramble out of the back door of Abrams and Friedman Quality Jewellers. Heading straight for their Kawasaki Ninja, the front runner leaps onto the seat almost instantaneously firing up the engine whilst the other scrambles behind him, riding pillion. Tyres screech struggling for traction on the cobbled side alley causing the bike to jolt. Almost thrown off, the passenger manages to save himself by desperately grabbing onto the driver's jacket. Speeding through the town centre and then into the side streets of Ramshill, an adjacent suburb, the pair ride to safety whilst a police car approaches the jewellers in the opposite direction.

"For fuck sake Doyle, you told me you'd disarmed the alarm. What happened?"

"Dunno, the code we were given worked. We got in, didn't we? Maybe it resets automatically after a while."

Kelly eyes his partner with seething scepticism but holds his tongue whilst Doyle shuffles uncomfortably on the rotted stump. Five long, wordless, minutes pass and no sign or sound of a police presence prompts Doyle to renew their conversation to lighten the mood.

"I'm telling you mate, I put in the code correctly, it must've been reset. Anyhow we got the diamonds, didn't we? They were exactly where we were told they would be."

Kelly holds up the two black velvet pouches. "We got some of the diamonds, mate. McCarthy was expecting a lot more than this little lot. He's not going to be best pleased now, is he? Half of them is scattered on the floor when you panicked and dropped the bags, you muppet. What you don't seem to realise is that we are in a heap of shit. I don't know what's worse, getting caught and doing some time or rocking up to McCarthy almost empty handed."

Doyle opens his mouth to speak, then decides that discretion is the better part of valour. He stares intently at the ground until he senses movement from his partner. Scooping up the pouches, Kelly climbs back on the motorcycle.

"What are we going to do now?" asks Doyle.

"Just get on the bike, we need to get out of here. It'll be light in a few hours, and we will stick out like a sore thumb if we don't make ourselves scarce, get rid of the diamonds and get out of this ridiculous gear."

Once they are clear of the woods and reach the edge of the road, Kelly slams on the brakes unexpectedly. Losing his balance, Doyle lists sideways and puts his foot down to prevent falling off the pillion. Kelly ignores Doyle's swearing and points to the eastern side of the Mount. Headlights flicker through the trees as a car makes its way up the winding road that leads to the top.

"Shit Kelly, is that the coppers?"

Kelly swings the bike around to make his way down the western side. "Doubt it, but we aren't hanging round to find out."

They wend their way down a series of bends eventually reaching the main thoroughfare, Seamer Road, and are presented with a straight choice. Turn left and go back into Scarborough or right and eastwards inland. Without hesitation Kelly turns right.

Back at the jewellers, the owner, Manny Abrams, surveys the scene outside his shop with some dismay. A police car is parked outside the main entrance, its lights flashing illuminating two constables stood by the front door. One is nearing retirement and the other is barely out of police school. They stare at the owner in disinterested silence as he approaches them. The older one speaks first.

"And who might you be sir?"

"I am the owner, Manny Abrams. What's happened here?"

"Well sir, I am afraid you've had a break-in and it looks like they got away with some of your stock. On the plus side, it also looks as though the alarm disturbed them and it is clear, judging by all the valuables strewn on the floor, that they scarpered off sharpish leaving a fair bit behind."

"Can I go in, and see?"

"Before you do, sir, can we see some ID? Better safe than sorry. I am sure you understand."

Muttering irritably, Abrams digs out his driver's license from his wallet, shows it to the constable whose nod indicates he is satisfied. A repeated request to enter the shop is only met with a shake of the policeman's head.

"Better not to just now, sir. We like to secure the premises and leave as much undisturbed as possible. It is important so that the crime scene can be examined thoroughly and not be contaminated or compromised by having any Tom, Dick, or Harry tramping around everywhere."

"I am not exactly any Tom, Dick or Harry am I?" snaps Abrams irritably. "I thought that was the point of showing you my ID?"

The older constable had heard it all before. "Yes, I understand sir, but it is for your own benefit. Detectives will be assigned to the case in the morning and will examine the scene. Rest assured, I'm sure they will wish to speak with you on several matters."

"Matters. What sort of matters?"

"Yes sir. Matters such as if you have any thoughts as to who might have done this?"

Hackles rising, Abrams responds. "What are you saying? Do you suspect I bloody well did this myself?"

"We are not making any judgement, sir. All avenues must be explored, and the detectives will want to talk to you and work with you to get the best outcome," added the young constable having just learnt the importance of getting good outcomes on his recent course.

"Talk to me? Work with me? What are you implying for God's sake?"

The older constable gestures to his young colleague to be quiet before the discussion deteriorates further. He smiles at Abrams. "Well sir, they will want to ascertain what items have been stolen by accompanying you into the shop to review your stock. I'm sure they will also want to map your whereabouts this evening and all sorts of other information – such as who has access to the alarm code."

"Alarm code?"

"Yes sir. We suspect they gained entry some time before the alarm tripped. All the rooms appear to have been ransacked and a few cabinets, including the safe, are open. They must have been in there for at least a few minutes before the alarm tripped."

"Are you saying this is what you lot call an inside job?"

Unable to hold himself back, the younger constable chips in. "Looks like you've watched a lot of detective stuff on telly sir."

The older constable once again puts out his hand to quieten his colleague and intervenes. "Talking of an inside job sir, is it possible that Mr Friedman is responsible? I can see he is not here."

"Y'know Mr Abrams, like an insurance jobby," adds the younger constable.

With increasing incredulity and exasperation, Abrams spits out his response. "Insurance jobby! Masterminded by Mr Friedman! Highly unlikely I would say. Not unless he is Jesus Christ, and this is the third coming. Mr Friedman died four years ago, and I bought out his share of the business from Sarah, his poor wife."

"Thought you lot didn't believe in Jesus," offered the young constable.

"What?" Exasperated and seething, Abrams balls his fists.

"And it is the second coming sir, not the third," explains the young constable, missing Abram's sarcasm but conscious that, on his inclusivity course, he needed a good working knowledge of all the major religions practised locally. "I thought you lot didn't believe in that stuff."

Abrams exploded, "You lot! What do you mean by 'You lot'? What on earth are you talking about? Are you just a bunch of racists fixated on Judaism? I have had my livelihood threatened and you're going on about bloody Jesus coming."

Suspecting his young colleague was about to delve further into the relative merits and complexities of religious belief systems, the older constable decided it was time to calm down the situation. "I am sorry sir, I appreciate it is very upsetting but believe me, if we follow protocol, we have the best chance of catching whoever did this. Let us secure the shop, take your details and when detectives have been assigned in the morning, they will be in contact with you."

Slightly appeased, but still unhappy, Abram was determined to have the last word and responded testily whilst staring pointedly at the younger constable.

"I suppose that's fine, as long as they don't send anyone else from the cop kindergarten."

•┅•

1.20 A.M. 2ND JULY 2022

"Jeez Billy, look how late it is. It's gone midnight. If Dad catches us, he'll go ballistic." Ben stares at his watch as if, by doing so, it will turn back the time.

"Don't sweat it. Dad was out for the count when we left and with the amount of lager he's sunk, he won't be awake until gone breakfast time, will he?" replies Billy to his brother.

"It's been bloody funny though ain't it?" sniggers Ben.

"Yep a real laugh just like the other night. We can do it again, but we had better get back now 'cause don't want to push our luck. It won't be so easy to sneak out late on other nights if Dad catches us this time. He'll be on his guard."

Gathering up their paraphernalia, the Messruther twins cut across the south field of Higginbottom's farm jogging past the sleeping herd. Muttering an expletive that would have earned him a clip around the ear if he had been in his father's earshot, Ben grinds to a halt without warning. Billy, who was following close behind, bumps into his brother almost bowling him over and mutters the exact same expletive. They both sit down, rubbing their heads, each looking accusingly at the other.

"Why did you stop, you idiot?" snaps Billy.

Still rubbing his head whilst lifting and then pointing

45

to his left foot, Ben replies, "'Cause I stood in a massive cowpat. Why did you run into me?"

"I was running behind you … dickhead. How was I to know you were going to bloody stop?"

"Look at my new trainers, they're sodding *Lacoste Neo's* – and ruined," moans Ben.

Impatiently, Billy springs up and jogs on the spot shifting his weight from leg to leg whilst urging his brother to get a move on.

"Just wipe it on the grass you moron, we've gotta get going or we're buggered if dad gets up for a pee or something and sees we're not in bed."

Ben follows his brother's instructions, dragging his shoe back and forth along the grass until he is satisfied that he has jettisoned most of the cow dung. Having awoken with curiosity at the noise created by the boys, a cow lifts its head and moos loudly which spooks them. They increase their jogging pace to a sprint to make a speedy exit across the field. Neither of the boys notice two shadowy figures, partially lit by the half-moon, crouched near the tree line less than a hundred metres behind them.

Slowing as they reach the hedge, the boys search for the opening that they originally came through. Ben spots it, shouts to his brother and points, once more breaking into a sprint. Arms pumping, they run as fast as they can, gasping for breath and grunting, until they reach the gap in the hedge. With a messy flurry of arms and legs, they squeeze through and pop out, like a cork from a champagne bottle, onto Forge Valley Lane. Pausing to catch their breath they each bend double, hands on their knees, sucking in large quantities of oxygen. They both rest. Once recovered, they look at each other and their expressions of exertion transform into wide grins then laughter. Happy at their night's work, they make their way down the lane arm in arm.

Other than the sound of a single car in the distance, the village is quiet, eerily so. With the high hedge which provides the boundary to the farm field to their left and the dark sinister shadows of Forge Valley trees looming to their right, the boys walk in silence. Their mood gradually transforms from light-hearted joviality to growing uneasiness.

"Quiet, ain't it Billy?"

"Yep Ben, can't even hear the birds, wonder what's happened to them."

"Guess they are sleeping."

"Do birds sleep?" asks Billy.

"Yep."

"How do they sleep?" asks Billy.

"They stand on the branches and fold their right wing over their heads, so it's dark enough for them to get some shuteye," explains Ben.

"Why?" enquires Billy.

Ben looks at his brother "Why what?"

"Why can't they sleep when it's light? And for that matter what stops them falling off the branches when they fall asleep?" asks Billy in a challenging fashion.

"I'm joking, you moron. Seriously mate, you need to sharpen up a bit."

Ben chuckles to himself at the stupidity of his brother until he thinks about it and wonders exactly, how, and where, birds go to sleep. If he thought about it, to be honest he didn't know either.

Billy was also thinking about the birds and attempts to construct a telling retort to his brother. Abandoning the idea of a witty riposte, he opts for a straightforward insult. It was never delivered. His attention is drawn to a rustling in the hedge a few yards behind them. Simultaneously they swing round to locate the source of the disturbance. They see movement amongst the leaves and branches which gradually intensifies into vigorous shaking until two figures come crashing onto the lane. Gaping in astonishment and fright, the twins freeze and try to take in what is in front of them.

A cloud passes over the half-moon making visibility even poorer which prevents them discerning much detail. The two strange figures seem to be thin and smooth with no sign of any hair on their heads. Straining to see through the darkness, both boys can make out large almond shaped dark shadows where the eyes should be. It seems impossible because the beings can clearly see them. One figure points at them and the other shakes its fists becoming increasingly agitated. When they start to move towards them in a threatening manner, the boys let out a squeal of fright.

Turning tail, the twins run down the lane towards the village not daring to look back. Their fervid imagination creates all sorts of images in their minds. Pictures of aliens, in pursuit on small rocket powered discs aiming laser guns at them, fuels their fearful visions. They speed past the castle which seems more sinister and spookier than ever. Hearts race, legs pump and their brows sweat with exertion and fear. The row of trees either side of them seem to be conspiring with the aliens. Closing in, threatening and endless.

A potential saviour appears in the distance. But escape becomes a forlorn hope. Reaching the first sign of civilisation, in the shape of the Henson's house, offers no more comfort or sanctuary than the Castle. Not a single light in the house is switched on and the blackness of the windows stare back at them, like pools of pure dark evil.

They sprint on, until finally there is genuine hope. Their hearts lift as the security lights of the Old Plough eventually come into view heralding a possible haven. Only when they arrive at the High Street do they stop and dare to look back down the lane. To their relief, they can see nothing sinister or threatening. Just still darkness beyond the lights of the pub. No aliens in pursuit and no laser guns. Only the, now benign, parade of trees reaching far down the lane disappearing into the depth of the valley.

With a gradually slowing heart rate, the boys amble along the High Street making their way to the eastern side of the village. Their home is in a small housing estate just south of the river Derwent which runs parallel along the main road.

"Jeez Billy, what was that we just saw?"

Billy shakes his head. "I dunno, but they looked like those aliens that were on the telly the other night. Did you see their eyes?"

"Couldn't see any eyes, it was too dark. All I could make out was dark patches as big as my hand. But yer right, in the dark they looked like those aliens on the telly. Can't be though, can it?" asks Ben doubtfully.

"All I know is that they didn't look local," jokes Billy.

Sniggering, Ben adds, "I reckon you're right, perhaps they're southerners, maybe from London. But to be honest, they scared the living crap out of me."

"Me too. Reckon we would have got the Olympic Gold medal for the four-hundred-metres," says Billy whose smile then turns into a frown. "Do you think we should tell someone?"

"About what? The aliens? Like who?"

Scratching his head, Billy processes a list of possibilities. "Maybe the police, our teachers, Auntie Norene or Dad."

Ben shakes his head. "Are you bonkers? How are

we going to explain why we were out this late? We'd get grounded for months and, besides that, who would believe us anyway? We'd get sent to the Looney bin, wouldn't we?"

Giving his brother a friendly tap on the head followed by a shove, Ben walks on ahead. Billy catches him and returns the compliment before they amble, side by side, with renewed confidence that they are now safe. It is short lived. The High Street is bathed in light but shrouded in silence which begins, once again, to make the boys uneasy. Not a word is exchanged. A scavenging fox upends a bin, startling them and they increase their pace, occasionally glancing back over their shoulders.

To their relief the sanctuary of home is in sight. They cross over the footbridge and into the side road that leads to their house. Creeping up to the front door they are relieved to find that there is no sign of activity or noise from within. All the lights are switched off, which is a good sign. Ben lifts the front door mat. Billy grabs the key, carefully slots it into the keyhole and turns the latch slowly before pushing the door open. They creep through the living room and up the stairs to bed accompanied by cacophonous snoring permeating through their father's bedroom door. Ten minutes later the twins are in their own beds, sound asleep adding tenors to their father's rich nasal baritone in the nightly symphony of the Messruther household.

Six hours later Ben is on Mars being probed by extra-terrestrials. Arms pinned to his side by metallic straps he is helpless as he lies on a cold steel table. Three aliens surround him, each holding what look like intergalactic medical instruments. One looks viciously sharp, causing Ben to yelp. Another is tubular, with a mechanical pincer at the end and the third appears to be a silver syringe. A fourth, larger alien, looms over him, grabs him by both shoulders and begins to shake him. A scream catches in Ben's throat, he has no voice.

"C'mon get up yer lazy little bugger. Yer gonna be late fer school and I've got better things to do than act as yer butler."

The blurry large alien transforms into his father who, seeing that his son is beginning to rouse, stops shaking him. Rubbing his sleepy eyes, Ben looks over to the other bed, but it is empty. An instant panicked thought grips him. *Billy has been abducted.* "Dad, Dad, where's Billy?"

"He's downstairs eating Weetabix. Now get in t'shower, stop asking stupid questions and get a bloody move on."

Dressed in his school uniform, with unruly damp blond hair leaving water spots on his shirt collar, Ben joins his brother at the breakfast table. Plonking a bowl of cereal in front of him, his father barks out a gruff command.

"Now 'urry up, yer need to get going in five minutes." Obediently, Ben starts shovelling the breakfast into his mouth whilst his brother munches on toast. Loading the dishwasher, his father addresses him.

"Yer brother says yer both saw some strange blokes in suits 'angin around the woods last night?"

Ben's heart misses a beat, and he looks accusingly at his brother. With an unconcerned smile, Billy speaks before Ben has a chance to respond and inadvertently get them into trouble.

"Yeah Ben, I was telling Dad that we got home around nine-thirty then went straight to bed but didn't want to disturb him as he was already asleep. I told him about the two blokes we saw that looked like they were dressed in space suits or summat."

"Highly bloody unlikely," grumbles their father. "It's bloody months before Halloween. Yer must 'ave imagined it. And fer the record, if you ever come back that late again, you'll be getting a clip round the ear, and you won't be going anywhere fer weeks. When I say nine, I mean nine, not nine-fifteen nor nine bloody thirty. Yer both lucky I decided to 'av an early night otherwise you'd have been in trouble."

"Sorry, Dad,"

"I'll bloody give yer sorry Ben. As I just told yer brother before yer came down, it's out of order but at least you told me the truth. If it 'appens again then yer in big trouble. It's only because Billy told me you were both so scared that you 'ad to hide in the bushes for a while until those blokes left, that I 'ave let you off this time. I'll be talking to the police 'bout what 'appened. They could've been murderers or paedos for all you know."

"But Dad, they could have been aliens. People have been seeing strange lights 'an all. It wasn't our fault, honest." protests Billy.

"Aliens my arse," grunts their father. "Aliens, my fat arse. Don't bloody push it or there will be trouble. Just do as I say and bugger off to school or you'll miss the bus."

Sat side by side on the bus stop bench swinging their legs, the boys discuss the night's adventure and agree to hold off on any more night-time excursions into the woods.

"Don't reckon they were pedos or murderers," says Billy.

"Nor me, I reckon they were aliens. I know it was dark, but they looked like aliens to me." Ben passes his mobile phone to his brother who takes it and examines the screen whilst Ben explains. "Look what I googled. See, I reckon I'm right. Look at the picture I reckon that's exactly what we saw."

Staring intently at the screen Billy nods in agreement and reads, in a mechanical tone, the words printed underneath the image.

"This is an artist's impression of a 'Grey' as described by Mr Seymour Bush of Boulder, Colorado. Mr Bush claims to have been abducted by aliens in December 2021. According to Mr Bush, they are approximately five foot tall, hairless and have large almond shaped dark eyes."

"Told you so," said Ben seeking affirmation of his theory.

Rubbing the back of his neck Billy thinks about it. "Don't really know bruv. It says here that they were approximately five foot tall. I reckon the ones we saw were bigger."

Undeterred Ben pushes home his point. "Maybe so, but why should they all be the same height? Humans aren't, are they?"

The school bus pulls up and Billy quips as he climbs the stairs. "Maybe they sent their basketball team down to earth." They sit in the back seat of the bus laughing all the way to school.

⋅╍⋅

10.15 AM 2ND JULY 2022

Being called to Detective Inspector Parkins' office rarely yielded a positive outcome so the expectations of Detective Sergeant Hardy and Detective Constable Stanley were exceedingly low.

Hardy knocks and hearing a muffled, "Come in," he pops his head round the door to be greeted with Parkins smiling and gesturing for the two detectives to sit. Hardy eases his increasing middle-aged spread into the chair and Stanley sits next to him looking like a stick insect on a leaf.

"Well detectives, thank you for coming, I have a favour to ask."

Heart rapidly sinking, Hardy stares suspiciously at a frozen rictus of a smile adorning the face of his boss.

"No need to look so gloomy gentlemen. This should be a walk in the park following your success in solving the Dibley case. You brought the killer to justice and everyone in West Ayton can now sleep soundly in their beds."

"Thank you, sir," replies Stanley acutely aware of the hint of sarcasm in the Inspectors voice, "but it was over a year ago."

"Indeed, I am glad you brought that up. From what I can see things have been very quiet and, how should I phrase it, low key. Your hit rate of solved cases, bar a few minor crimes, seems to have dried up over the last twelve months. Time for you to get your teeth into something meaty."

Warily Hardy nods, anticipating further clarification.

"So, detectives, have you heard of a shop called Abrams and Friedman in Scarborough?"

"Yes sir," replies Stanley. "It's a jeweller. I got my girlfriend a necklace from there a few weeks ago."

"Well, it's a good job you weren't planning to go the whole hog and pop the question today because the shop was burgled last night. It seems the thieves got away with a reasonable stash."

"How much sir?" asks Hardy.

"I am told that the owners were holding an unusually large stock of uncut diamonds which were being assessed for a client before being shipped onwards to Amsterdam. Apparently, they got away with about half, but were disturbed and the rest ended up strewn across the back-office floor. Seems like the alarm was tripped, they must have panicked and grabbed what they could from the shop cabinets on the way out."

After pausing to let the information sink in, Parkins adds, "It seems a mystery as to how they got in and then subsequently set off the alarm."

"Any idea how much the stolen items are worth?"

"Still being assessed, but the current reckoning is around half a million. Anyway, I need my best men to take on the case but unfortunately DS Hocart is on, how shall we say ... gardening leave. Apparently can't keep his hands to himself with the local WPCs. If that's not bad enough, DS Deanmore is on an effective communication course. He is being taught to smile as he scares the victims of crime more than the bloody perpetrators with his miserable attitude. But I digress. Looking at your current caseload it seems you have some time on your hands given the distinct lack of homicides around the place. So off you go. You can start by questioning the owner of the shop. A Mister Abrams. He is getting increasingly angsty for some sort of response by the police as well as complaining about some racist local constables not giving him the attention he merits because he is Jewish. So, hop to it but tread carefully."

The two detectives do not get beyond the office door.

"Oh, I almost forgot, I have another favour to ask."

Slowly, they both turn back to face Parkins.

"I would like you two to pop by West Ayton and make your presence known. Ask a few questions, that sort of thing. I was talking to a friend of mine at the Bridge Club, Councillor Mandelson. Seems that there is a spate of weird events which are terrorising the locals. I promised Jeffrey, that is, Councillor Mandelson, that I would send some people over to see what they could do."

"What kind of events?" asks Hardy.

"Well, various locals are reporting that they are being terrorised and, in some cases, almost assaulted."

With information to impart, Stanley pipes up. "I heard something about that. A reporter I know has been talking to locals in the village for a few days now. All sorts of weird crazy stuff such as UFOs and Sasquatches." Parkins nods, non-committing, at the young detective and looks over to Hardy for a comment. Hardy obliges.

"You want us to investigate UFOs and Sasquatches, are you kidding me? What are we now, the bloody X Files?"

"Don't be so damn flippant, Hardy. Of course not. I have no doubt it will be local idiots playing up. You just need to show a presence and ask a few questions to deter whoever is involved. Community policing, it's the new way. Now bloody well get on with it."

Back in their car Hardy hesitates and checks his phone before turning on the ignition.

"What's up boss and what's the plan?"

Exhaling in frustration, Hardy looks across at the expectant expression of Stanley. "Well, I will tell you one thing. In our list of priorities, we won't be putting either Bigfoot or close encounters of the third effing kind on top of our hit list. The desk sergeant at the Scarborough station has just texted me to let us know that Abrams is coming in at 11 a.m. So, let's get a shift on."

Nearing the outskirts of Scarborough, the two detectives leave Racecourse Road taking a more circuitous, but quicker, route to their destination. Open fields give way to large Victorian houses which rest in grandeur in a leafy affluent suburb inhabited by lawyers, accountants, doctors, and the more successful local businessmen. In doing so they avoid the A64 which serves as the main route into the town. Being the height of the holiday season, it is crammed with lorries, caravans and day trippers in cars bursting with excited children.

Weaving through the back streets they eventually arrive at the familiar ugly architectural monstrosity of concrete grey pillars with orange rendered panels.

Having parked at the back of the Police Station, they make their way into the foyer to be greeted by the desk sergeant whose welcome is edged with his usual degree of sarcasm. After their success in bringing the murderer of the Reverend Peter Dibley to justice, the banter is lower key. No longer does he whistle the Dance of the Cuckoos. The theme for Laurel and Hardy being an unsubtle reference to the similarity of the names and physical profile of the two detectives. Recent events have provided him with a new avenue of taunting.

"Well, well, well, it's the BFRO," chuckles the Sergeant.

"What?" asks Hardy with a scowl.

"The BFRO," explains Stanley, on the grinning Sergeant's behalf. The desk sergeant nudges his colleague behind the counter realising that the junior detective has taken the bait.

"What?," snaps Hardy, redirecting his irritation to his partner.

"BRFO. It stands for Big Foot Research Organisation. It is a TV program about a load of yanks who wander around the forests of America trying to prove that Bigfoot exists." Stanley gives a beaming smile, pleased that he can enlighten his boss.

Hardy stares coldly at the desk sergeant. "I see that news travels at great speed in these parts."

"Like the Bigfoot apparently, or is it the Yorkshire Yeti?"

"Very funny sergeant, but unlike you, we have work to do. Is Mr Abrams here yet?"

Reaching below the counter, the sergeant presses a button which is followed by a loud jarring buzzing sound as the security door to the side of the reception desk clicks open. Directing the detectives to Interview Room 3, he gives a workable impression of the eerie sound of the X Files TV theme tune as they pass through the door.

"Hilarious," mutters Hardy as the door clicks shut behind them. They make their way down the windowless corridor to the interview rooms.

They find Abrams sitting at the only table in the room with a mug of coffee in front of him next to a recording device. The room is depressing. No natural light, yellowing white paint, smell of damp, claustrophobic, uninviting.

Hardy introduces himself first and then Stanley whilst they settle into their seats. Opposite them, Abrams runs his hand over shiny black hair, tidying his widows peak whilst assessing the detectives through piercing dark brown eyes. A black Armani suit, perfectly moulded to Abrams body shape, matched with a white open neck Loro Piana shirt, gives the jeweller a casual elegance in direct contrast to sartorial taste of the detectives.

Looking disdainfully, Abrams chooses not to share his thoughts on Hardy's worn brown corduroy jacket which was clashing offensively with a black checked shirt. Shuffling to make himself comfortable, Hardy's shirt is embroiled in a wrestling match with his girth as the lower buttons threaten to burst free. Staring at the pair in front of him, the jeweller's musings remain private. As first impressions go, Abrams was not pinning his hopes high on a successful outcome.

At least the cheap suit worn by the young detective almost fits him, as it hangs limply over his bony shoulders. Hopefully, one should not judge a book by its cover. *Looking at these two, if I do, then I can kiss goodbye to the diamonds.*

"I see you have been availed of our renowned station hospitality," says Hardy, attempting to lighten the mood and establish a relaxed tone in the hope of putting the interviewee at ease. It falls on deaf ears; Abrams is not in the best mood. The coffee is, and would remain, untouched, ultimately consigned to the plughole in the station's kitchen sink.

"Can we please get down to business DS Hardy. I am keen to get things moving to recover everything that's been stolen. That is once your colleagues have examined what they nicely term as 'the crime scene'."

"We just have a few questions and then perhaps you can accompany us down to your shop so we can have a look at the, er, crime scene, and try to ascertain what has been taken. First things first, who else besides yourself works in the shop?"

"Tamar and Shira."

"Come again?"

"They are my nieces and before you imply otherwise, they are entirely trustworthy."

Hardy resets himself physically by shuffling in his chair and mentally by reminding himself of the benefits of politeness and patience.

"Sorry, Mr Abrams, they are unusual names. Never heard them before."

"They are traditional Jewish names, not that it's of any relevance."

"Yes, sorry. Do they have the codes to the alarms? I understand the alarm initially was not triggered."

"Of course, they do, that's how they open the shop every morning. What are you inferring?"

Stanley joins in the questioning. "Are all the goods insured Mr Abrams?"

"Yes, they are. Well, I say they are insured but who knows when you are dealing with those paper shuffling sharks. They'll probably come up with some esoteric clause in the policy to avoid paying."

Abrams' brow furrows in realisation. "But what are you implying? That bloody racist schoolboy masquerading as a constable last night kept going on about the insurance. Kept talking about 'an insurance jobby.' Is the whole of the North Yorkshire Police force populated by incompetent racists?"

Seeing that Stanley was adding fuel to the fire, rather than dousing it, Hardy struggles to regain control.

"Excuse my colleague Mr Abrams, but we need a full picture of who works at the shop, their background and an understanding of vital information including who was able to access the shop without apparently tripping the alarm. Can I ask who set the alarm yesterday?"

"I did. And, in fact, I do it every day unless I am on holiday or away on business. And, before you ask, I was in the shop yesterday at closing and I set the alarm."

"Are you sure?" presses Hardy.

"Yes I bloody well am sure. What's more, we can check the security application to confirm this. It's on my phone."

Tapping and swiping his phone until he gets to the record of activity, Abrams smiles triumphantly and holds up the phone screen in front of the two detectives. Squinting as they try to decipher the activity log on the small screen, Abrams explains. "If you look at the third line from the bottom you can see that it says the alarm was set at 5:43 p.m. and the user was me."

"Anything else recorded yesterday evening?" asks Hardy. This prompts more tapping and swiping until Abram's olive complexion pales slightly.

"Yes, it does, it looks like the alarm was disarmed at 11:37. It says 'user unknown'. It also records the alarm tripping again at 11:47."

"Why would that happen?" asks Stanley.

"Not entirely sure but if you do not press 'confirm' twice the alarm resets after a short period, presumably after ten minutes by the look of it. I suspect that's what may have happened. I have to say that this feature has never been triggered before because I guess we all know what we're doing."

Forehead wrinkled revealing scepticism, Hardy gives out an involuntary "hmmmm." Stanley seeks further clarity on the sequence of events. "So, who informed you about the break-in Mr Abrams. I understand you turned up unexpectedly at that late hour. How so?"

Abrams eyes Stanley with a mixture of suspicion and irritation trying to decipher the intention and inference behind the questioning. "It feels to me that you both seem to be pursuing a line of inquiry that puts me directly in the firing line. Are you both implying that I have robbed my own shop?

"Not at all," says Hardy, "just trying to assimilate information. Who has access to the code? Who is familiar with the layout of the shop? That sort of thing. It helps us to piece together the events of the evening. Perhaps you can answer DI Stanley so we can get on with the investigation and act quickly as you have requested."

"What was the question?"

Stanley obliges. "How come you came to the shop around midnight to find there had been a break in and the local police were present?"

"Oh. Well, I didn't know at that point that there had been a break-in, but the security application buzzes an alert on my phone telling me the alarm had been triggered. This happens on occasion, usually either a glitch or some drunken youths walking by and banging on the doors. Either way I want to avoid complaints, so I come out to reset the alarm when this happens. I was a bit taken aback to find the police there, lights flashing and the doors wide open."

The Information gathering continues for several minutes until Hardy and Stanley have exhausted all the questions and angles they can think of. They suggest to Abrams that they go to the shop to see if the scene of crime officers have anything to show them and to compile a list of what has been stolen. Abrams is directed to the toilet before they go, leaving the two detectives alone in the room.

"Well boss, what do you think? Seems like he isn't involved."

"Why do you think that?" asks Hardy.

"Well, that alarm thing. If it was him or someone working for him, they would have known about the alarm thing."

"What thing?"

"That you must press 'confirm' twice to avoid the alarm resetting."

"Maybe, or maybe not. He isn't stupid, and perhaps that's just his way of taking the heat off himself or his accomplices. Maybe he is too clever by half."

Stanley shakes his head doubtfully. "Not sure boss, seems genuine to me."

5

AT THE WESTERN end of the village high street in the Old Plough, Ken and Dolly Wilkes prepare the pub ready for opening. Hands on her wide hips, Dolly stares at the large stuffed Koala that sits permanently on a chair in the corner. In a homage to the large bear-like landlord, the Koala was named Kenneth by locals.

"I do think he is beginning to look the worse for wear – Ken."

Engrossed in cleaning the pumps the landlord responds without looking up.

"Who dear?"

"Kenneth … he's beginning to look threadbare, showing his age."

"Bit like his namesake," chuckles Ken, which also makes Dolly giggle.

Smirking to herself, she unlocks the main door for the lunchtime session "Yer daft apeth. Still, I may have to take a needle and thread to him in due course."

They go about their duties with no other words exchanged until the silence is eventually broken. Traffic noise leaks through the front entrance, followed by two tall men. Ken surveys the odd-looking pair with interest before addressing them when they reach the bar.

"Ow do, gentlemen, what can I get you?"

The older man responds in a slightly affected upper class English accent, which lacks authenticity. "Could we have two pints of your local ale?"

"Certainly, two pints of Tetley's it is then." Ken chats as he pours the beer. "You don't sound as though you're from around 'ere. On holidays or 'ere on business?"

The older man's grey curly locks wiggle as he searches for the wallet in his tweed jacket and then places it on the counter. Waiting patiently for the pint glasses to fill, he stares directly at the landlord, stroking his moustache and goatee beard with one hand whilst the other rests in the pocket of his plaid waistcoat. His younger companion in contrast is dressed conservatively in an ironed navy polo shirt and freshly creased trousers, with a haircut as sharp as a knife.

An odd pair, muses the landlord. *In fact, a bloody funny looking and unlikely twosome if ever I have seen one.*

"Actually, we are here on both," replies the older man. "Especially given your rich history in this sceptred isle, but our primary reason is business."

"Sorry, what did you call our isle?"

"Sceptred ... Mr?"

"Wilkes, Ken Wilkes. Call me Ken."

"Sceptred Isle. A quote from your very own Shakespeare. Richard II, I think, if my memory serves me. It is how this wonderful old country of yours is described through the pen of the great bard."

"I think I've now placed your accent. You sound American."

"You win a cigar, Mr Wilkes."

"Ken," says Wilkes, as he watches his customer take a long draw of his pint followed by a histrionic flourish of his hand to remove a speck of froth from his goatee.

"Sorry, Ken. Whilst, having just tasted your ale, it is

exceptional, I must admit that this is not the only reason I have come to this fine village. Perhaps you could assist in our venture. But firstly, let me introduce myself. My name is Septimus Harcourt and my colleague here is Sherman MacArthur the Third."

Ken appraises MacArthur. "You look as though you're fresh out of the military, Sherman."

MacArthur reflexively gives a crisp salute raising his hand to his forehead and holding it perfectly horizontal against his blond crew cut. "Yes sir, thank you sir. I was in the Marines, then transferred to the United States Air Force ... security division. We are mainly here on business sir."

"I see," replied Ken, who clearly didn't.

"Let me explain," offers Harcourt. "I am here because I am a cryptozoologist. That is, I specialise in studying and searching for creatures that conventional science does not recognise as even existing."

Intrigued by the conversation, Dolly sidles up next to Ken who puts his beefy arm round her whilst introducing his wife to the two Americans.

"Sorry, I don't understand," interrupts Dolly.

Smiling with a slight air of condescension, Harcourt clarifies. "Well madam, our aim is to dispel the myth that certain creatures do not exist."

"Don't you mean the myth that they do exist?" enquires Dolly.

"No, Mrs Wilkes, the myth perpetuated by so-called scientists is that they DO NOT exist, even though they have been seen by many thousands of witnesses over several centuries. There is documentation all over the world on local native art, written records, newspaper reports, cave paintings et cetera. The evidence is overwhelming."

"So what creatures are you talking about?"

"Well, Mrs Wilkes, allow me to clarify. Primarily my studies have focused on the Bigfoot or Sasquatch as many call them. But there are many wonderful creatures sighted around the world. Even here you have the Loch Ness Monster on your doorstep, do you not?"

With a slight squint of scepticism Ken joins the discussion. "If I am getting where you are going with this, you've come to West Ayton because of the nonsense in the newspapers about a big monkey in the forest?"

"Precisely," huffs Harcourt with a victorious sweep of his hand. "We have been over here for two weeks following up reports of sightings of Bigfoot around England. There was in fact a recent one only about thirty or forty miles from this village, near a small town in Cleveland. Drawing breath to comment further, Harcourt's flow is interrupted.

"Nurse, nurse … what on earth does an old Queen have to do to get a drink here?"

Dolly looks over to one of her favourite locals. "Ooh sorry Donald, I didn't even hear you come in. I was so engrossed by these gentlemen here. They're American and monster hunters y'know."

Hitching up his neatly pressed trousers, Donald clambers onto his bar stool. Adjusting his navy-blue jacket and shuffling his posterior to get comfortable, he looks over with a withering expression.

"All I can say Dolly, my love, is that I have had a dreadful night with those infernal lights floating all around the village and, can you believe it, outside my window. No monsters, just a monster of a headache which can only be cured by a gin and tonic. A very large one, at that."

"Excuse me sir, did you say you have seen the mysterious lights?" asks Harcourt, whose interest had been aroused.

Taking in the incongruous pair stood across the bar, he gives Harcourt a puzzled look. "Well, my dear man, I suppose the answer is, yes. I certainly don't know what on earth they were." He takes a sip from the glass that Dolly had just set down in front of him.

"These gentlemen are investigating the strange 'appenings Donald," clarifies Ken who introduces the two Americans.

"Indeed," confirms Harcourt. "I am a cryptozoologist."

"Sounds painful," replies Donald, who is now waving his glass for a refill and Dolly quickly obliges.

With the comment flying above his head, Harcourt explains. "I am looking for the large creature that has been spotted near the village. We believe it to be part of the Sasquatch genus."

"Sasquatch?" replies Donald, raising his left eyebrow.

"Yes. They are big hairy ape-like creatures. Have you seen one locally?"

"Unfortunately, I have not been close to anything big and hairy for quite a few years now … so no," quips Donald.

Ken bursts into laughter causing Harcourt to swing his attention from Donald to the landlord. Suspicious that he is not being treated seriously, with a tone of mild annoyance he asks Ken if he has seen the creature.

"Sorry, Mr Harcourt, the only hairy animal I have seen is Kenneth."

"Pardon," snaps Harcourt with increasing exasperation. He looks in the direction at which Ken is pointing.

"Kenneth the Koala," blurts out Ken, as his six-foot-four frame shakes with mirth.

MacArthur can see his colleague rapidly losing his temper and restores order with a change of tack. Addressing Donald he says, "Sir, please, you mentioned lights, can you describe what you saw?"

Playing with the swizzle stick in his drink, Donald gives

it some consideration then speaks. "I thought you were after hairy monsters, not lights. I think all I can say is that there seemed to be four lights in a horizontal line moving in a very odd fashion but in perfect unison. Up, down, sideways … even diagonally. Never seen anything like it. And, before you ask, it was not an airplane or helicopter or anything light that. As far as I could tell, they made no sound at all. I take it you are not a cryptologist or whatever it's called, are you some sort of light fetishist?"

"No sir," interrupts Harcourt. "Sherman's expertise is in the extra-terrestrial. He was in the United States Air Force working in Nevada, in Area 51. You may have heard of it?"

"United States? Nevada? Area 51? I've lived in the United States."

"Really? Where exactly?" asks MacArthur, who soon wishes he hadn't.

In New York. Area 51! No. Now – Studio 54, that would be a 'yes'. It was the late seventies when I was in my heyday, so to speak. Manhattan, what an era and what a nightclub," replies Donald wistfully.

"Okay, understood sir," says MacArthur, who didn't. "But did you see anything else near the lights? Maybe men in bodysuits, perhaps even space suits?" ventures MacArthur, keen not to lead the potential witness too much, but failing miserably.

"There were a few in gold and silver body suits in Studio 54," chuckles Donald, waving to Dolly for a refill. He adds, adopting an American accent, "Burrt sadly, none in little 'ol West Ayton." He eyes MacArthur with a mildly lascivious smile. "So, tell me more. You say you were in the Air Force. Bet you have seen a few men in bodysuits in your time. I saw that film with Tom Cruise the other day. Marvellous it was."

MacArthur shuffles uncomfortably on his feet, unsure as to how to respond leaving Harcourt to pursue an ultimately fruitless line of questioning. After a series of dead ends in his exchanges with Donald, Harcourt gives up.

"Well, thank you landlord. Finally, may I ask if you know of where we might find a bed for the night in this quaint little hamlet."

"Hamlet. Are you back on to Shakespeare again?" jokes Ken. Seeing from Harcourt's puzzled expression that he is not on the same wavelength, Ken moves on and offers up a solution. "That's easy. We have a couple of rooms above the pub if that is of interest to you. Dolly here also does an excellent full English."

"Pardon me. What's a full English?"

"A cooked breakfast," explains Dolly. "Eggs, bacon, black pudding, mushrooms, fried bread ... the works."

Turning to MacArthur, Harcourt throws him a bunch of car keys. "Sounds excellent. Would you mind getting the bags Sherman, whilst I fill in the paperwork?"

Ken calls back as he disappears into the back office. "I will get you the room keys and register you."

"Marvellous, we intend to stay a few days and conduct a night hunt or two in the local woods. Is there anyone else in the village who you know has witnessed this phenomena, Mrs Wilkes?"

"Call me Dolly."

"Yes Dolly. Has anyone else seen strange lights or other unusual things recently."

"Quite a few actually. The Addinalls, who live along the High Street, have seen lights, like Donald over there." Donald raises his glass in acknowledgement. "Oh, and I know Purple and Colin have seen something that sounds like one of them Sack Watches."

"Sasquatch," corrects Harcourt. "You said 'Purple.' Who or what is Purple?"

"Yes, sorry Mr Harcourt, Purple is the nickname of a local villager. His real name is Phil Hayes," explains Dolly.

His confidence now visibly growing with the number of potential witnesses, Harcourt asks if any other villagers have reported sightings.

Scratching her rosy cheek, Dolly gives it some thought. "Mmmmm, yes, well, let me think. There are two boys, but I don't know how reliable they will be. I have heard that the two Messruther boys claim to have seen two strange beings who they reckon look like those aliens in that film that was on the telly. No hair, skinny, big head, oval eyes and all that sort of thing. Sounds ridiculous to me, I have to say."

"Greys," announces MacArthur, returning with the bags. In Area 51 we called them 'Greys', Mrs Wilkes."

"That may be the case. I don't know what colour they were, but God only knows what the Messruther boys saw. Assuming of course that they saw anything at all. I would not necessarily put all my trust in them. Those boys do have a reputation for being pranksters."

Completing the guest register whilst also gathering the addresses of the assortment of potential witnesses, the two Americans make their way to the side door which gives access to the rooms above. Before they pass through the door Donald shouts "good luck" which is echoed by Ken and Dolly. Harcourt ushers MacArthur through first and looks back to shout out his thanks.

"The game is afoot," he calls back jovially, his mood now lightened at the prospect of solid witnesses in the village.

"Is that Shakespeare again?" Ken shouts back.

"No, Conan-Doyle," replies Harcourt as he starts to climb the stairs.

"Odd couple," says Ken.

"Neil Simon," responds Donald.

"What?" says Ken.

"Neil Simon, he is the man who wrote the Odd Couple."

"Another, gin?" asks Dolly.

"That will do nicely."

Large teeth revealing a beaming smile buried underneath his bushy beard, Ken makes an announcement to Dolly and Donald. "It certainly will my lovelies. It certainly will do us very nicely; I've just had a brainwave."

"Brainwave?" asks Dolly.

"Brainwave?" echoes Donald.

"Yep, bloody genius."

"Ooh do tell," encourages Donald.

Battering the bar top with his enormous hands in a workable impression of a drum roll, Ken announces his idea with great gusto. "A theme night for Friday to drum up business." Once he gives a more detailed explanation Dolly and Donald both clap with excitement. Over the next half hour, the three put the meat on the bones of Ken's idea and develop a plan of action, with Donald offering to be a willing publicist.

"Well, we've only got three days before we do it, so we'd better get it out there to the villagers but more importantly we need to run it by our two guests. We don't know yet if they are up for it." Betty places her hands on her hip to emphasise her point but Donald, excited at the idea, gives her a chastising look and waves away her negativity.

"Course they will be Betty love. Course they will be. It's in their best interests after all. A chance to talk to all the witnesses in one place," says Donald.

Grateful that he has a supporter for his idea Ken nods in agreement with Donald and is about to promote it further when Betty shushes them.

"Listen, I can hear them coming down the stairs. Let's see if we can grab them on their way out."

They wait in anticipation until the door opens from the back stairs and the two Americans appear but stop in their tracks. Both look over, slightly perplexed at the attention from the three villagers. Dolly, Ken, and Donald stare at them expectantly. Ken seizes the opportunity.

"Hope you made yourselves comfortable gentlemen and that the rooms suit you. We were just discussing your venture and thought we may be of assistance. I have an idea which is of mutual benefit."

Raising an eyebrow, Harcourt's interest is piqued but his colleague responds.

"Yes sir, thank you sir, we'd be much obliged to hear what you have in mind," says MacArthur.

"Agreed," confirms Harcourt.

"Then take a seat," replies Ken pointing at the bar stools next to Donald and then waits for the guests to settle themselves in.

Dolly pours them both two pints of beer and replenishes Donald's drink.

"On the house," beams Dolly as she places the glasses of amber liquid on the bar in front of them.

With a broad grin, Harcourt thanks Dolly. "Very generous. It appears the much-vaunted hospitality of English publicans does indeed have veracity," he announces with a stroke of his grey moustache. MacArthur gives a reflexive half salute which ends up being more like a tip of his short blond forelock to acknowledge his own gratitude. "So, please enlighten us," adds Harcourt.

Dolly and Donald defer to Ken, the originator of the idea.

"It's like this gentleman. Most Fridays we like to do something different to keep the locals interested and get a few other customers in from round abouts."

"A roundabout? Isn't that what the English call our traffic circles?" asks Harcourt, perplexed.

Ken laughs, realising the confusion. "No, sorry, it's a local expression. When we say 'from round about' we mean from near here. I just mean that we like to do something to encourage others from nearby villages to come to the pub for a good time. So, some Fridays we might have a local band, y'know, live music. Anyway, we thought that, given your own investigation into what locals have seen, we could kill two birds with one stone so to speak. We could host an event and call it something like 'Twilight Zone Night.' When people come to the pub, you could invite them to tell their stories and then ask them all your questions. We could offer incentives such as a prize for the best story, or even the best costume if anybody wanted to come in dressed for the theme. Some locals like an excuse to dress up and this would be perfect."

"Sorry sir to sound both ungrateful and disrespectful," replies MacArthur who is frowning, "but to Mr Harcourt and myself this is a serious matter and not something to be made a laughing stock."

Showing his massive palms to placate the Americans, Ken explains further. "No, no, Mr MacArthur, no disrespect is intended. It's just a way to get people in and encourage them to tell you what they have seen without being embarrassed. It's the English, well at least the Yorkshire, way. If we make light of the whole thing, then it will encourage people to speak up and not worry what others will think. Ensure that other people won't think they're 'nutters.' If you pardon my French."

"Sir, excuse me sir, are you saying there will also be French people present?"

"No, no, Mr MacArthur, sorry again, more English expressions. It's just a saying," replies Ken, not wishing to be sidetracked with another detailed explanation of colloquial English.

Having processed the proposal, Harcourt speaks up. "I think I can see some merit in this idea," and turns to address his colleague.

"I think Sherman, this will be an effective way of gathering all the intelligence from local people and may even encourage others, those who have hitherto not come forward. I have to say, it is an idea that I have warmed to and, Sherman, what if people want to dress up and have fun. Well … what harm can it do?"

"To be honest Mr Harcourt, I doubt we would get too many doing the dressing up thing anyway. Just a few keen for free drinks but it will all add to the fun of the night and 'opefully you will get what you need in the bargain. Winners all round, so to speak."

Together the group discuss the themed night further, determine the format for the evening and assign roles. Donald agrees to design and print a few fliers from his home office. The Americans agree to help him deliver the fliers to houses around the village. Dolly agrees to talk to local business owners like the butcher, Stan Proudfoot and Betty who owns the grocery store and persuade them to put up the fliers and tell their customers about the event. Dolly also tells the Americans that the author of the newspaper article is the niece of the butcher, and she will ask him to let her know in case she is interested and wants to come along. Who knows, she may even write a follow up article.

6

UNLIKE THE GROWING momentum of the Americans investigation, that being conducted by the police to date could be described, at best, as pedestrian, and at worst, fruitless. It had not been a good week for Hardy and Stanley. They were no nearer to apprehending the perpetrators of the break-in and theft of the local jewellers. Not one shred of evidence had been obtained in their first avenue of enquiry which was largely based on the premise that it was an inside job to get an insurance pay out. Abrams, and his nieces who were employed at the shop had a clean record, and nothing concrete indicated their involvement in any form of wrongdoing. Monitoring the bank accounts of the suspects had not yielded any suspicious activity so, as far as the detectives could tell at this stage, they were all in the clear.

Disappointingly, the scene of crime team had not come up with any earth-shattering physical evidence to give rise to any meaningful leads or alternative avenues of inquiry. Security video and CCTV in the area was poor but what was clear was that there were two perpetrators. Blurry images revealed little more than this fact. Although hard to decipher from the footage, it seems both perpetrators were dressed in a similar fashion. They had covered their faces with some sort of mask, but this was also hard to interpret any detail from the images, even when paused to a shaky still.

Initially, they had not ruled out that the two thieves, who seemed to be dressed in some sort of jumpsuit, could have been Abram's nieces. However, when this was shown to a colleague who had recently trained in Kinesiology, the study of body movement, the conclusion was that the likely gender of the thieves was male. That aside, the nieces seemed to have a strong alibi. Even the fact that they caught footage of the thieves escaping on a motorbike became an exercise in lost hope. The number plates had been removed and the best guess of the analyst was that they were probably riding a Kawasaki. None of the stolen jewellery or diamonds had been recovered.

Respite from the case, in Stanley's mind, drew near when Friday arrived. Relishing the prospect of a weekend free of duty, Stanley, for one, was breathing a sigh of relief.

His older colleague, whose more advanced age is becoming increasingly evident in a relentlessly growing spread of his midsection, is less enamoured by the prospect. Single, bored, and disillusioned, both with his career and his private life, the weekends held little more excitement than the working week. Like a neap tide, Hardy sees his prospects of promotion receding into the dark distance along with his social life, which consists of drinks with other police colleagues interspersed with occasional forays into on-line dating. The latter being as unsatisfying for him as it tended to be for the woman sat opposite. Most venues, selected by the dating website for romantic hopefuls, were generally soulless and full of middle-aged singles reeking of desperation.

Stanley on the other hand still clung onto the enthusiasm of youth, albeit on the wane as he approached thirty. Friday evening looked promising. He had arranged to meet a newly qualified police constable, Agnes Hope, for a drink. Anticipation with a hint of nervousness built up in the young detective as the day of his date had arrived. It was his first since his ex-girlfriend had broken up with him.

With the working day reaching its end, Stanley chews on a pen, daydreaming about Agnes.

"What's with the moon face, love struck, expression? You look like love's young dream?" asks Hardy with suspicious curiosity, tinged with the prickly thorn of jealousy.

Hands behind his head, Stanley leans back precariously on the two back legs of his chair with a smug expression. With his feet on the desk for balance, he replies with evident self-satisfaction.

"As a matter of fact, boss, I am looking forward to the weekend. I have a date with Agnes."

"What, that new WPC? That Agnes?"

Stanley nods, giving a knowing look and taps the side of his nose. He offers no more information, but Hardy cannot let it go.

"WPC Agnes Hope. Well, well, my, my ... hope springs eternal. Let's hope so anyway and I also hope your date wasn't for tonight, because you have a date with me."

Hardy runs out of hope references whilst Stanley's mood cascades like an avalanche. Complaints fall on deaf ears. Hardy rebuts protestations and suggests to his younger colleague that he rearranges his tryst for the following night.

Seeing the writing on the wall, Stanley reluctantly texts Agnes. He waits nervously but receives no immediate answer. Despite looking repeatedly at his phone, no icon appears indicating a received message. With increasing desperation, he stares intently at the screen.

"If I can wrest your attention away from your mobile for a minute, I will tell you why you have hit the jackpot of an evening with DS Hardy."

Dejected, Stanley looks up and his boss explains his thinking. "It's clear we will have little to report to Parkins about the jewel theft, but he also asked if we would look into the assaults, or whatever you call them, in West Ayton. You may not know it, but his best buddy is the local Councillor. I reckon if we can at least report some sort of progress on this it may take the heat off the jewel heist for a bit." Confused and unclear as to the urgent need to visit the village on a Friday evening, he stares blankly at Hardy which prompts further explanation.

Feeling guilty, Hardy softens his tone and addresses his junior by his first name. "Look Keith, sorry about tonight but it so happens that there is an event at the village pub called 'Twilight Zone Night'. People are being invited to talk about their experiences and alleged encounters with aliens and monsters. Now we in the Yorkshire Constabulary do not, of course, believe in aliens and monsters, but at least we get to show a presence as per Parkins' request. And, who knows, we may glean some useful information and even sort some of these matters out. So put on your glad rags and I will see you at the Old Plough around seven tonight, when it seems that all will be revealed through the stories of the villagers."

Patting his younger colleague on the shoulders, he adds, "I'll be Mulder, you can be Scully because you clearly have the bone structure and blond hair for the part, judging by how you get little Agnes' knickers in a twist."

Sulkily Stanley replies. "Looks like your little spanner in the works has untwisted them boss. I texted her apologising about tonight, but she seems to have ghosted me."

"Ghosted, how appropriate. Good to see you are getting into the Twilight Zone theme. Enough with the pet lip, she'll come round once you've flashed your lovely blue eyes at her, but for now, she'll have to go on the back burner."

By seven that night, the Old Plough was bursting at the seams with the whole village crushed into the bar, augmented by residents from nearby villages and a group of students from York. A cocktail of noise reverberates around the small pub. Underlaying the excited chatter and laughter around the tables, the juke box plays 'There's a ghost in my house,' an old hit by R. Dean Taylor. It takes the landlord back to his youth frequenting Northern Soul clubs when that song filled the dance floor.

Accompanying Kenneth the Koala in the back corner, the Addinalls are positively shaking with anticipation and the evening is all the more improved when they persuade their handsome neighbour, Chris Ashton, to join them for moral support. They plan to put up their hands to recount their story to the visitors from overseas who are stood at the centre of the bar, waiting for the optimum moment to start proceedings.

On the table next to them are five nerdy looking individuals who all sport the pale undernourished look of first-year university students. They are all wearing the same dark blue tee-shirt with silver stars and a logo in yellow writing which spells out 'YETIS.' Ashton leans over to engage them in conversation.

"I take it you are all here for the 'Twilight Zone Event' and that you are all part of some club."

They eye Ashton suspiciously. There is only one young woman in the group, who fiddles awkwardly with the silver hair bands on her pigtails before responding.

"Yes, we are," she smiles with polite nervousness.

Returning the smile, Ashton says, "I assume you are all interested in the stories about the Bigfoot, that people have seen in the area."

"Why do you say that? That's not the case. It is not our area of interest."

Pointing to the logo on her tee-shirt, Ashton replies. "It's just that you all have the word YETIS on your tee-shirts, so I assumed you were interested in a Yeti because of the talk of a Bigfoot in the area. Isn't a Yeti another name for a Bigfoot? Obviously, I'm mistaken."

"Oh, I see, Mr…? "

"Call me Chris."

"I see what you mean Chris. No, it is the logo of our club. It stands for 'Yorkshire Extra Terrestrial Investigation Society.' Our interest lies in proving that Extraterrestrials visit Earth. We all go to St John's University in York, but we just had to come to check all this out given the press coverage and publicity the village has received." She laughs dismissively and adds, "No, of course we're not silly enough to believe in Yetis or Bigfoot, that's just fiction. We believe that intelligent alien life exists and visits Earth to study humankind." Her four male companions all nod in support.

"Oh, well that makes much more sense then," responds Ashton, tapping his temple before turning back to the two sisters who had overheard the conversation.

"See Chris, we told you. Those lights we saw must have been alien spaceships. If clever people like university students believe it, then it must be true," chirps Freda.

The familiar call of "nurse" floats across the bar where Donald holds up his glass for a replenishment of gin and tonic. Dolly acknowledges him by lifting her tea towel, which she is using to polish the glasses.

"On second thoughts Dolly love, get me two doubles,

it looks as though it is going to be mayhem this evening and a major drama to get oneself a drink."

"Okay love but you are in pole position in your seat, so no need to worry. Love the hair band by the way."

His belly laugh causes his coiffure to shake which makes the glittery baubles on springs attached to his gold hairband jiggle.

"One's got to make an effort my dear Dolly, especially as you and Ken have put on such a marvellous event."

"But what are you meant to be?" chuckles Dolly.

"These, my dear, are my alien antenna. I'm from Uranus," he narrows his eyes wickedly.

Near the door Hayes and Hendricks have settled in for the evening and look forward to the entertainment as well as a chance to take centre stage. To their knowledge they are the only ones to have seen the Bigfoot, so they are expecting to play a significant role in the discussions. Arthur Messruther is sat with them.

"Have you seen any weird stuff, Arthur?" asks Hendricks. Skilfully, he places three full pint glasses on the table. Without a single drop spilt, Hendricks had carried them through a jostling crowd, by securely jamming the glasses between his tobacco-stained hands.

"Cheers," says Arthur taking a sip. "I've seen nowt lads. But my kids reckon they have. Keep going on and on about seeing aliens."

"How many? Where?" asks Hayes.

"Up Forge Valley Lane in Higginbottom's field. A bit beyond the Castle. They reckon there was two of 'em."

Both men stare at Arthur with evident scepticism as they concentrate on emptying their glasses. Arthur takes another small sip and puts his glass down. "Lads, I'm with you, it's all a load of bollocks in my 'umble opinion. Just kids being kids. Active imagination 'an all that."

"So why did you come then?" asks Hendricks.

"Nowt else to do and I thought as the kids aren't allowed in 'ere, I could come along and tell these yanks what they said they saw. Y'never know, might be some cash in it. A sort of reward for information leading to the capture of aliens, monkeys or whatever they end up catching out there."

"Fat chance," mutters Hendricks, emptying his glass and tipping it towards Arthur, indicating it is his round. Studiously ignoring the hint, Arthur picks up his own glass which is still half full. Peeved, Hendricks grabs his tobacco pouch and announces he is going out to the back of the pub for a roll-up.

Sitting directly in front of the Americans, Mandelson occupies the table in pole position which the parish Councillor had consciously assumed was appropriate given his status within the local community. His long-time friend, Ronald Neaves, joins the Councillor at the table. They had known each other since they went to school in Scarborough. In those early days they developed a symbiotic relationship whereby the bullish prop forward of the school team provided physical protection for the studious unpopular Mandelson who in turn completed Neaves' homework assignments with aplomb. Their relationship dynamic had evolved and changed as they progressed through adulthood. Mandelson had used his position of power to assist Neaves, whose own business had stuttered, mainly due to an unfortunate run in with another Scarborough 'businessman', Trent McCarthy. Unfortunately for Neaves, his nemesis was a man whose business interests bobbed like a weighted cork slightly above and frequently below the legal waterline.

Contradicting the relative physicality of the two men, Mandelson now dominates the relationship in direct contrast to their schooldays. Habitually deferring to Mandelson, Neaves remains grateful for his friend's political power and influence which helped drag the construction company from the commercial mire of near liquidation. They are currently embroiled in a scheme seeking council approval for the development of a hotel in the village. McCarthy, constantly on the lookout for legal money laundering outlets, is also a partner, albeit an unwelcome one. He was reluctantly taken on board to fulfill a debt owed by Neaves. Matters are further complicated by the disastrous shambles of the church renovation. After winning the tender for work on the west wall, courtesy of the influence of Councillor Mandelson, the project had not gone well. Disquiet as to the quality of the work, led to increasing acrimony between the administrative hierarchy of the clergy and the builders. Shortly after the murder of the vicar over a year ago, the troublesome west wall collapsed during an unusually heavy rainstorm and a plan to build a hotel next to the Church came under scrutiny given the involvement of Neaves Construction. Councillor Mandelson, Chair of the Planning Committee, had oiled the approval process for the hotel but the increasing scrutiny of the Council's auditors threatened to reveal the, hitherto hidden, commercial relationship between Mandelson and Neaves. Although the murder of the Vicar shocked the village to the core, it did provide a serendipitous distraction, enabling the issues of bodged construction and conflicted interests in the planning approval process to fall under the radar. One year later, the proposal for the hotel was back on the table and the church renovations had proceeded with a much better outcome.

Wrapping bony hands around his glass of red wine, Mandelson takes a drink. Transfixed, and slightly nauseous, Neaves tracks the deep maroon liquid filtering though his friend's livery lips. Noticing Neaves staring, but misinterpreting the reason, Mandelson asks if he would like a glass of the excellent burgundy.

"No, I'll get myself a beer and another one of those for you while I'm there." Rising from his chair, Neaves' bulky frame casts a shadow which momentarily engulfs his friend. For a moment, the normally tormenting, intimidating manner of the Councillor is dispelled, taking Neaves back to their schooldays when the balance of power in the friendship favoured him.

Villagers are scattered around the bar area, some standing at the back but most sitting at the tables which had been carefully arranged to accommodate the event. Betty, the owner of the grocery store, sits with Jenny who owns a cottage in the woods at the north of the village.

"Long time, no see. How's your psychic thing going Jenny? I'd have thought this sort of stuff would be right up your street."

Patting her dyed pink hair self-consciously, Jenny replies. "Not really. None of this has anything to do with spiritualism, herbalism, or wicker craft. Don't think I personally believe in aliens and Bigfoots. Too farfetched for my liking." She fails to read the slightly ironic smile of her friend.

On the table next to them are the Hensons. Julia sits gracefully sipping white wine with her customary elegance. Her accountant husband, Sebastian, is sat opposite, his paunch straining and stretching the middle of his Ralph Lauren polo shirt. It did not sit quite as well on his body as it did on the young model in the on-line catalogue, where Julia had ordered it. His, often overt, insecurity coupled with gossip that his beautiful wife was having an affair with the vicar, placed him as a murder suspect in the minds of some villagers. Had they been aware of his business association with the likes of McCarthy, they may well have considered their suspicions confirmed. Over a year had passed since the case was closed and the killer jailed, but some still had doubts about Henson's innocence.

Had he paid the killer? Someone must have.

When the two detectives enter the pub, they scan the room and quickly realise all the tables are taken. Hardy points to two stools at the end of the bar and they weave between the tables to claim their seats. "Jeez, this place is rocking," says Stanley. "It's a hell of a turn out."

Hardy gestures to the landlord for two pints and they quickly appear in front of them just as the Americans step forward from the centre of the bar clapping and raising their voices. Despite this they struggle to gain the attention of the audience. "Here we go," comments Hardy and Stanley nods, lifting his beer to his mouth.

Two cries for attention from Harcourt fail to quell the noise and chatter of the crowd, so Ken intervenes by ringing the bell at the bar which is usually only used to call 'time.' His booming, stentorian roar brings the place to a respectful silence.

Raising his hands to draw their attention away from the landlord, Harcourt speaks. "Ladies and gentlemen, your attention please. Firstly, I would like to thank you sincerely for taking the time out tonight to talk to us about what you have been experiencing in the village. My name is Septimus Harcourt and my colleague here is Sherman MacArthur."

MacArthur gives the audience a half salute.

"Now, Sherman and I have visited England to pursue our research and it appears that there are hitherto unexplained events in and around this village which may be of interest. With the assistance of our kind hosts, Ken, and Dolly Wilkes, we have tried to add some fun to the evening, and I notice a few of you have dressed accordingly. But, and I emphasise the word 'but' … there is a serious side to what we are trying to achieve. I am a cryptozoologist. That is, I study and seek creatures whose very existence is disputed by science. We are interested in the Bigfoot, which is also known as a Sasquatch, or even a Yeti."

Harcourt pauses for potential questions, but the crowd remain silent. So he introduces MacArthur who takes two paces forward to address the now hushed audience.

"Thank you. I am ex-military and have had many different roles, but these include security at a US military installation called Area 51 which I am sure many of you will have heard of."

This receives a few nods around the room, the most vigorous coming from the table of students who form the club, YETIS. MacArthur gives their table a half salute recognising their evident enthusiasm.

Continuing, MacArthur explains further. "Whilst I share Septimius' interest in Bigfoot, I also have a specialist interest in the extra-terrestrial, given my experiences with the military. So, I am also keen to hear about the sightings of strange lights and other phenomena that many have experienced."

Exchanging positions with his colleague, Harcourt regains the floor. "Thank you, Sherman, so before we begin, are there any questions?"

No one raises a hand, so Harcourt begins to speak, only to be interrupted by a tap on the shoulder by MacArthur who spots Donald sat at the bar with his hand in the air. After seeing where his colleague is pointing, Harcourt invites Donald to speak. Donald stares mischievously at the two Americans.

"So, you spend your life looking for large hairy men. I am thrilled to hear that someone in this place has a similar interest to me." The bar erupts in laughter with Donald milking the applause by raising his glass. Patiently waiting for the noise to die down, Harcourt forces a smile to disguise his irritation. With a manufactured good-natured laugh, he gestures for silence by moving his hands downwards. Further 'shushing' from Ken, reduces the raucous laughter down to a murmur.

"Marvellous to see we are all having fun and the famous British humour is alive and well. Now down to business. Let's start with the hairy men as the colourful gentleman in the blazer at the bar calls them. Or 'Bigfoot' as they are termed by cryptozoologists. Who thinks they may have seen or even just heard one in this area?" Several hands fly up around the room and one by one the witnesses recount what they believe they have seen and heard. All the stories are sporadically punctuated by Harcourt with 'yes, yes, yes." MacArthur knows from experience that this indicates his companion is unconvinced and is trying to move them on, in the hope of a more credible account from another audience member.

With the Americans reaching the point of lost faith, Hayes and Hendricks' come to the rescue when they recount their story. Giving a satisfying degree of detail they purposely omit revealing what they were consuming at the time, lest it promotes doubt in their veracity. Listening attentively with encouraging murmurs, Harcourt shows a keener interest in this account and patiently waits until Hayes runs out of steam.

"Let me just recap on the description, Mr…?"

"Hayes, Phil Hayes and my mate here is Colin, Colin Hendricks."

"Quite so." The moustache gets a tweak whilst Harcourt formulates his question. "You both say the creature is large, broad and its neck is practically indiscernible. You also say you saw strands attached to its body which you think was matted hair. What about height? What would be your best guess?"

Scratching his head through his own thin blond strands, Hayes gives it serious thought. "To be honest I can't be certain. Too dark and a bit too far. Nothing nearby to compare it with and give us a reference point. But if you pushed me, I would guess it was between six and seven feet."

MacArthur whispers to Harcourt. "Mmm, Sherman here thinks it sounds as though it was an adolescent and I have to say I tend to agree. Sightings of adult beasts back home range from seven feet upwards."

"Did it have acne spots, an attitude, and glued to its mobile phone? If it did it was definitely a teenager," shouts a wag from the back of the room which is greeted by a roar of laughter.

Once more Harcourt waits for the mirth to die down, finding it increasingly difficult to maintain his outwardly jovial demeanour. Giving MacArthur a brief nod, his colleague holds up a large Ordnance Survey Map of the surrounding area.

"Perhaps Mr Hayes you could point out on our map the exact locality where you saw this creature."

"Can do better than that. We can take you there tomorrow," answers Hendricks with Hayes giving the thumbs up in agreement.

Gesturing for MacArthur to put the map back on the bar, Harcourt gives a roar of approval. "Excellent, Sherman here will take your details and we'll be in touch. Perhaps you can join us in our night investigation."

A voice to the left calls out. "Excuse me…"

"Yes sir, and you are?" inquiries Harcourt.

"Detective Sergeant Hardy."

Smiling and surveying the audience, Harcourt

announces, "Great to have the local police involved. If the police are interested and taking this seriously, then the rest of you good folk should be. Good to see."

Hardy interjects to correct Harcourt's assumption. "Whilst we don't necessarily take seriously claims of mysterious large animals wandering the Yorkshire Moors, we are concerned for the safety of the public. If local people are being accosted whilst on their evening stroll, going about their lawful business, then it is a matter for the police."

DS Hardy gives a sceptical sideways glance in the direction of the table occupied by Hayes and Hendricks. "As for your intended night investigation, I'm not sure if it is wise to go wandering around in the dark looking for trouble."

"Are you saying it is against the law, detective?" asks Harcourt.

"No, you are free to go on your walks. It is just my duty to advise of the danger," responds Hardy, not pleased with the tone taken by the American. "Anyway, why do people in your, errr, how should I say, profession, always do your investigations in the dark. What's wrong with doing it in daylight?"

Now Harcourt feels challenged but is equal to the task. "Two reasons, the first being that these creatures are known to actively avoid contact with humans and therefore do their hunting at night."

"Hunting what?" asks Stanley.

"Looking for food, things like berries or small animals."

Oozing scepticism Hardy follows up. "And what is the second reason?"

"For what?"

"For doing what you call '*a night investigation*'?" clarifies Hardy.

"Well, listen to the stories we have already heard tonight, Detectives. All the sightings, including the very close encounter experienced by Mister Hayes and Mister Hendricks, have all occurred at night-time," replies Harcourt triumphantly. "And talking of close encounters, this brings me neatly on to the next part of our evening. Sherman here would like to know who has seen any evidence of alien activity or even spacecraft. We understand there have been quite a few sightings. Hands up please."

Several hands are raised, and MacArthur leads the process of encouraging people to recount their experiences. There are many stories of mysterious lights. The consistency of the observations encourages MacArthur, who becomes increasingly convinced that there is some genuine activity around the village.

He turns to Harcourt. "Well, Septimus, I believe there is plenty going on to merit a night investigation."

Harcourt addresses the room. "Couldn't agree more Sherman. Does anyone else have anything to add?"

"We have," shouts Hayes pointing to Arthur Messruther sitting next to him. "Our mate here has a story much better than a few lights in the sky, he's seen aliens."

"Really. How very interesting." Speaking directly to Arthur, Harcourt asks, "Excuse me sir, could you give me your name and tell me what you've seen?"

Slightly displeased by Hayes, who has placed the spotlight on him, Arthur gives his companion an irritated glance before addressing Harcourt. "People know me around here, the name's Arthur 'an to be honest I 'avent seen owt. It's my kids. And before you ask, they're not 'ere. Too young to be 'anging around in pubs."

Sherman straightens his back in expectation of the story he is about to hear. "Thank you, sir. Much appreciated and fully understood. Please tell me what they saw."

"Look, they are a canny couple of buggers. Just a couple of young lads with active imaginations but I reckon they saw summat."

"Summit? Are you saying that they saw something on the top of a hill?" asks MacArthur.

"An 'ill, wot are you on about?" replies Arthur, confused.

Donald, a little worse for wear by now, calls out from the corner of the bar. "Perhaps I may interject to facilitate clarity. My fellow villager, Mr Messruther, is Yorkshire born and bred."

"True," calls out Arthur, "Yorkshire born, Yorkshire bred, strong in arm, thick in head."

MacArthur is now totally lost, but Donald saves the day. "Mr Messruther, in his own inimitable style, employs the Yorkshire dialect. That is, when he says the word 'summat,' he does not mean the highest point of a hill. He means he genuinely believes his sons saw 'something.' Hope that clarifies."

Gratefully, MacArthur confirms it does. "So, Mr Messruther, what was this 'something' they told you they saw?"

"I am not saying they did, mind. But they told me they saw them aliens. Like those you see on TV. Those bald, skinny things with big dark eyes."

"Not my type at all," quips Donald which receives chuckles from around the room.

Ignoring the comment, MacArthur presses for more information. "You mean Greys?"

"The boys didn't say what colour they were, but there was two of 'em."

Several questions later, having received increasingly uninformative replies, MacArthur lets the interrogation rest. Arthur agrees to join the night investigation that the

Americans are proposing and promises to allow the twins to show them the exact spot where they saw the aliens.

"Thank you for your co-operation, Mr Messruther, you are most kind," says Harcourt.

"It's all fine, but I can't let you take the little buggers on any night investigation, they are too young and 'ave school in the morning."

"Fully understood and agreed Mr Messruther," assures Harcourt. "Now does anybody else have anything to share?"

Slowly, Freda Addinall puts up her hand. "We have," she says, pointing to her sister and then back to herself. After a hesitant start, the two sisters work together to recount, with gusto and in detail, all the events they had witnessed. Twenty minutes later, they have finished, much to the relief of the audience, whose increasingly loud background conversation indicates a growing level of disinterest.

Ashton backs up their story and assures the Americans that what they saw was no plane or helicopter. Eventually the other stories recounted from around the bar peter out. Armed with a notebook, which is now full of reported events, the Americans systematically obtain all the contact details of the witnesses they feel are credible. Announcing the date for the night investigation they get a half-hearted cheer from the crowd which turns into raucous applause when they add that they are standing a round of drinks for the whole bar.

With closing time imminent, the villagers, now fully fuelled from the nights drinking session, raise another loud cheer when the prize for the best costume is announced. Stan Proudfoot stands up from the table he shares with his niece, Lois, the young reporter who has also taken copious notes of her own to submit a follow-up article to her editor.

"I am pleased to announce that the prize is sponsored by Proudfoot Family Butchers." He holds up a large tray of meat bulging through clingfilm. It is adorned with steaks, pork chops, his home-made sausages, and a leg of lamb. Excited babble is hushed by Dolly from behind the bar, allowing Stan to announce the winner.

"And the winner is ... Betty! Stand up love, so everyone can see you."

The grocery store owner obliges and eases her large frame from the chair. An evening wearing a tight silver spandex suit was beginning to take its toll on her and beads of perspiration mottle her forehead.

"Betty came as Barbarella," shouts Dolly over the applause, as Betty gratefully accepts the meat tray from Stan.

"And now it's about closing time and, as all the locals know, closing time is Sinatra time. Join me in our traditional song. Take it away Frank," booms Ken.

Everybody, except the Americans and the two detectives, start to rock from side to side as the opening bars to '*My Way*' are played. Familiar with the protocol, the locals wait for Ken to sing the first verse before they join in where they can.

"And now the end is here,
And so, I face the final curtain,
My friend I'll make it clear
I'll state my case, of which I'm certain ..."

By the time Ken reaches the final few lines of the song most of the villagers have joined in and give a rousing finale. They hammer out the last lines together and even Harcourt sings as the song draws to a close.

"Not to say the things that he truly feels
And not the words of someone who kneels
Let the record shows I took all the blows
And did it myyyy waaaay."

When the cheers and clapping dies down, Ken's final call of 'time please' precipitates a scraping of chair legs across the wooden floor as the patrons rise and ease their way out of the pub, laughing and chatting happily. Donald is the last to leave, half stumbling as he exits, but manages to recover his balance. He looks back at Ken and gives him a shaky wave goodnight.

"Go easy mate," calls Ken, as he collects the glasses from the tables, but Donald is already through the door and wobbling up the street. Bolting the door, Dolly looks back towards Ken and blows out a sigh of relief, which Ken returns with a histrionic wipe of his brow.

"I am knackered Ken, let's clear up in the morning."

"Great night love, and you get off to bed, I'll finish up," replies Ken, continuing to collect glasses from the tables and place them on the bar counter. She waves in thanks and disappears through the door to their living room at the back. Smiling at the prospect of counting the night's takings, he continues to clear up whilst humming the Pink Floyd classic, 'Money.'

7

BACK TO THE NIGHT OF THE ROBBERY
12.20AM 2ND JULY

SIPPING WHISKEY IN his favourite booth at the back of his nightclub, Dukes, McCarthy glances at his watch. If everything is going to plan, Mr Abrams of Abrams and Friedman Quality Jewellers, is being relieved of his most valuable stock. Regarding valuable gems, Dukes is his own jewel in the crown. His other clubs exist for one purpose, and one purpose only, to make money either through the revenue they generate or the money they launder. On the other hand, Dukes, despite barely wiping its feet financially, is his happy place. A little oasis of yesteryear, taking him back to his youth. A time when he was starting out, making a name for himself, planning the empire that he had now established. An oasis of proper music. No incessant mind-numbing bass pumping out all night, no house, hip hop, techno trance or breakbeat, but a home for his passion of jazz combined with old school entertainment – magicians, impressionists, burlesque, and comedians. But not modern comedians whose acts are hidebound by political correction and the fear of cancel culture. Not for McCarthy. Not for Dukes.

Tonight, his old friend and favourite, Benedict Bunton, is top of the bill. Bunton's claim to fame is hosting a game show which aired for one season in the 1970's under his since jettisoned stage name of Benny B. The show was discontinued due to shrinking ratings, and a growing concern from television executives that Bunton's borderline alcoholism was becoming increasingly evident on screen. Added to the fear that his material was skirting close to the boundary of what was comfortable for the executives, Bunton's career became confined to nightclubs and working men's clubs. Even these institutions began to dry up as a source of income for the ageing comedian whose material had not evolved one iota beyond his halcyon decade.

Luckily, Benny B had a benefactor in the form of McCarthy, his biggest fan. Even the regular clientele at Dukes had warmed to him over the years and it was only when "blow-ins" entered the club, that the risk of offence multiplied exponentially.

Shuffling on stage, engulfed in a suit that his ageing, shrinking body no longer filled, the audience initially observe what they believe is a physically frail man. Regulars to the club who are familiar with his act, know better. His mind and wit remain as razor sharp as it was in the 1970s. Most giggle in anticipation, but the few who have never seen his act feel nervous on his behalf. He surveys the audience and picks out a familiar face.

"I see we have a celebrity in tonight," he smiles at a tough looking wiry man at the front table. "It's Tommy Hardcastle. Our very own local lad who is now the British Bantamweight champion. Congratulations on your title win Tommy."

The boxer lifts his hands in acknowledgement and Bunton raises his voice. "Come on you lot, give him a round of applause. We have a local lad who is a British champion for God's sake." Applause echoes through the small club. "Yeah, well done Tommy, great effort. Tell me, do you know why boxers don't have sex before a fight?"

The boxer shakes his head.

"Because you are both so ugly you don't fancy each other."

Hardcastle, along with the audience, burst into laughter and applause.

"Funny thing – sex. When I was a young kid, I remember overhearing my mum tell her friend that the best time to ask my dad for anything she wanted was during sex. Anyway, I locked this thought in the young Bunton brain bank and waited for my moment. When I heard my dad at it, I burst into his bedroom and shouted at him, as loud as I could. 'Hey Dad, can I have a new bike?' He was very upset, but his secretary was surprisingly nice about it."

Laughter rebounds around the room, then dies down.

"I got the bike."

Renewed laughter.

"In fact, given the circumstances I got the best bike in the shop."

More giggles.

"I'm getting on a bit, nearly eighty, so I went to the doctor, and he gave me Viagra. He was a wee bit patronising. Felt the need to point out the instructions, which said 'keep away from children.' I was outraged, so I said 'what kind of a man do you think I am?'"

Guffaws from the crowd eventually die down.

"When you get to my age, sex is different. I was in bed yesterday with the wife and we were in the plumber's position."

A member of the audience shouts, "What's that Benny?"

Keeping his deadpan expression, the comedian looks at the caller straight in the eye. "Thank you, sir. It's the plumber's position. You stay in all day, but nobody comes."

Applauding at his table, McCarthy gives a nod over to the head bouncer at the far end of the room, who immediately makes his way across the club, squeezing his large frame between the gaps in the tables. He accidentally knocks the elbow of a heavily tattooed arm belonging to a skinhead drinking with three friends. Swinging round to voice a complaint, the skinhead's eyes meet the steely greys of the bouncer. He immediately re-thinks his response, keeps quiet and waits for the bouncer to speak.

"My apologies sir," says the bouncer, in a flat tone. Neither his eyes nor facial expression are consistent with a man being contrite.

"No worries, mate, no harm done," replies the skinhead, able to save face, even after the bouncer's insincere apology.

Lumbering through the remaining gaps, the bouncer finally reaches McCarthy's table.

"Any news?" asks McCarthy, examining his Rolex.

"Nothing yet."

"It's almost one o'clock. Try to get hold of them and if they are not here by closing time, I want you to track them down. Try Doyle's place first."

"Okay boss, I'll give it until then. If he doesn't answer his mobile, I'll get myself round there."

Back on the stage Bunton was in full flow and most of the audience were enjoying the act.

Still smarting from the spilt drink, the tattooed skinhead with his group of friends, was getting restless and decided Bunton looked like an easy target. Cupping his hands to the side of his mouth he calls out. "Get off you old fart." His friends laugh out of loyalty, but the remainder of the audience remain silent.

Not missing a beat Bunton responds. "Last time I saw a face like that I fed it a banana." A peal of laughter echoes around the club.

The skinhead's face reddens as the audience laughs at his expense. Struggling and failing to come up with a retort, he tries to stand, but a heavy hand on his shoulder keeps him in his chair. The bouncer whispers in his ear. "Settle down sir or I may have to ask you to leave."

The remainder of Bunton's act goes uninterrupted. Leaving the audience to appreciative applause and a few random whistles, he is replaced by Betty Boobs, a local drag act who sings a series of gay anthems opening with '*It's Raining Men*' and closing the act with a rousing rendition of '*I Will Survive*.'

Almost apologetically the final act of the evening creeps on to the stage. Colin the Conjurer takes the audience through a series of old-style tricks involving the appearance and disappearance of pigeons and rabbits. Around the club, the volume of chatter increases as the magician struggles to generate any interest.

Barely registering that the last act had taken the stage, McCarthy sips whisky, checks and re-checks his watch, deep in thought, questions simmering in his mind.

Where the hell is Kelly and that idiot Doyle? Did they get caught? Why haven't they called?

Polite but sparse applause occasionally rises to the surface for Colin, but when the manager walks on the stage to announce that closing time is imminent, it is practically an act of artistic mercy. The manager claps as the Conjurer leaves the stage, indicating to the audience that they should follow his lead, which a smattering of customers do, out of politeness.

Encouraging the clientele to finish their drinks, the manager switches on the main lights transforming the atmosphere from a cosy, welcoming semi darkness to a jarring, discouraging, clinical glare.

The club gradually empties, leaving the bar staff

and manager to collect glasses and tidy up. McCarthy sips his drink sulkily, a solitary figure in the now empty room vacated by the departed audience. Private thoughts are interrupted by the vision of the bouncer weaving his substantial body through the gaps in the tables, occasionally shoving aside an errant chair that blocks his path. Smiling, as he approaches his boss, he announces the good news.

"Hey boss. They just got back."

"Good, where are they?" McCarthy's expression brightening.

"In the office."

"Why didn't you bring them straight to me?" McCarthy asks irritably.

"Thought it was best to keep them out of sight. You'll know what I mean when you see them."

Easing his way out of the booth, McCarthy walks rapidly to his office with the bouncer close behind moving at a surprisingly quick pace given his bulk. Giving a sardonic laugh, McCarthy takes in the scene before him and walks round his two guests, to sit behind his large oak desk. Once settled, he lets out another hollow, humourless cackle and surveys the pair sat side by side on two thin wooden chairs. McCarthy stares at them, shaking his head. To their relief, the tense silence is broken when McCarthy finally speaks up.

"Well if it isn't the Spidey twins. Spidey Dick and Spidey Head … the Spidey dickheads."

Doyle and Kelly sit, heads slightly bowed, feeling a mixture of embarrassment and fear, adorned in their muddied, slightly ripped, Spider-Man costumes. They both subconsciously wring the head masks held tightly in their hands, which are resting on their laps.

"Okay, I cannot bear the suspense, you are gonna have to tell me … why the fuck are you both dressed as Spider-

Man? Had they run out of Batman and Robin costumes?"

"No boss," they answer together.

"So, you couldn't decide who would be Batman and who would be Robin then?" snarls McCarthy rubbing the scar on his right cheek. This, the bouncer knew, was a clear sign that his boss was trying hard to maintain his composure. Straining to hold his ever present streak of menacing violence in check, McCarthy runs his hand over his closely shaven head. The room fills with a scream from the gangster, banging his fist on the table. The Newton's Cradle on the corner of his desk rocks back and forth.

"Look you morons, open your sodding mouths, and tell me where the hell you've been. And more important, where are the fucking diamonds?" He shifts his icy gaze back and forth between the two men, who look more and more like frightened naughty schoolboys fearfully awaiting their punishment. Leaning back in his leather chair McCarthy loudly exhales, visibly attempting to calm himself, and orders them to respond.

"Speak."

"We got into the gaff, no problem boss, no dramas. We disabled the alarm and were in there in no time at all. It was all going well for the first few minutes, and we got to the diamonds as planned. Problem is … the alarm tripped." Kelly looks over to Doyle, who decides silence is the safest option.

"Well, how did that happen?"

"Honestly don't know boss, no idea, none at all," replies Kelly with Doyle at his side nodding in agreement.

Suddenly deciding he has the courage to speak, Doyle finally suggests, "Maybe a glitch in the system boss … "

"Glitch, what fucking glitch? What the hell does that mean?"

Doyle only manages a limp, 'dunno' in response.

Deep calming intake of breath enables McCarthy to attempt to get an understanding of the events of the evening through reason rather than threat.

"Alright, muppets. Firstly, why are you both dressed as Spider-Man?"

"Disguise boss, no identifying factors, not even clothes that someone could identify," answers Kelly. "Anyone seeing us would just look at the costume. They wouldn't be able to give any description of us."

"Well two dickheads in Spider-Man suits is pretty fucking identifiable." Privately, McCarthy thought the costumes were not bad thinking, but he was not going to share his approval with the two idiots in front of him.

Examining the damage to their muddied costumes, he pursues his line of questioning. "Okay, well you both look as though you got dragged through a hedge or something. What happened when the alarm went off?"

"We had to gather what we had and scarpered sharpish on the bike. The cop shop is only a couple of hundred yards from the jewellers."

"Go on Kelly, go on," says McCarthy.

"Well, we managed to get out of the town centre and went up Olivers Mount. It gave us a good view of what's going on and there are several exit routes if the coppers came looking for us."

"I don't need a fucking geography lesson, just get on with it."

Swallowing nervously, Kelly continues his story.

"And when we thought it was safe, we went down to the bottom and headed off out of town towards West Ayton. Y'know, away from the town and the cops."

Once again McCarthy, in his private, unshared musings, had to grudgingly admit that what they did made reasonable sense.

"So, here is the sixty-four-thousand-dollar question. Did you get any? Where are the diamonds?"

"We got some boss, but we were interrupted by the alarm," replies Doyle, warily.

"Doyle, you just shut the fuck up and let Kelly do the talking. I can only cope with one idiot at a time." McCarthy stares down Doyle, almost daring him to speak. Doyle sits deeper into his chair in a vain attempt to make himself invisible. Inside his head he repeats, *just keep your mouth closed, let Kelly do the talking.* Being told to keep quiet was one instruction he was more than happy to comply with.

Dismayed at his own position, now well and truly back in the firing line, Kelly hesitantly continues. "I reckon we got almost half boss, but we haven't had time to sit down and check it out."

"Very well, let's check it out now then, shall we?" Looking them up and down, McCarthy adds, "From what I can see, you don't look at though you have much on you. So where are they?"

"Well boss, we went to West Ayton to keep out of the way of the cops and that's where we left the diamonds, 'cause if we were stopped, we thought it best not to have them on us."

"WHAT … DID … YOU … DO … WITH … THEM?" McCarthy could feel the burning anger and red mist grow rapidly inside him.

Looking across to his friend, Kelly desperately seeks support, but none is forthcoming. Purposely avoiding eye contact with his friend, Doyle stares down into his lap, leaving Kelly hanging high and dry. Paddleless up the proverbial creek.

"We buried them, boss."

Exploding in anger, the gangster rises to his feet and leans over the desk causing Kelly to recoil involuntarily.

"You buried the diamonds? What the hell are you doing burying the diamonds? Are you both having a fucking crisis of identity? I thought you were Spider-Man, not Long John-*fucking*-Silver! Who or what the fuck do you think you are now? PIRATES?"

Wisely, neither of the two men speak. McCarthy draws breath.

"I am surprised you both didn't go on a nice little cruise around Scarborough fucking harbour, with the skull and fucking crossbones flying high as you both set sail on the Jolly-*fucking*-Roger."

Wisely, Kelly decides not to point out that the erstwhile popular tourist attraction, the Hispaniola, was no longer operating. Nor did he choose to correct the gangster, that the Jolly Roger was the name of the flag, not the faux pirate ship.

"And where is your fucking parrot? Did you bury it with the fucking treasure as it squawked 'pieces of eight'?"

Having mentally punched himself out, McCarthy slumps to his chair with frustration. It had been a long day which had just become longer. Moving beside his boss, the bouncer replenishes the whisky glass and gets a nod of appreciation in return.

Sensing the moment is right to appease his boss, Kelly speaks up whilst McCarthy empties his glass. "Don't worry boss, it'll be safe. No one saw us burying them."

"Yeah right, do tell me. Where exactly did you bury them?"

"A field behind the main street of a village. It's a farmers field so no one is likely to wander there, except the cows," responds Kelly with growing confidence. It appears McCarthy has expended all the anger he had, at least for the time being.

"And how exactly are you going to remember where

you buried the diamonds in a sodding field where one bit of grass will look much the same as another? I presume X marks the spot and you drew a treasure map."

"No, we thought of that Boss. Not the map obviously, but how we were going to find the place we buried the diamonds. We buried it on the edge of the field next to the tree line."

"And?" asks McCarthy with increasing doubt.

"We marked the tree alongside the spot we buried it."

"Please don't fucking tell me you carved out an 'X' as in, 'X' marks the spot."

Oblivious to his boss's sarcasm, Kelly cheerfully confirms the supposition. "Yeah boss, you're right, we did mark the tree with an 'X.' Just a little one mind, no one would notice it."

"For fucks sake." McCarthy mutters to himself and glances at the poker-faced bouncer who offers no comment or contribution other than a dismissive shake of his cube like head. Kelly and Doyle await instructions and McCarthy obliges.

"Right, here is what you do. Leave it for a few days and let all the attention, and whatever, die down. Then, when it is no longer a TV news headline or featured on page one in the Scarborough Evening News, you will go and get me my diamonds. My advice is, do not come back here unless you have them safely tucked into your Spider-Man costumes. Got it?"

They both nod in the affirmative and having then been told to 'bugger off,' do so gratefully and without hesitation, relieved that the ordeal was over.

8

IT IS LOVE'S young dream. Billy Messruther ached from an emotional void. His brother had boxing lessons three times a week and he needed a 'Ben replacement' which came in the form of Sharon Corner. Shazza to her mates. They walk hand in hand up Forge Valley Lane in a comfortable silence save for the chomping of chewing gum, which was ever-present in Shazza's mouth. Their physics teacher, Mr Pratt, had declared in class that he was going to notify the Royal Society that he had finally discovered, in the shape of Shazza's oral cavity, a true example of perpetual motion. Shazza was confused but pleased to be the subject of something important, she did not want to ask for an explanation lest she appeared stupid. On the other hand, Billy was full of questions such as 'what is the Royal Society?'

Mr Pratt explained that it is a learned society furthering and supporting the development of scientific knowledge. In fact, Mr Pratt explained, it is the oldest existing scientific academy in the world. 'Sharon here,' he declared, 'may have unwittingly violated the first and second laws of thermodynamics and created something that was hitherto believed to be impossible.' Revealing this made Shazza burst with pride and sit up straight to pay attention to the remainder of the lesson for the first time ever. As did Billy, who bathed in reflected glory once he was confident that violating the laws Mr Pratt was talking about wouldn't get her in trouble.

Birds cheep, twitter, and warble in the trees as the early evening sunlight flickers through the tree branches, occasionally bathing Shazza's dyed blonde hair in golden radiance. Always keen to follow fashion, she had tied her hair back into a ponytail as tightly as humanly possible giving her a slightly Asian appearance with what was known locally as a 'Council house facelift.'

Overcome by teenage adoration, Billy surreptitiously steals sideways glances and marvels at her beauty. *Much better than boxing'* he thinks. Through a gap in the hedgerow, a spot well known to Billy and his brother, the pair of lovers make their way across the field, observed by the disinterested cow herd lethargically chewing their cud. Having reached the tree line at the eastern edge of the field they sit underneath an oak tree side by side but twist their necks awkwardly to face each other and kiss. Reluctantly, they separate for air. This allows an opportunity for Shazza to reach into the pocket of her jeans and dig out a fresh strip of Wrigley's chewing gum. She unwraps and pops it into her mouth. The old one was lost in their passionate embrace. Unknown to Shazza, Billy had inadvertently swallowed the chewed gum ball, but was too polite to mention it.

Staring at his love, Billy desperately attempts to construct a meaningful sentence to enhance the romantic moment. Observing her pretty mouth and the rolling motion of her jaw, he notes the striking similarity of the movement to that of the cows munching on the grass a few yards away.

"Guess what Shazza," his eyes light up.

"What?" replies Shazza mechanically.

"It's a special day, today."

Turning her head to face Billy, she says "Do tell."

"It's our two-month anniversary."

"Is there such a thing as a two-month anniversary?" she asks doubtfully. "Though if it is then it's a record for me. The longest I've ever been out with a boy is about a month."

"Me too," replies Billy, who was new to the girlfriend business but did not want to appear inexperienced. "I reckon we should do something to celebrate it."

Suspiciously, she crosses her arms over her breasts and asks what he has in mind. Her brow furrows when she sees him reaching into his back pocket. Pulling out a penknife, he declares his intention. "I am going to carve our initials on this tree."

"Bad idea," replies Shazza, leaving Billy crestfallen. "If you carve our initials, then we'll get into trouble, won't we? If Higginbottom finds it, then he is going to know that we did it. Think about it."

Looking at the blank expression of her lover, she decides to spell out her concern. "He'll know who we are from the initials you've carved. We'll get done for trespassing. My dad is on probation and if he gets in trouble 'cause of something I've done, he'll kill me."

"Okay," agrees Billy, carving into the tree.

With a cry of alarm, she shouts out. "Billy, Billy what are you doing? I just told you not to do that."

"It's okay, it's okay, I have just carved a small cross, no one will see it. It's my kiss to you, so our love will last forever."

Smiling with relief and enjoying the compliment, she gives him a peck on the cheek. "Forever?"

"Well at least until the end of the summer's holidays. I guess we had better get back," announces Billy, pleased with the success of his romantic gesture.

"End of the summer holidays? Maybe," adds Shazza.

They get up, kiss, and walk hand in hand along the tree line. Neither notice that the sixth tree they pass also has a small cross carved into the trunk, which looks strikingly similar to their own public statement of love. By the time Billy gives Shazza a final kiss goodbye at her door and makes his way home, the evening sun had surrendered to the night and was replaced by streetlights, which struggled to push back the darkness.

Back in the woods the night's activity, announced by the hoot of an owl, has just begun. A light wind whistles through the branches and rustles the leaves in the trees, disguising the sound of footfalls as Doyle and Kelly make their way through the woods.

"Are you sure this is the right way?" asks Kelly, who is following closely behind his friend.

"As sure as I am about the idea of wearing these sodding Spider-Man suits again."

"Stop whinging Doyle, at least if we get seen we can't be identified. If we mess up again, we are toast. McCarthy will kill us. And I mean literally. And while we're at it, what is that on your arse?"

"It's a patch, the suit got torn last time when we went through those bushes. The missus patched it up, but only had black material with white spots."

The question was begged, so Kelly had to ask it. "What exactly does your missus think you are doing, wandering about at night in a sodding Spider-Man uniform?"

"I just told her we all must dress up on some days at work. That the company is raising money for charity."

Kelly considered going down the line of enquiring

about which charity was supposedly going to be the lucky recipient but decided not to enter the world of Doyle. Without further discussion, they reach the end of the woods and find themselves in the open field and can make out the shadows of the cows, laying in a huddle on the ground in the south-west corner.

Looking up and down the tree line, they both try to assess their location in relation to where the diamonds are buried, finally agreeing that they have entered the field too far north. Armed with torches and short handled shovels they slowly creep southwards down the field shining their beams of light on each tree they pass.

Doyle stops abruptly after a few yards and keeps the beam of his torch trained on an oak tree. In a stage whisper, he tells Kelly that he has found the tree. He scuttles to it, leans with his back to the trunk and purposefully takes three paces in a measured fashion. Both men fall to their knees and start digging furiously but become increasingly anxious as their hole deepens and widens but fails to reveal the black bags containing the diamonds. They stop digging and sit back, breathless.

"Are you sure you got the right tree?"

Shining his torch on to the trunk to reveal the small cross carved on it, Doyle responds. "Yeah, look. There's the cross."

"You sure this is your cross?"

"Well a cross is a cross; what are the chances that another tree has a bloody cross? Zero – I can tell you."

"Okay, are you sure you just took three paces?"

Exasperated by the questions, Doyle hisses out his answer. "Yes mate, of course I'm bloody sure. Do you think I'm an idiot?"

"No comment," says Kelly irritably. "Well, they are not here now and that means we have a major problem on our hands."

Their argument is cut short by the noise and lights of a vehicle coming down the field. They freeze, watch, and listen. The engine noise becomes louder, and the lights grow larger and brighter as the vehicle bears down on them. Grabbing up their shovels, they flee into the woods and do not stop running until they reach the main road to Scarborough.

In the field, the quad bike ridden by Higginbottom comes to a halt. Climbing off, the farmer completes his evening check on the herd and, satisfied that all is well, pats the nearest cow, returns to his vehicle, and drives back to the farmhouse.

Jogging up the verge of the road Kelly and Doyle head for their Kawasaki Ninja hidden in the bushes. Before they reach the bike, a Mini Clubman, owned by the Addinalls, passes them on its way back to the village. Freda, who is driving, shouts out to Mary in the passenger seat.

"Oh my God, did you just see that?"

"I think I did, Freda."

"I didn't get a good look, it's too dark and I was concentrating on my driving, but they looked strange."

"I know, human but not human. You know what they made me think of?" asks Mary rhetorically.

"I think I do. They were like those aliens that Arthur Messruther said his boys saw when we were at that Twilight Zone night in the Old Plough," answers Freda.

"One hundred per cent. It was just like Arthur said. Thin bodies, no hair, and big eyes."

Freda nods in agreement. "I have to say, I didn't really believe those boys saw anything at all. They're always up to mischief. But credit where credit's due, it looks like they were telling the truth."

Both sisters agree that they must strike whilst the iron is hot and head straight for the Old Plough to report their sighting to the Americans. Within minutes they are pulling up excitedly into the car park. Greeted by Ken Wilkes as they walk through the pub door, they head straight to the bar.

"Oh Ken, have you seen the Americans?"

Seeing their excitement, Ken walks straight over to join them at the corner of the bar. "What's going on ladies, you look like you've lost a penny and found a pound?"

Letting out a squeal, Freda spills the news. "We must see Mr Harcourt and Mr MacArthur. We've just seen something that they'll be extremely interested in. We think we have seen what they are looking for."

"What, the Bigfoot creature?"

"No Ken," replies Mary. "The other thing, the aliens. The ones that the Messruther boys saw."

Turning to his wife, Ken asks Dolly if she knows if their guests are in. Dolly tells the twins that they have been out all day but came back a short while ago and went up to their rooms. She offers to go and knock on their door, which they urge her to do. Dolly returns with the two guests who are directed to sit at the bar next to the two sisters.

"Good evening, ladies, I understand from Mrs Wilkes, that you have important news to share," says Harcourt in the smoothest most charming voice he can muster. He strokes his goatee whilst he waits for the two sisters to gather their thoughts. Sitting next to Harcourt, MacArthur smiles and nods to the sisters.

"Well, we don't have too much to tell because it all happened so fast," says Freda.

"Yes, very fast," confirms Mary.

"Take your time," purrs Harcourt.

"Well, we were driving home from Scarborough. It's our shopping day but it was very busy in town and got late so we treated ourselves to fish and chips on the foreshore. And then." Freda nudges Mary to get to the point, which prompts Mary to shorten her tale.

"Oh! Sorry I am going on, aren't I? Anyway, you don't want to know all that. But as we drove home this evening and came to the outskirts of the village, we saw, or at least we think we saw, two aliens. They looked like those described by him the other night in the pub." Mary points in the direction of MacArthur.

"You mean the Greys?" asks MacArthur.

"Yes, indeed! They looked like those Greys you described. But we were in the car and driving quite fast and it was very dark. Although we got just a glimpse, I have to say that it certainly looked like them. Big eyes, no hair, skinny," confirms Freda.

"That's very interesting, thank you for reporting it, ladies. How do you feel about taking us to the place you saw them, now?" asks Harcourt. "I realise it's late, but we should strike whilst the iron is hot."

"We'd love to, our car is just outside," replies Freda.

Crushed into the Mini Clubman, the two Americans, are shoehorned into the back of the car, whilst they are driven at speed to the site where the sisters saw the 'aliens.' Mary shouts for Freda to stop, worried that she will drive past the exact location. Slamming her foot down hard, Freda just manages to retain control of the vehicle as it skids along a muddy path at the side of the main road. A rare expletive escapes from the mouth of MacArthur but the 'goddamn' is barely audible. Only Harcourt hears it and gives his partner an admonishing glance.

Both sisters immediately climb out of the front seats, release the levers, and pull them back as far as possible, allowing Harcourt and MacArthur to squeeze their large frames out through the narrow gaps. They pop out of the car like two corks from a bottle.

Flicking the switch of her torch, Freda scans the beam of light up and down the muddy path then over the line of trees in front of them. Gently prising the torch from Freda's hand, MacArthur runs the torch beam carefully along the track.

"Can't see any footprints Septimus, though up there I can see a partial tyre track, which could be from the wheel of a car which has veered slightly off the road, or possibly even a motorcycle. But no large footprints or unusual tracks as far as I can tell."

Continuing the search, Harcourt and MacArthur go about their business but discover nothing of interest which would support the presence of aliens. Defensively, the two sisters plead their case and the two Americans assure them that they believe that they saw something. Afterall, they are not the first villagers to witness the presence of unknown and unidentified beings, alien or otherwise. Checking his wristwatch and the lateness of the hour, Harcourt calls a halt to the search.

"Okay ladies, I think we should call it a night and Sherman and I will return in the morning. Perhaps daylight will reveal something rather than scrabbling about in the dark with a torch. If it is acceptable to you ladies perhaps you could drive us back to the Old Plough?"

Disappointed and slightly embarrassed, the two sisters trudge back to the car. They pull back their seats allowing the two Americans to squeeze themselves through the narrow gap once more and wedge themselves into the back seats. On the journey home, Mary peers out of the passenger seat window hoping that she sees something that she can point out to the two passengers. Nothing out of the ordinary appears and Harcourt, once he has escaped from the confines of the Clubman, thanks the sisters graciously as does MacArthur, with a brief salute. Before Freda drives away to make the short journey home, Harcourt calls over to them from the front door of the pub.

"Thank you once more ladies, and do not be disillusioned. Keep your eyes peeled and whatever you see, however unlikely, please call us. Many people spend years searching for what you have seen tonight and never are as fortunate as yourselves." As the Clubman turns left out of the car park, Harcourt gives a final wave to the sisters.

"Do you think they saw something, Septimus?" asks MacArthur, still waving until the car disappears out of sight.

With a sly, sideways sceptical glance, Harcourt responds. "I doubt it, Sherman. A couple of local spinsters with little to occupy their minds and an overactive imagination. All I could see was a tyre track. Maybe they saw a motorcyclist and they thought the crash helmet was part of a spacesuit or something. Nevertheless, in the interests of scientific study, I think we should investigate in the morning in case we missed something."

"I agree," replies MacArthur. "Still worth a look and, don't forget, we have an interview tomorrow evening on the radio. Might get some leads from callers and the word out there to encourage other witnesses to come forward."

Entering the bar, they are greeted by Dolly. "Any luck lads. Did yer catch any aliens?" she asks good naturedly.

"I am afraid not Mrs Wilkes. Probably a false alarm but we will check out the location in the morning. It's been a long day and there is much to do tomorrow before we carry out the night investigation on Friday. We also have an interview on a local radio station tomorrow evening. A show hosted by a Mr Riders. Do you know of it?"

"Never listen to it personally Mr Harcourt. But I hear that he can be challenging and, I'm told, a bit rude at times. I think you call them Shock Jocks in America, don't you?"

Sherman responds. "Yes madam, we do have them and, don't you worry, we know how to handle them. We hope people will call in with their experiences and give us some leads. Still, with thanks to you and the residents of West Ayton, we have plenty to go on already. For now, we will bid you goodnight."

Once they have left the main bar and made their way upstairs to their lodgings, Dolly turns to her husband who is busy cleaning glasses. "They're not that bad I reckon Ken, for foreigners. It's been quite nice having them here."

"And, good for business," adds Ken.

Business is not good for Kelly and Doyle who have secreted themselves safely back in Kelly's flat in York. His home overlooks common land called the Knavesmire, situated near the racecourse where Kelly spends a lot of his spare time. In dire need of a fresh coat of paint, the one-bedroom flat is sparsely furnished. A TV, sofa, coffee table and side chair populates the small living room which has a poorly insulated sash bay window that rattles when the wind swirls over the Knavesmire. Doyle is on the sofa and Kelly in the chair, each with a can of Tetley's Smooth ale in front of them. Their Spider-Man costumes are piled apologetically near the door to the room. 'Who wants to be a millionaire' is playing on the TV but the sound is muted.

"That was a sodding disaster," declares Doyle, before taking a sip of his beer.

"That is a major understatement," replies Kelly. "What the hell happened? Are you sure you got the right tree and took the right number of paces?"

"Mate, the tree had a cross on it and, yes, I took three paces. The diamonds should have been there."

Kelly snarls. "But they weren't, were they, you muppet? If you're certain there was a cross on the tree and that you only took three paces, then there is only a couple of possibilities."

"Which are what?"

"That someone came and took the diamonds, or there is another tree with a cross on it and we got the wrong one. Which frankly leaves us with only one option."

"Which is what?" enquiries Doyle as he empties the can of beer.

"That we go back and check all the trees to see if another one has a cross that you marked it with. Because if this is not the case, we are well and truly screwed. If someone else took the diamonds, we have no hope of finding them and getting them to McCarthy. I, for one, will be re-locating down south if we can't find them and will not be attempting to explain the unexplainable to him."

"Bugger."

"Bugger indeed Doyle. What I will say is, that I'm not convinced that they've been taken because when we were digging around, like pigs in shit, it didn't look as though that ground had been touched. I don't think it was the original spot or even, for that matter, that someone dug them up and nicked them."

"Didn't think of that," replies Doyle.

"No Sherlock. Thinking isn't your strong point, is it?"

"What do you want to do then, shall we go back now?"

"I think we need to leave it for a day or so to let things calm down. I don't know if the bloke on the quad bike was coming down because he saw us, but I do know we were clocked by some old biddies in that ancient motor that drove right by us. Luckily, we had those on." Kelly points to the costumes on the floor.

"Fair enough. What's your thinking? When should we go back?'

"Friday, I reckon. Now I need some kip and you need to sod off home to your Missus. See yerself out. We'll meet back here on Friday around nine. By the time we get to West Ayton from here, it should be dark and late without a soul in sight. Most of the village should be tucked up in bed."

9

CLOSING CREDITS FOR the late afternoon show begin to fade and the Producer points to the DJ signalling they are live on air.

"Weeellllcome listeners. Welcome to *Riders Brings A Storm*, the coolest show on the East Coast. We have a packed show tonight and I can promise you three hours of fun, cool music, and incisive commentary on the current issues in North Yorkshire. By way of introduction to our first item I'm gonna play for you a song from the sixties by Bobby Pickett. The older listeners amongst you will surely remember the Monster Mash."

Pressing a button on his console, Riders leans back to enjoy the music, his faded Black Sabbath tee-shirt rides up over his paunch. On the airwaves, a short drum solo leads into the song.

> *"I was working in the lab, late one night*
> *When my eyes beheld an eerie sight*
> *For my monster from his slab, began to rise*
> *And suddenly to my surprise*
> *He did the monster mash*
> *The monster mash, it was a graveyard smash*
> *He did the mash, it caught on in a flash*
> *He did the mash, he did the monster mash ..."*

Opposite the DJ, Harcourt and MacArthur sit stony faced. Not discouraged by their demeanour, Riders smiles at them and pumps his arms up and down to the music. Harcourt whispers across to his friend. "I get the impression, Sherman, that this gentleman is not going to take us very seriously. To be expected I suppose."

"I agree," replies MacArthur, "we just need to remain professional and at least we have a chance to get the message out there and maybe someone will call in with useful information."

They sit patiently. When the song draws to a close, Riders gestures to them to put on their headsets whilst the producer switches on their microphones. The last lines of the song repeat and fade out. 'Wa hoo, monster mash, wa hoo monster mash, wa hoo monster mash.'

Leaning forward Riders makes direct eye contact with Harcourt whilst addressing his unseen audience. "Now it seems that we may have our very own local monsters. Regular listeners may recall in our show last week, that we had several guests reporting all sorts of strange happenings in, and around, sleepy little West Ayton. Were they all conspiring to create a clever prank to fool us all? Well, it's not April the first and it seems that we have two experts from across the pond who have come over to investigate these claims further. Mr Septimus Harcourt and Mr Sherman MacArthur. Welcome gentleman."

Both men thank Riders for the opportunity to speak on the subject after giving a general hello to the listeners.

"Thank you, gentlemen, for sparing time in what must be your busy schedule to talk to us. Perhaps before we start, and possibly take some calls from listeners, you could both explain your own qualifications and background."

As the two Americans give a potted history of their

work to the listeners, Riders looks down at his notes but nods politely to indicate he is listening. Once they have finished, Riders looks up and asks his guests to clarify, for the benefit of the audience, what cryptozoology entails. Once Harcourt has finished his explanation, Riders asks MacArthur to give some detail about Area 51. Both Americans confirm that they are happy to answer questions from the listeners, allowing Riders to invite the audience to call in.

"Okay gentlemen, the switchboard is already alight like a starry night. Before we take any calls let me explore what you believe is going on. Let's start with the alleged sighting of this big hairy creature you call Bigfoot. Have you seen it yourselves?"

Adjusting his waistcoat, Harcourt leans into the microphone. "If you mean, have I ever personally seen a Bigfoot, I believe I have had glimpses on three occasions when investigating in the Appalachians. Added to that, I certainly have seen footage which is very convincing. I have also examined a wealth of evidence including footprints in the ground, casts taken by other witnesses and photos of footprints from eyewitnesses around the world. There is also an extensive library of vocalisations which I possess, both from my personal investigations as well as those from others who work in the same field."

Smirking with a sceptical glint in his eyes, Riders asks, "Vocalisations, are you saying these creatures can talk?"

Waving away the suggestion and giving a good-natured laugh, Harcourt replies. "No, no, no Mr Riders. No one believes they speak English or French, Chinese, or Russian for that matter. It is, however, thought that they have their own form of communication which linguists would recognise as a form of language. By vocalisation, we mean recordings of sounds that cannot be attributed to any other animal or even humans in the vicinity."

"You say that, but couldn't these sounds just be other animals such as bears, coyotes, wolves or the like?"

With a forced chuckle of condescension, Harcourt responds. "There are many wildlife professionals who have become experts at classifying and understanding the acoustic repertoire of animals. Highly educated members of the scientific community have examined recordings given to them. There are even software applications that have been developed for this purpose. Whilst certainly many recordings, when subject to analysis, are revealed to be a case of mistaken identity ..."

Smelling blood, Riders interrupts, "Such as ... what examples do we have, which animals?"

Irritated at the interruption to his flow, Harcourt regains his composure and responds. "A few, for example, coyotes are often identified as the culprits. But my point is, setting aside the known errors and claims from over-exuberant investigators, a significant body of recordings are classified as unknown. In other words, no known animal can be identified as creating the sound."

"Okay, fair enough, but surely if these creatures exist, they would have been discovered with all the technology we now have at our disposal. There would have to be large numbers of these creatures to ensure that their survival is viable and therefore would surely be discovered by now. How do you explain that?" challenges Riders.

Unperturbed, Harcourt leans back casually to settle into the discussion. "You'd be surprised how much remains unknown and undiscovered. Hundreds of species of animal and plant life are discovered for the first time every year."

Riders laughs off the comment. "Yeah, maybe bugs and plants may go unnoticed in remote areas but not eight-foot creatures stomping around the place. Come on Mr Harcourt, really?"

He had seen and heard it all before. With engineered calmness in his voice, Harcourt fires another condescending smile at the DJ. "Yes, really, Mr Riders. In 2017 the Tapanuli orangutan was discovered in a Sumatran forest. These are not bugs or plants, they can grow to almost five foot and weigh up to two hundred pounds. In my own homeland there are vast areas of remote and barely explored wilderness across the American continent."

"Okay Mr Harcourt, you may have a point, but we are in the United Kingdom. We are not the Amazon or the Appalachians. We are a little island. We don't have a jungle over here. So why would you waste your time in England?"

"I believe that intelligent thinking retains an open mind. If something has been seen and there is no rational explanation forthcoming, then any investigation should proceed without prejudice. I accept that England is a small country, but new animals are discovered even here. Setting that aside, there are others in my field that have more esoteric theories."

"Such as?"

"Well, Mr Riders, some believe that Sasquatches are from another dimension. A well-known researcher of paranormal activity, a Mr William Hall, began his research on UFOs and aliens now contends that many classic signs from these encounters, including Bigfoots, have startling similarities."

"Such as?"

"Sudden appearance and equally as sudden disappearance. Fast movement of beings or unidentified objects, strange lights, orbs and so on. Many believe that these creatures enter through multi-dimensional portals.

Even NASA has recognised that magnetic portals may be real."

With exasperation and disbelief evident in his voice Riders says, "You have got to be kidding me, Mr Harcourt – *portals!*" He is momentarily distracted by the gesturing of the producer.

"Okay listeners, now you have heard it all. My lovely producer has pointed out that our board is alight with calls. On line one we have a Mr Duncan Holden. You are on air Duncan, what's your opinion?"

"Bloody ridiculous, Norman. Never heard so much claptrap in my life. Big hairy creatures coming through portable toilets. The man's a bloody idiot. Is he for real?"

Scratching his head, Riders tries to process the comment. "Sorry Duncan, what's this about public toilets? I think I missed that."

"It's what that Yank said, 'e reckons that they appear in port-a-loos. Never mind other blooming dimensions, what universe is he from?" asks Duncan with righteous indignation.

"Duncan my friend, thank you for the call but I think you have the wrong end of the stick. To be fair to Mr Harcourt he was not talking about portable toilets, he said portals, not port-a-loos."

"Portals my arse," exclaims Duncan in a final act of defiance before he is cut off.

Not missing a beat, Riders goes to another call. "Alright, on line four we have Len Legget. You're on Len. What's your thinking?"

"Cheers Norman. My thinking is that it's all bollocks. It's either an escaped monkey from a local zoo or a bunch of silly buggers prancing around in costumes. Much more likely than inter-demented beings messing around scaring people. If they had the power to go between different worlds they would hardly nip into some woods in North Yorkshire, scare a couple of gullible idiots and then bugger off back to whatever world they came from. Now, would they?"

"Inter-demented? I think you meant 'inter-dimensional,' but you are clearly a man who talks sense. At last, the voice of reason. Good point Len. Any comment on this Mr Harcourt?" asks Riders.

"Well Mr Legget, I would say that we, as well as a local reporter, have looked into the escaped monkey theory and it seems that, according to officials at the nearest zoos and wildlife parks, that no animal has escaped."

"They would say that, wouldn't they? Scared of losing their jobs," retorts Legget.

"I really cannot comment on that, Mr Legget. I can only report what I have been told in, what I assume is, good faith. As to your other point about people in costumes, it's certainly possible, and we're not ruling anything out when we undertake our night investigation. We've been known to catch a few pranksters in our time."

Riders interjects, "Unlike Bigfoots."

"Pardon?"

"I am just pointing out that you may have caught pranksters, but you don't seem to have caught what you are looking for in these night investigations which to people, such as myself and Mr Legget, is no big surprise. Anyway, let's move on. If people think the idea of hairy monsters roaming around the Yorkshire Moors and Dales is ridiculous then what about the other claims. Skinny beings with large eyes from outer space. What are your thoughts on that? I understand you are the expert in this area Mr MacArthur." An expression of smug cynicism cloaks the face of Riders.

Half saluting, MacArthur takes up the mantle. "Yes sir, thank you, sir. I would be happy to answer any questions."

"Listeners would probably be interested in your background. I understand you are a military man who has worked in the infamous Area 51. For our listeners out there, Area 51 is the epicentre for aliens. Or at least the epicentre for conspiracy theories. Until recently the US Government even denied the facility exists."

"I am duty bound to comply with regulations limiting my ability to disclose certain details, but I can reiterate the information that has been declassified and released into the public domain. Is that acceptable Mr Riders?" Riders nods and MacArthur continues.

"I worked in security at the facility and can confirm some of the program work examined unusual phenomena. In particular, the Pentagon has made public the knowledge that Area 51 does exist and within it a government funded program is active to analyse anomalous aerospace threats. A team of trained analysts have interviewed test pilots who, whilst flying state of the art military aircraft, claim to have seen strange anomalies in the air space above the facility. Many pilots captured video evidence of these anomalies with their on-board cameras to back up their claims thus proving what they saw was not just a trick of the mind."

"Trick of the mind?"

"Yes Mr Riders, these pilots are placed under significant stress when flying test aircraft at high speed."

"I see," says Riders, "sounds cool. It seems we have a young lady on the line who is keen to talk, her name is Nina. Go ahead Nina."

"Thank you, Mr Riders. I am the President of a university club called YETIS."

"Whoa, hang on Nina you are too late. Looks like you missed the bus. We have moved on from Yetis, Bigfoots and Sasquatches and are now discussing little green men."

"No, no Mr Riders, that is what we are interested in. YETIS stands for Yorkshire Extra-Terrestrial Investigation Society."

"Okay, my mistake, go on Nina. What's your question or comment?"

"Evening Mr MacArthur. I notice you use what sounds like military speak and I want to be sure that the government is recognising the existence of alien life. You referred to anomalous aerospace threats. This is government speak for alien aircraft is it not?"

"No ma'am. It is nearer to what members of the public might term unidentified flying objects rather than a definitive statement that what was seen by pilots, and captured on camera in some cases, was an alien aircraft."

Undeterred, Nina pushes the point further. "Have you seen any of the footage and, if so, would you tell us what you saw?"

"Yes ma'am, happy to. One video captured by the gun camera of the aircraft shows a white oblong object, perhaps twelve metres long and four metres thick performing a series of tumbling manoeuvres that in the opinion of analysts defy the laws of physics. There are many reports referenced by the government describing alleged UFO sightings including those produced by the Advanced Aviation Threat Identification Program."

After fielding a few other calls, mainly from listeners claiming to have seen monsters and aliens, Riders brings the session to a close to accommodate his next guest. DS Hardy brushes past Harcourt and MacArthur as they exit the studio and takes one of the seats that they occupied. Holding up three fingers, Riders indicates to Hardy that the advertisements have about three minutes to run before they are back on air. Slipping on his headset, the detective patiently waits for his cue from Riders who is busily shuffling through his program notes.

An excited teenager enthusiastically recommends a visit to Cowsheds Burgers which brings the advertising segment to a close prompting Riders to leap into action.

"We are back folks with a new guest. He is no stranger to our show and a regular on our weekly segment, *Cooperate With Our Cops*. So off we go, let's cooperate. Evening DS Hardy, what do you have for us today?"

"Thank you, Norman. I want to put out a request for information relating to the robbery of a local jewellers. In the early hours of the morning of July the second, a local business, Abrams and Friedman Quality Jewellers, was broken into and thieves escaped with uncut diamonds and assorted rings, necklaces, and bracelets. Camera footage indicates there were two suspects, wearing some sort of full head mask and bodysuit, who escaped on a motorbike. One was riding pillion."

"So, what are you looking for? How can our listeners help?"

"To date Norman, no witnesses have come forward so if anybody was in the area of the jewellers that night and saw anything suspicious – anything at all – please get in contact with us."

Riders announces to the listeners, "The number will be read out at the end of this item and can be found on our website."

"Yeah, thanks Norman. People may have seen the two men on the bike and may be able to give us more to go on. Even a description of the two thieves. I know they had masks but even details such as their size and body shape may help. Possibly a good description of the vehicle. Details such as size, colour, make and model. Maybe, someone saw them riding in a specific direction. Literally, anything people can think of could be vital."

"Anything else on the robbery, DS Hardy?"

"Yes. Your producer has kindly agreed to upload images of the stolen jewellery and if anyone recognises, or sees these, please get in touch. Some of the designs are quite unique. We have also put an image of the uncut diamonds on your website, but these are far less unique and recognisable from any other raw stones."

"Thank you, DS Hardy, and listeners, you are our eyes and ears to help keep the community safe. If you know anything, please get in touch. It is now time for the eight o'clock news."

Reaching up to remove his headset, Hardy notices Riders holding up his hand indicating he wishes the detective to remain. He settles back into his stool and Riders mouths a 'thank you' giving him the thumbs up. With the microphones switched off whilst the newsreader goes over the headlines next door, Riders mouths another 'thank you' and holds up one finger which tells Hardy that there is one other thing that he wishes to discuss. With a first date arranged at a local wine bar through a website, 'Mid Life Singles,' Hardy was hoping to do his bit and get out quickly, but it clearly was not to be. Frequent glances at his watch makes the three-minute news slot seem like an eternity.

"Hola folks, we are back. Listen people, I have asked DS Hardy to hang fast because he may have something to say about our earlier item. Word on the street, DS Hardy, is that you're in the monster and alien hunting business yourself. That you have been in West Ayton making your own enquiries. Tell us all, does the Yorkshire Constabulary have a secret section that investigates the X Files?"

The phrase '*for fucks sake*' drifts across Hardy's mind as he steels himself to answer with false bonhomie.

"Ha, ha, very funny Norman. But seriously, we have been asked to keep an eye on events."

"Oh, so the rumours are true DS Hardy. Perhaps you can catch the Bigfoot. Looks like the Americans have failed to date, ha ha."

Forcing a smile, Hardy responds. "Ha ha ha. No Norman. It's more a matter of community safety. If people are wandering around jumping out of bushes and scaring people, we need to be sure that the perpetrators have nothing more sinister in mind other than practical jokes. One or two villagers have been quite scared, so we're keeping an eye on things."

Hardy takes off the headset and taps his watch indicating he must leave. In response Riders gives him the thumbs up. Frantically texting his date to let her know that he is behind schedule, Hardy rushes through the studio door, winding his way along the labyrinth of corridors and eventually out onto the street. Studying his phone, he sees that his date has texted him back. No words, just an angry face emoji. Meanwhile, oblivious to the spanner he has put in the works of Hardy's predominantly barren love life, Riders continues with the show.

"Aaaand so – on with the show, listeners. I've dug out a classic by my favourite punk poet, John Cooper Clarke and what else would it be given tonight's discussion … yes siree, it's '*I Married A Monster From Outer Space*'."

Eerie rhythmic music precedes the strong northern accent of the poet, whose metronomic voice beats out the words.

"I fell in love with an alien being
Whose skin was jelly – whose teeth were green
She had big bug eyes and the death ray glare
Feet like water wings – purple hair
I was over the moon – I asked her back to my place
Then I married the monster from outer space …"

10

SITTING QUIETLY IN the passenger seat, DC Stanley has assessed his boss's mood very quickly. He has barely buckled his seat belt when Hardy speeds off with a slight screech of the back tyres. A curt 'hello' accompanied by a sullen expression and what was proving to be slightly aggressive driving, were enough signals to indicate to Stanley that he should avoid too much conversation.

Two miles from West Ayton, Hardy overtakes the Addinalls in their Mini Clubman startling them to the point where they almost veer off the road.

Stanley struggles for a neutral topic to ease the tense atmosphere, blissfully unaware of the angst his boss was feeling following the date last night. In fact, there was no date. The woman in question had decided that her potential suitor was not worth the wait and left shortly before Hardy rushed through the door of the wine bar, twenty minutes late.

Unable to bear the stony silence any longer, Stanley bit the proverbial bullet. "So, what's the plan boss? Why are we heading back to West Ayton?"

"We're going to do some good old fashioned detective work."

Struggling to formulate an appropriate and uncontroversial response, Stanley is beaten to the mark when his boss decides to elucidate.

"It seems that a couple of witnesses have come forward and saw a pair on a motorbike heading from Scarborough directly to the village on the A170. They were riding at high speed in the early hours of the morning. As we have precious little else to go on, I thought it would be worth making a few enquiries. You never know, someone may have seen them and can tell us more. Whilst we're here, we can also show a bit more community presence to keep the illustrious DI Parkins and his councillor mate happy."

Pulling into the carpark of the Old Plough, the detectives climb out of their car to begin what proves to be a fruitless and frustrating morning going in and out of local businesses, door knocking houses and accosting unsuspecting residents as they make their way along the High Street. They get very little information of interest other than ramblings about sasquatches, aliens, and mysterious lights. It becomes clear that the whole village is obsessed. At least they had shown their faces and provided a visible police presence as DI Parkins had requested, even if no one could offer any information relating to the two suspects on the motorbike.

Defeated, Hardy suggests they go to the Old Plough to get a bit of lunch before heading back to the station. Entering the bar, they are greeted by the landlord, Ken Wilkes. "Morning officers, you seem to be spending a lot of time here lately. What can I do for you?"

"We've popped in for a spot of lunch. What do you have?" asks Stanley.

"Steak pie, chicken pie, shepherd's pie, fisherman's pie … all with chips or salad," replies Ken.

"Anything other than pies?" asks Stanley hopefully.

The landlord shakes his head and stares expectantly for a decision. Both detectives order the steak pie and half a pint. Watching the beer being poured, Hardy, with the glazed look of a defeated man, decides to have one last attempt at getting a lead for the case.

"I wonder if you could help Mr Wilkes. We've been asking around the village if anybody has seen two individuals on a motorbike on the night of a robbery of a jeweller in Scarborough. Apparently, they headed to the village at high speed in the early hours of the morning on the second of July. Did you see or hear anything?" Shaking his head, the landlord flicks off the beer tap with the glasses full to brimming.

Placing the drinks on the bar in front of them, he gestures over to the table next to where Kenneth the Koala resides. Looking over his shoulder Hardy recognises the pair sat huddled together in front of a laptop and deep in conversation.

"Those two might have something useful to tell you. The Addinall sisters came in the other night all excited saying they 'ad seen something going on at the edge of the woods near the Scarborough Road. Those two over there went with them to investigate. Might be worth asking 'em? The pies'll be ready in about five minutes."

A faint glimmer of hope lightens Hardy's mood. "Cheers, appreciate it. I'll pop over for a chat."

"No problem."

The detectives take their drinks and sit at the table next to the two Americans. Engrossed in a document on the screen of the laptop, neither of the Americans notice their new neighbours. Leaning across, Hardy grabs their attention.

"Excuse me gentlemen, I wonder if you could spare me a minute."

Slightly startled, they both look up and acknowledge the detectives. "Of course, we saw you at the event the other night," says MacArthur. "What can we do for you?"

"I understand from the landlord that two ladies approached you, having seen some unusual activity in the woods near here."

"Yes, they did. It was the Addinalls. They came into the bar very excited and asked us to accompany them to the woods because they claimed to have seen two strange beings. Their description matched that of the two boys who reported a similar sighting. The boy's father told us their story in here the other night. I think his name was Mr Messruther and he recounted how his boys claimed to have seen extra-terrestrials."

"Did you find them?" asks Hardy, with a barely disguised hint of sarcasm.

Ignoring the tone of the question, Harcourt explains what transpired. "The ladies took us to the location where they saw the two figures. It was a short muddy layby on the side of the road. Whatever they saw, or thought they saw, was no longer there. All we found was some sort of tyre tread. Either from the wheel of a car or possibly a motorcycle."

With the suggestion of a motorcycle, Hardy's hopes rise. "Can you describe exactly where this is?"

"Yes sir," answers MacArthur. "As you leave the village onto the main road which I believe leads to Scarborough, the layby is about three hundred metres on the left just after a speed limit sign. You can't miss it."

Bingo, thinks Hardy. After thanking the two Americans, he returns to his barstool just as Dolly brings out their food. She places the steaming pies in front of them. Intuitively, Dolly guesses which order belongs to each detective. Hardy has the chips side order and Stanley the salad. Quickly dispatching their lunches, the two detectives drive out of the village and pull up to the layby. Hardy eases his car to the edge of the track and brings it to a halt, consciously trying to avoid driving over any tyre marks already there. With the passing of time and rain since the Americans examined the area, there was very little to see, but Stanley is convinced he can make out the remnants of a tyre mark.

"I think this is a motorcycle tread. It looks too thin for the wheel of a car."

Hardy agrees and they scour the layby for any further evidence, but the search proves fruitless. Taking a picture of the tyre mark using his mobile phone camera, Hardy turns to his partner. "Whilst we're here let's have a good look round."

They spot a clearing in the trees, finding that it leads into a well-used trail which they follow, scouring the ground and trees for anything unusual or out of place. No luck, so they decide to head back to their car. Stanley leads the way but, without warning, stops abruptly a few metres from the opening to the layby and holds up his hand. Gingerly he steps through the mud and reaches for a thin branch which is broken but still attached to the tree by a thin layer of bark. He examines it closely, with Hardy stood behind craning his neck over the shoulder of the young detective trying to see what is so interesting. Stanley turns round and holds up a clump of hair between the thumb and forefinger of his left hand. In his right hand he shows Hardy a thin strand of something they both find unrecognisable.

"What is that ... another hair or something else?" asks Hardy.

"Well, this is definitely hair, but it isn't human," says Stanley holding up the small clump between his finger and thumb. "But I've no idea what this is, it could be hair as well" he says, showing the unidentified strand.

"Good work Stanley. Someone or something has been through here. It's certainly an odd place to be wandering around so we may as well find out what this is. Keep them and we'll get the forensic boys to look them over."

Raising his eyeballs in exasperation, Stanely replies, "Dealing with Morgan again. That will be a joy."

⋅┼⋅┼⋅

Desmond Morgan manages the forensics laboratory and his irascible manner had led to a run-in with Stanley, who was investigating the murder case of the local vicar some eighteen months earlier. Older and wiser, Stanley had learnt that cajoling the scientist produced better results than his previous approach. Making petulant remarks about lengthy time taken to provide a report on their findings had not ended well for Stanley. Coming off second best, Hardy had to intervene to secure the scientist's co-operation. This time, Stanley follows protocol and steels himself to wait patiently for the results. Having done so, he is somewhat surprised to get a phone call the same day.

"Is that DC Stanley?"

"Yes," replies Stanley.

"Desmond Morgan here."

"Yes, Dr Morgan, I wasn't expecting to hear from you for some time. I know how busy your teams are."

"I have the samples you sent through for analysis in front of me but want some clarity as to what it is you need to know. What is the context and what are you hoping to find? Indeed, what exactly are you looking for?"

"Yeah, sorry Dr Morgan, let me clarify. We're undertaking an investigation into a robbery of a jewellers in Scarborough. The perpetrators may have made their escape through to West Ayton and possibly hidden in local woods. When conducting a search in the woodland, we found the samples we sent you and hoped that it may shed some light on the matter. Maybe down the line this may link these items to the perpetrators and the location, if we manage to apprehend them. It also happens that residents of the village have witnessed a few strange events in the area and thought if these samples were not relevant to the jewel theft case, then they may be connected to these events."

"And what exactly are these strange events, pray tell me?"

Heart sinking in the realisation that the conversation could go rapidly south, Stanley braces himself. "Well believe it or not Dr Morgan, locals claim to have seen aliens and Bigfoot. DI Parkins specifically asked us to investigate it."

"Bigfoot! You mean the mythical creatures that an unhealthy number of moronic Americans believe inhabit their wilderness?" asks Morgan with incredulity. "Are you telling me that you are using our resources to try to prove the existence of Bigfoot and that this is sanctioned by the Detective Inspector?"

Desperate to de-escalate the situation Stanley adopts a passive tone and tries to clarify. "No Dr Morgan. I don't believe DI Parkins gives any credence to these claims. He is more concerned about the incidences with villagers and wants to be sure that there is nothing more sinister than practical jokes or genuine misidentification."

"Well, you will be pleased to know that regarding the clump of hair we already have an expert opinion. No tests necessary because we have a zoologist on our team."

Unsure how to proceed with the discussion, Stanley asks "So, with the sightings that people are reporting, we wondered if they're seeing something like an ape that's escaped from the zoo?"

"No DC Stanley, not an ape."

"Or is it that the sample cannot be identified. Maybe an unrecorded creature. Maybe something like what they call Bigfoot?"

Morgan's hollow laughter echoes through the phone. "Bigfoot? No. It is not a Bigfoot. Not unless your Bigfoot wears a fox fur coat."

"Sorry, I don't understand."

"My team member instantly recognised the hair sample. She did her post graduate dissertation on the breeding ritual of Canis Vulpes and has spent hours watching hungry foxes work their way through local rodents, squirrels, and birds after an active session of 'how's your father'."

"Oh, I see." Desperate to change the subject, Stanley asks about the strand and Morgan is a little more circumspect.

"The other item is a little more challenging and we'll run tests to confirm but we think it is skin," says Morgan.

"Human skin?" asks Stanley, hopeful of a potential opportunity for a DNA match if the thieves are caught.

"No DC Stanley, neither human nor Bigfoot for that matter. We think it may be skin from the jute plant."

"Jute plant? Sorry, Dr Morgan, I've never heard of it."

"You may better know it as hessian. That rough material used for sacks amongst other things. It's hard wearing and used to transport produce such as tobacco, tea, and coffee. It has hundreds of other applications so I can't say what it might have come from."

"Oh, I see, hessian, of course, I understand" replies Stanley who didn't really understand what it was doing hanging from a tree branch. "Well thank you for calling so promptly, Dr Morgan. I will pass all this information on to DS Hardy."

"Good luck with your monster hunting," says Morgan facetiously, before ending the call.

Staring into space, whilst slumped in the chair at his desk, Stanley ponders the information he has just acquired from the police scientist. It seems that the harder they try the further they get from progressing, let alone solving the jewel robbery or even the bizarre events in the village. His rumination is brought to a jarring halt by Hardy who places a plastic beaker containing a muddy liquid that originated from the office urn marked 'Coffee.'

"Here you are, this should perk you up. You look as though you're daydreaming about young Agnes Hope," scoffs Hardy.

"Naw boss, just thinking."

"An encouraging development, we'll make a detective of you yet."

Forcing a smile at Hardy's not so humorous jibe, he takes a sip of coffee which causes him to wince. "Jeez boss, this stuff gets worse every day. Anyway, I just had a call. Believe it or not it was Morgan."

"What, forensics?"

"Yep, he was actually relatively civil and what's more, he had an answer to our queries about the bits of hair we found."

"Don't tell me. It's from a beast hitherto unknown to science and we have discovered the effing Bigfoot," says Hardy in mock wonderment.

"Not quite boss. That clump of hair is from a fox."

"Bugger, what about that weird long strand of hair?"

Scratching his pointed chin, Stanley replies. "They don't even think it is hair. They're not entirely certain at this point, but they think it is hessian. Y'know that rough stuff used to make sacks."

"Yes Stanley, I am aware of what hessian is. It's hippy cloth. So, another bloody dead end."

"Looks like it," replies Stanley, slumping further into his chair, "unless the Bigfoot's a hippy."

11

UNWITTINGLY, THE DATE of the night investigation oozes cosmic significance. Ancient culture assigns different names to the full moon throughout the year to track the months and seasons. In tune with the agenda of the investigation team, the moon obliges, offering up the Claiming moon, sometimes called the Harvest moon. Celtic lore names this moon to reflect the time of the year when communities gather herbs to use as dry remedies. Anglo-Saxons named it after the time for harvesting hay. It is the perfect moon for gathering and reaping what nature has to offer or, in the case of the investigation, evidence of the terrestrial … or extraterrestrial. The moon did not disappoint, and by the end of the night, the search for evidence bore some fruit.

Expedition night arrives, and it proves to be a long and eventful one for all concerned. And 'all concerned,' comprises of more than the two visitors from across the ocean. Four members of YETIS are present along with the Addinalls and Chris Ashton. Despite several attempts at a gentle push back, Ashton's neighbours were not going to take 'no' for an answer and had got the bit between their teeth having seen the alien lights. Overcome by the indomitable will and logic of the sisters, Ashton, who had also seen the lights when they dragged him to investigate a week earlier, had skin in the game. For Ashton's part, he eventually yielded to their entreaties, more so because he felt he could not live with himself if anything happened to them. He had no expectation of encountering aliens. More likely a stalker or even worse. It is going to be a few hours, he would never get back, but, in the end, he is happy to do it.

Gathering in the Old Plough, a few minutes before the allotted meeting time, the team sit patiently at two tables reserved by Dolly for the expedition. Next to them, Kenneth the stuffed Koala, seems to appraise them critically with his black beady eyes. Arriving precisely at 7.30 p.m., Harcourt and MacArthur sit at an adjoining table, and everyone shuffles their seats to face them.

"Welcome, welcome," says Harcourt brimming with positive energy and receiving murmured responses from the expectant hunters. MacArthur gives everyone a salute and then smooths his crew cut with a large, meaty palm. Satisfied everyone is present, Harcourt gets down to business.

"I seem to recognise everyone here from our previous event, but perhaps Sherman and I can refresh our memories with your names. I think I know you two ladies, the Addinalls."

"Yes, Mary my sister and I am Freda," replies Freda then points to Ashton who shrinks slightly in embarrassment at being drawn into the whole escapade. "And this is Chris Ashton, our neighbour, who has kindly offered to join us for security and protection," adds Freda with a chuckle of delight. Self-consciously, Ashton gives a subdued greeting.

"Chris also saw the same lights that we saw," says Mary as if to further validate their neighbour's presence.

"Excellent," declares Harcourt, whilst indicating for the people at the other table to speak.

"I am Nina, President of YETIS," and she gestures to the three young men at the table to introduce themselves.

"Scott."

"James."

"Zeltron."

Blinking in surprise, Harcourt does a double take. "Sorry, did you say 'Zeltron,' young man?" In contrast MacArthur stoically retains a straight face. Ashton smirks at the young man, who gives him a sideways wink in return.

With a wobble of his double chin, the largest member of the group sporting a complexion so pale it does not look as if it has been exposed to sunlight since birth, responds. "Yes, I was christened Brian but changed my name to Zeltron by deed poll." Noting Harcourt's confused expression, the student clarifies, "Zeltron is a Klingon name. I am also a member of the Trekkers Club at Uni. Y'know, Star Trek … James T. Kirk … beam me up Scotty and all that stuff."

"Aaaahh … oooh!," responds Harcourt momentarily stumped for words.

However, the 'Zeltron' can of worms had been opened and the young student had the bit between his teeth. "I can speak Klingon."

"Pardon," responds Harcourt.

"TlhIngan Hol Dajatlh'a?" asks Zeltron.

"Errr , sorry?" is the most Harcourt can muster.

"It means, 'Do you speak Klingon?'"

Keen not to discourage a willing team member, Harcourt responds. "Err no, but that will be useful if we encounter alien life forms, and they are Klingons."

"BIlughbe" responds Zeltron

"Sorry?"

Smugly Zeltron replies, "It means 'You are wrong.'"

"Oh, why is that?" responds Harcourt with increasing confusion.

"There are several dialects in Klingon. I can speak Krotmag, but if it's Morkan or Tak'ev then I have to say we are buggered." Zeltron sits back in his chair, smugly self-satisfied with his superior knowledge. Stunned, Harcourt stares at him.

With the momentary pause in discussion, MacArthur exploits the opportunity for a change of topic. He turns to the female group member. "Hi Nina, I think you told us that your group investigates extraterrestrial activity!"

"That's right, we're the Yorkshire Extra Terrestrial Investigation Society," confirms Nina.

Back in control, Harcourt takes the floor. "My first observation is that it seems to me that our team is well supported for those interested in the extra-terrestrial activity, but no one here seems to have an interest in the Sasquatch side of things. Where are those two men, I wonder, who claim to have seen the creature?"

In the hope of bringing the meeting to a close and getting, whatever they are supposed to do, done and dusted, Ashton clarifies. "You mean Phil Hayes and Colin Hendricks. On a nice warm summer night like this, I would guess they are in the copse on the west side of the field behind the pub. Quite possibly sampling the local horticulture. Before you ask, I mean the magic mushrooms which grow there. The worst kept secret in West Ayton."

Rising from his chair, Harcourt suggests, "Let us all take a quick bathroom break and then I will set out what we're going to do considering their unfortunate absence."

"I had a bath before I came out," says Zeltron.

Increasingly irritated with her team member's wit and fearful of getting the Americans offside, Nina gives a huff of exasperation. "I think that's enough Brian. They mean the toilet."

Retreating to the quieter sanctuary at the corner of the bar to discuss strategy, the two Americans are quickly deep in conversation. Ashton looks over to them smiling and then leans over to Brian. "I am guessing that you were taking the piss out of the Americans, or do I call you Zeltron?"

"Nah. Just wanted to get a rise out of them because they look like they are one hundred per cent Donald Trump supporters. I hate Trump. Added to that, Americans don't do irony, so it's entertaining to see them trying to cope with it." This prompts a wave of giggles from the rest of the group except Nina who tries to get them back on track. "That said, Mr Ashton, we do believe in the existence of alien life forms."

"But not Klingons?"

"Nah, not Klingons," replies Brian, who gestures to indicate that the Americans are returning and taps the side of his nose.

Having got the attention of all the expedition members, Harcourt announces the plan whilst dipping his hand into a rucksack that MacArthur is holding open for him. "I think we'll have three groups. Sherman and I will investigate the western side of the farm. I believe this is where the copse is located and the place, I am told, where our two friends who saw the Bigfoot seem to spend their time. The YETIS group should investigate eastern woods to the north and the Addinalls and Mr Ashton, you take the southern area of those same woods."

He pulls out two Walkie-Talkies. "I have only three so that is one for each group to share." Nina and Ashton step forward being the leaders of their respective groups, and each takes a device. Ashton confirms he has used one before and Nina gets a brief demonstration from MacArthur.

Harcourt continues his briefing. "Tonight is all about eyes and ears. We need to both keep a sharp eye out and, equally as important, listen for noises that are unusual and unrecognisable."

"Excuse me Mr Harcourt, what sort of noises?" asks Mary.

"It could be howls or wood knocks on trees which is a form of communication used by Sasquatch. If you see or hear anything unusual, take pictures and record noises on your phones. Then alert the other groups for support. Now, if we have no more questions, let's go hunting."

•|••|•

At the same time as the hunting expedition files out of the Old Plough, Kelly locks the door of his flat in York. He makes his way to the communal garage of the flats finding his partner, Doyle, sulkily waiting for him. Wheeling his bike out of the garage he gestures to Doyle to close the door behind him. Petulantly, Doyle slams the garage door shut. "Why do we have to wear these sodding Spider-Man suits again?" moans Doyle as Kelly mounts his Kawasaki Ninja.

"Just stop moaning and get on the bike. I know it's unlikely that anyone is going to be wandering around West Ayton woods at this time of night, but better safe than sorry. If we do get clocked and we're not disguised, then you'll be wearing a prison suit instead."

Clambering behind his partner, Doyle mutters to himself as the engine fires up and they speed off into the night.

•|••|•

All three groups involved in the night investigation split up when they reach the southwestern tip of Higginbottom's field, which they accessed through a gateway at the back of the garden behind the pub. The YETIS group and the Addinalls immediately head eastwards along the southern tip of the field, until the YETIS group then peel off making their way further north to their allotted search area. The Americans head directly towards the copse on the western edge of the field. Seeing the others disappear into the darkness, Harcourt taps Macarthur on his shoulder.

"I think, Sherman, it's time to break out the thermal camera."

Heeding his partner's instructions, MacArthur sets his rucksack on the ground, unbuckles the flap, and fishes out a camera. He switches it on and waits for it to power up. Once he examines the image created on the screen, and is satisfied that the camera is functioning, he gives Harcourt the thumbs up. They proceed through the lush, damp grass. In smooth, measured, sweeping movements MacArthur scans the field and soon calls for his partner to stop.

"Hold on Septimus, I've got a hit here, I can see large figures laid on the ground and they look big." Eyes screwed in concentration; Macarthur attempts to decipher the images on his screen which become clear when one of the beasts stand up from its prone position.

"False alarm Septimus, it's cattle. There are lots more. I can now see there is a whole herd out there to the northeast."

"Good work Sherman, keep the sweep going and let's head on further until we get to the copse where the Sasquatch was seen by Mr Hayes and Mr Hendricks."

"It is very quiet Septimus. I would have expected to hear more wildlife."

"I know but we're not back in the States, they don't

have coyotes here. We both know back home that unusual silence has often indicated that Sasquatch is in the vicinity but – less so, I think, over here. They simply don't have the volume and animal diversity that we have."

Affronted by the suggestion, a barn owl hoots and the cows moo in response. Three yards in front of MacArthur, Harcourt holds up his hand to halt progress and tilts his head to the side to listen more intently. "Can you hear that in the distance?" hisses Harcourt. "Sounds a bit like a scream and then a dog barking but somehow different. It does sound a bit like a coyote, but it can't be. Are you recording it on your camera?"

"Yes Septimus, I can hear it and it's being captured on the audio but there's nothing on the thermal."

Once more silence descends on the woods as the animals settle down. The pair press on until eventually they are within fifty metres of the copse.

"I think we are here, Sherman. Can you see anything on the camera?"

Almost immediately MacArthur confirms the presence of two images.

"What are they? Are they bipedal?" urges Harcourt.

"Hard to tell, I think they are either sat or laid on the ground."

"Cows, perhaps?" suggests Harcourt.

"No, smaller I think."

"Okay let's proceed quietly with caution," advises Harcourt, adopting a crouched position as he creeps toward the edge of the copse and hides behind a large tree.

"Still there Septimus, I still have sight of them on the thermal," whispers MacArthur, as he draws next to his partner. They listen intently and eventually can distinguish what sounds like a language being spoken.

Sat against adjoining trees, Hayes and Hendricks are coming down from their magic mushroom trip to discuss matters of great significance.

"Whoa man, that was cosmic," says Hendricks.

"Freaky man, did you hear that noise? Like a banshee."

"I did man, but it was no banshee. It was a Basil Brush," answers Hendricks.

Massaging his pale temples, Hayes tries to process what his partner is talking about. "Basil Brush? What you on about, man?"

"The TV fox, it was a puppet," explains Hendricks.

"You need help man, what's a talking puppet doing in the woods at night? You need to lay off the mushrooms mate."

"Naw Purple, I mean the noise, the banshee noise, was a fox. I was just joking about Basil Brush 'cause he's a fox, ain't he?"

"No idea mate, but I reckon it's time to head off. Do you wanna get something to eat?"

Shaking his head Hendricks says, "No mate, when I'm on the mushrooms I lose my appetite. They're not like dope."

"Yeah, I know," agrees Hayes. "But I'm beginning to look like a refugee from Belsen."

"What?"

"Belsen, that Nazi concentration camp."

Hendricks tuts in disgust. "No need to get heavy, man. Let's go."

With no small degree of effort, the two friends haul themselves into a standing position, albeit shakily. Once on both feet, they sway like human metronomes. But they are dragged from their stupor by the baritone American accent of Harcourt, causing both to jump backwards and turn towards the voice.

"Good evening gentleman, apologies if I startled you, but I believe you are the two men who have sighted the Sasquatch."

"Jeez man, you almost gave us heart failure. And what is he aiming at us?" complains Hayes pointing at MacArthur. Harcourt turns to his partner indicating that he should lower the camera.

"Nothing to be concerned about, it is a thermal imager, we are on our night expedition trying to track down the creature you both saw. Hopefully get it on camera. You know, the Sasquatch. We just wondered if you have seen anything unusual tonight?"

"Plenty man," answers Hendricks, "but it was probably the mushrooms. We can sell you some if you're interested?"

With a dismissive wave of his hand, Harcourt presses further in the hope of getting information. "Have you heard any unusual noises? We thought we heard some earlier. It was a sort of screaming then barking sound."

"We heard it, it was a Basil Brush," replies Hendricks.

"Sorry, a what?" asks MacArthur joining the conversation.

"He means a fox," clarifies Hayes, keen to avoid a trip down the path of the previous conversation. "The woods are full of them."

Disappointed, Harcourt turns to MacArthur, "I think that probably solves that little mystery, Sherman."

⁕⁕⁕

Across the field, directly east, the YETIS group arrives at their designated search area. All four are what rural people call 'townies' and find surroundings devoid of pavements, buildings, and streetlights, disconcerting. Alone at night in the woods is a new and unsettling experience for all.

"This is bloody hard work," complains Brian whose

whole body undulates when he half tumbles onto the ground and, with an ungainly wriggle, eventually works himself into a comfortable sitting position. "I'm knackered. Need a rest."

"The only thing you need mate is a few less burgers a week," says Scott sarcastically.

"Let's do a deal, I'll eat less, and you get a personality," retorts Brian.

"Am I the only one who is finding this all a bit creepy?" asks James.

Keen to stifle the rapid deterioration of team morale, Nina trawls her brain for the core team working principles listed in her 'Young Women in Leadership' course. "Now come on boys, let's be nice, we all need to focus on our common objective and not be distracted by individual needs. We must remain mission focussed. Don't forget, teamwork makes the dream work. There is no 'i' in team."

"True," says Scott, "but strictly speaking there is a 'me'."

"Sorry, what do you mean Scott?" asks Nina, a little thrown by this revelation. This was not mentioned in the leadership course.

"There is an 'm' and an 'e', is there not? This makes a 'me'," replies Scott smugly.

Looking directly at Scott, Brian adds his wisdom with the dual objective of supporting Nina and getting back at Scott. "True Scotty boy, but there is a 'U' in Cu—" His last expletive is drowned out by a piercing scream. Two foxes screech at each other.

"Oh my God, what the hell is that?" whines James.

"Dunno, but I ain't going to hang around here to find out," declares Brian, desperately trying to get his bulk back into an upright position.

"Me neither," adds Scott.

"Oh my God!" exclaims Nina.

"Whaaatttt?" respond the three boys.

Pointing north into the sky, Nina shouts, "Look there."

All four stare in disbelief.

•┃••┃•

With a slight skid, Kelly brings his bike to a halt in the same spot that they parked previously. Just out of sight on the side verge of the road to Scarborough. They dismount with the expectation of a quiet night, devoid of interfering locals sticking their noses into things that do not concern them. It was to be a ten-minute job to find the right spot, dig up the diamonds and get the hell outta Dodge. After that, they would get them safely to McCarthy and get him out of their hair.

No words are exchanged as both weave their way through the woods, each carrying a short-handled shovel. Breaking through the tree line, they look up and down the open field to get their bearings. Kelly points south and they scuttle along, hunched, hugging the boundary, shining their torches on the trunk of each tree they pass.

Gesturing for Doyle to stop, Kelly shines his torch onto a tree illuminating a small cross carved into its trunk. Lowering the beam, he reveals the broken ground showing Doyle that this was the spot that they were previously digging. The shallow hole with churned up soil remained exactly as they had left it a few days before. Continuing along the tree line, they examine each tree until Kelly gives a grunt of satisfaction. He shines his torch beam onto Doyle's carving who, recognising his handiwork, fist pumps in triumph before he walks to the tree and rests his back against the trunk. Carefully measuring out the required paces, Doyle rips off his head mask, throws it aside and drops to the ground digging furiously.

"What the hell are you doing Doyle, what if we get seen and you don't have your mask on?"

"Mate, half the problem last time was that I couldn't see what I was doing in the dark through these bloody eye holes. It's the black mesh. It's hard to see through. Don't stress, I'll be quick, and we can get out of here."

Clicking his tongue, Kelly says, "Mate, it was nothing to do with the Spidey eyes, the problem last time was that you started digging near the wrong fucking tree. Just get on with it."

⋅┼⋅⋅┼⋅

Ashton motions with his arm for the two sisters to stop. He turns to them, finger on his lips to signal that they need to be silent, which proves to be far too challenging a task for Freda, who whispers, "What is it, Chris?" This is greeted with a more emphatic vigorous shake of his hand which achieves the desired effect. With a firm order to stay put, the sisters move next to the nearest tree as if it will provide security and protection. Ashton proceeds alone, walking stealthily towards the field. He clicks the speak button on the Walkie Talkie.

"Septimus, Sherman, can you hear me?"

"Loud and clear," responds Sherman.

"I need you to get over here. There is definitely some activity near the tree line on the eastern edge of the field."

"We can also hear you Chris," interrupts Nina who had listened in to the conversation on her own device, "We will head down as well."

"Okay, I'll sneak up and check out who or what is making the noise."

Edging closer, Ashton hears the murmuring of voices before the two figures come into view. They are scrabbling on the ground and digging with small spades.

"Evening, what are you lads up to?"

They freeze and look up to Ashton. Both spring to their feet. "What the fuck do you want?" snaps Kelly through his mask. Doyle, having discarded his mask on the ground, does his best to cover his face with his arm.

"I asked first, now don't be rude. It's a strange place to be holding a Spider-man convention. Not to mention you're trespassing on private land. Don't you know you've been frightening the locals?"

"And who are you, Old MacDonald who owns the farm?" snaps Kelly.

"Hilarious, but I suggest you disappear off, using your Spidey powers. I don't want any trouble."

Lurching forward, Doyle takes a haymaker swipe at Ashton with his spade but falls well short of the target. The momentum of the swing twists Doyle's body to the side presenting Ashton with an open target for a swift and powerful kick to the kidney which leaves Doyle writhing on the ground. Sensing danger, and then movement in his peripheral vision, Ashton weaves to avoid a blow but is only partially successful. Kelly's punch does not hit him with full force but glances his temple causing him to stagger back. Trying to press home his advantage, Kelly swings a kick which is easily blocked by Ashton using his elbow which digs painfully into Kelly's shin. Squealing in pain, Kelly takes three steps back and hauls up his partner from the ground. Breathless, they both face up to Ashton. Rubbing his side, Doyle snarls threateningly at his adversary, but Kelly's scowl of hatred is hidden under his mask. Realising that he had lost his own anonymity, Doyle covers his face with his arm once more.

"There's two of us and one of you, just fuck off mate and you won't get hurt," shouts Kelly.

"You two look like the ones who are hurt," replies Ashton, smiling.

Kelly edges forward menacingly, but stops dead in his tracks when a voice emerges from the darkness.

"Is that you Chris? It's Sherman."

"And Septimus," adds Harcourt, "who's with you? We can see three figures on the Infrared."

"Don't know them, but they're in fancy dress," Ashton shouts back, all the while keeping his eyes trained on his two opponents. He flinches and tenses when they move, expecting another assault. The pair turn tail and flee into the woods.

"Looks like they are done for the night, they've run off," shouts Ashton who is greeted by two concerned faces as Freda and Mary waddle towards him.

"Oh my, oh my, oh my, are you okay Chris? Who were those horrible men?" asks Mary.

The question is left unanswered, because the two Americans emerge from the darkness of the field and make their own enquiries as to Ashton's wellbeing. They are quickly joined by the YETIS members with Nina, Scott, and James, jogging side by side towards them, with Brian lumbering twenty metres behind. The last to join the group.

"What were they doing?" asks Harcourt.

Pointing to a spot on the ground a few metres away, Ashton responds. "Not sure, they seemed to be digging in the ground just over there." MacArthur walks over shining his torch beam along the ground. Before thoroughly inspecting the area, he is distracted, kneels, picks up the discarded mask and returns to the group. Holding it aloft he declares, "This is all I could find and there is a patch of disturbed soil, but nothing else. Surely, they weren't trying to bury this?"

"I doubt it, Sherman, it makes no sense," says Harcourt. Looking through the thermal camera attempting to track the two fugitives he adds, "Whatever they were doing here, they have gone now."

MacArthur suggests, "Perhaps, as we have all the groups together, we should discuss what we found tonight."

Everyone murmurs their agreement allowing Harcourt to open the discussion. "On our part all we found was Mr Hayes and Mr Hendricks, but they had little to tell us. We know what happened here but what about the YETIS group?" Harcourt looks over to Nina expectantly.

"We did see something. We saw strange blue lights, moving around the sky further north. They were not aircraft but they seemed to move in close formation."

"Excellent, did you, by any chance, record them on your phones?" asks MacArthur hopefully.

Raising his hand in the affirmative, Brian gives his report. "I got a few seconds, but by the time I got my phone working they were disappearing into the distance and then were hidden by the trees. After that, the SOS call came over on the Walkie Talkie and we all hot-footed it here."

Setting up the video footage on his phone, Brian then passes it around the group. Once everyone has had a chance to review it Harcourt reconvenes the impromptu meeting.

"Thoughts anyone?"

"That's exactly the lights we have seen," says Mary with Freda nodding in confirmation behind her.

Subconsciously rubbing a growing bruise on his temple, Ashton agrees with the sisters. "Yeah, they look very similar to the lights I saw when I was out here with Freda and Mary a few days ago."

"I agree with Nina, these lights are not from any conventional aircraft that I am aware of. And I would also agree that, if they are from some sort of craft, then it is not a piloted aircraft developed with current human technology. Problem is that the lights were too far away and there is no reference point to gauge their size." says MacArthur.

"So, are you saying the lights are definitely from an extra-terrestrial spacecraft?" asks Brian.

"I cannot definitively make that statement Mr, er, Zeltron. In any case we would define it as a UFO not a spacecraft. I would need to examine the footage much more closely to ensure it's not something that we can identify such as weather balloons, headlights from a car, or the landing lights on an aircraft. If you can send me the video I will have a proper look," replies MacArthur.

Harcourt addresses the group. "Overall, I believe, it has been a worthwhile and productive night. We have video footage of the lights which is exciting." Holding the Spider-Man mask above his head he adds, "And I suspect we've solved the mystery of the alien beings. What we do not know is, what those two gentlemen were doing. Pranksters I presume."

"Nobody saw the Bigfoot either, so the whole thing sounds a bit of a failure," snipes Brian.

Shaking his head, Harcourt counters the negativity, "I am afraid Mr Zeltron, I cannot agree. We have the video and we have also achieved another objective of our investigations."

"Such as what?" asks Brian sceptically.

"We seek to find the truth. This means obtaining compelling evidence of the existence of Bigfoot and extra-terrestrial life but also, almost equally as important, debunking claims either made in error or with the intention to deceive. Those two gentlemen in the costumes clearly fit into the latter category. It also, incidentally, proves those two boys saw something and, although they were duped, they were telling the truth. Overall, I think the evening was a success and we should decamp to the Old Plough for a celebratory drink."

"I'm afraid that we'll probably have to call it a night. It's past closing time at the Old Plough and I personally need to get home and take a couple of aspirin," says Ashton. Nursing his temple which was already showing signs of swelling, he chose not to share his opinion that the Spider-Men were operating on an agenda a bit more serious than playing pranks.

12

EXAMINING THE BRUISE on his head the following morning Ashton notices, in the mirror's reflection, his Beagle sat patiently behind him with expectant eyes. "I think this is going to ruin my natural good looks for a while, what do you think Barry?" Tilting his head slightly to the side, Barry wags his tail in response. "Ah, sorry, I forgot, I haven't given you your post walk treat." Barking in anticipation, the dog follows him to the kitchen where his owner grabs a dog chew from the shelf and pops it into the Beagles mouth. Barry immediately turns and scuttles off to find a quiet place to demolish the treat without interruption.

Earlier that morning he had spoken to DS Hardy and offered to meet him in the Police Station to hand over last night's trophy, the Spider-Man mask. He accepted Hardy's counteroffer to meet at Ashton's house when he was passing through the village.

The doorbell sounds and Barry jumps to his feet dropping the chew in his rush to get to the front door and resume watchdog barking duty. Ashton opens the door and ushers Hardy into the kitchen where they take a seat at the small pine dining table. An offer of a drink is declined by Hardy who has already worked his way through three coffees that morning. Realising Hardy wants to get straight to business, Ashton leaves the table, opens the bureau, and returns to Hardy with the mask.

"What exactly is this?" asks Hardy.

"A Spider-Man mask," replies Ashton, who then takes the Detective through the whole encounter the night before.

"To be clear, Mr Ashton, you were participating in a hunt for aliens or Bigfoot, and you came across two men dressed as superheroes wandering around the woods. They were then so angry that you had discovered them, that they tried to assault you but had to flee when the rest of the group came to your rescue."

"Pretty much. One of them tried to hit me with a small shovel, but whilst I dealt with him the other one took a swing at me. I ducked and luckily only got a glancing blow," said Ashton subconsciously touching his injured temple.

"I can see that," replies Hardy, eyeing the bruise.

"By the time I cleared my head, the other one was back up and they were standing together spitting out threats. But when the rest of the group came to help me, they turned tail and ran into the woods."

"I see. Looks like you know how to handle yourself. I recall when we interviewed you regarding the murder of Vicar Dibley, that you'd spent time in the military service."

"Yes, that's right," confirms Ashton. "I called you because I thought I should report an assault directly to you, as opposed to going to the police station. You said at the Old Plough event that you'd been assigned to look into the strange stuff happening in and around the village."

"Yes, the monster hunting event! That was an interesting evening. But you're quite right, we have been asked to keep a lookout given the strange reports. My superior, who is a friend of Councillor Mandelson, is concerned that the sighting could be a precursor to a felony. Looks as if he is right. I guess this also clears up the report of aliens with big black almond shaped eyes." Hardy taps the mask on the table.

Again, Ashton subconsciously touches his bruised temple. "I have to say that I am sceptical that these two were just playing a prank. Their response when I disturbed them was, what I would describe as, over the top. They were extremely aggressive."

"I tend to agree with you Mr Ashton. Let me take a few more details, then I will get out of your hair."

•┼••┼•

Having thought and agonised long and hard, Kelly and Doyle decide their best course of action is to do something they rarely did when faced with the risk of McCarthy's wrath. Tell the truth.

Controlling their nerves, they sit facing McCarthy in his office at Dukes. Preparations are underway for the evening. A vacuum cleaner noisily reverberates in the main bar, permeating through the office door which breaks the increasingly uncomfortable silence. Having heard the tale of woe, McCarthy is wrestling with the urge to cause the pair significant pain, whilst his enforcer stands behind him with a face as stony as the silence. It is three minutes since McCarthy last uttered a word and continues to stare at them whilst he is processing his next steps. But it seems like an hour. Doyle nervously eyes the enforcer, whose muscle-bound body strains the seams of his suit.

The left side of McCarthy's brain is processing logical thought and holding at bay his emotional right side, which is urging him to hospitalise the two idiots sitting in front of him. As usual he must do all the thinking for the morons who surround him and has set his mind to formulating the optimum pathway for recovering the diamonds. A loud exhalation from the gangster indicates a conclusion has been reached. Kelly and Doyle are conflicted as to whether this is a good or bad sign.

"I will summarise what I think you have told me, and I don't want you to interrupt because you need to know that my patience is paper thin."

Kelly and Doyle nod to indicate their understanding and McCarthy continues. "You went back to get the diamonds last night. By the sound of it you could not have picked a worse night because the place was crawling with nerdy idiots chasing imaginary fucking monsters. You were disturbed by one of them who managed to get the better of the two of you. I won't even ask how one nerd managed to do this. You then ran off when other idiots came to the aid of the one idiot, who had got the better of the two of you. You didn't get the diamonds but think the idiot, who got the better of the two of you, probably dug up the diamonds and now has them. It seems to me that if a nerdy monster hunting idiot can take on the two of you and come off best, that you are in the wrong fucking business. Is my understanding right?"

Silence. Fearful expressions.

"You both can speak now. I asked you a question."

Kelly answers, "Yeah boss, but he took us by surprise and before we could deal with him all his mates rocked up."

Nose pointed in the air McCarthy asks Kelly, "Do you know what I can smell?"

"No."

Sniffing theatrically, "It's bullshit I can smell. If you feed me any more, Jason here will knock it out of you."

The enforcer remains expressionless.

Kelly and Doyle remain silent.

Drawing in a deep breath McCarthy continues. "Now

listen up because here is what we are going to do. I presume you would recognise this nerd in the light of day?" Kelly nods in the affirmative. "Good," says McCarthy. "The odds are that he lives in the village, so I need you to go for a looksee and find out who he is and where he lives. Once you do that, we'll pay him a visit and persuade him to return the diamonds to their rightful owner."

"What? The jewellers boss?" asks Doyle.

"No, you fucking idiot … me. Now piss off, time is short as will be your lives if you come back empty handed."

Rising from their chairs, the pair make their way to the door but are brought to a halt by McCarthy. "And one more thing, lose those bloody costumes. Now you've blown your disguise you'll get lifted by the cops in seconds."

"Yes, boss."

•┼••┼•

"Don't just sit there like a couple of melons, update me." DI Parkins leans back into his chair with low expectations. Stanley looks across to Hardy waiting for his boss to take the lead.

"We are making progress sir, but we are not there yet," replies Hardy.

"Go on," says Parkins, screwing his eyes doubtfully and scratching his pointed nose.

"As you know we've been keeping a high profile in West Ayton. Just as you requested. We were contacted by a resident, Chris Ashton, regarding an incident at night-time involving an assault in the woods behind the village. Two individuals appear to have been disturbed by Mr Ashton. It is unclear as to what they were doing but their response was violent which leads me to think that they were up to no good. After a scuffle they left behind this, which I think is of interest on two counts."

Digging into his jacket pocket Hardy pulls out the Spider-Man mask and places it on Parkins' desk. Shuffling forward Parkins snatches it up and examines it. "Go on Hardy."

"Firstly, we believe that these two characters, being dressed in Spider-Man costumes, are probably responsible for the sighting of aliens. Extra-terrestrial beings. The description given by local boys was of two figures with smooth bodies which matches how these men, dressed in these costumes, may appear in the dark. As you can see from the mask, the eyes holes are covered in mesh and are almond shaped. Again, in the dark they would appear as large shadowy eyes. They wouldn't see the whites of the eyes through the mesh."

"Okay, vaguely interesting and I am sure Councillor Mandelson will be relieved that his village is not being overrun by little green men from outer space, but I assume we don't have the individuals in custody to find out what they were doing. Perverts, muggers or whatever they are, they are still running loose. I suppose at least the fact they have been exposed may deter them from further nocturnal activity."

Leather squeaks as Hardy slides his weight to the edge of his chair. "But what is more interesting sir, is I think there's a connection between these two characters and the robbery of the jewellery store in Scarborough."

This causes Parkins to sit upright, his interest piqued. Impatiently, he gestures for Hardy to continue.

"You may recall sir that we obtained CCTV footage, and two individuals were seen riding at speed but there was not a great deal to identify them because of the quality of the picture. But, that said, they seemed to be wearing one-piece suits with no other distinguishing features. We've examined the video closely and I'm about seventy per cent sure that the two on the bike were wearing these costumes. I can't be certain because of picture quality, the light, and the speed they were riding. But they were heading in the direction of West Ayton. I think it is too much of a co-incidence and I believe they were possibly returning to Ayton because this is where they hid all the stuff they stole. Admittedly, it's a bit of a long shot but well worth following up."

"Mmmm, I wonder," replies Parkins, trying to process the facts and Hardy's theory. "I agree it's a bit of a long bow to draw but you did say their encounter with Mr Ashton was quite violent, which suggests that they have something to hide and the stakes are high. Your theory is certainly not out of the question. Good work. I think it is worth running this through forensics to extract DNA which may be useful as the case unfolds. Good work Hardy."

Beaming at rare but welcome praise from Parkins, Hardy exchanges glances with Stanley who finally chooses to contribute to the briefing. "We thought that it's possible, as the two suspects fled after their encounter with Mr Ashton, that they didn't finish their business and therefore the diamonds may be hidden somewhere in the woods. If this theory is correct, they'll almost certainly return."

Hardy takes over. "DC Stanley is right sir, so we are going to keep an eye on the village. We will ask around and encourage locals to report anything unusual. So, if they see two strangers are around the place with no obvious reason to be in the village, then we will encourage them to call us directly."

"Well done detectives. In the meantime, once the DNA is harvested from the mask let's see if it is matched to a profile on the National DNA database. You never know. If they've been involved in the robbery, then they're probably professional. They may have a profile on the database from a previous conviction. It's another long shot but worth a try I think."

"Anything else sir?" asks Hardy.

"Yes, one other thing. Get the boffins to scan the crime scene for DNA and see if any can be matched to that from the mask. Again, the chances of a match are slim, given the scene will now be highly contaminated with all sorts of DNA, but you never know."

13

LOST IN THE afternoon play on Radio 4, Betty sits behind her counter and barely notices the tinkle of the bell above her shop door. With the elegant demeanour of an ex-model, Julia Henson glides over to the counter and addresses the shopkeeper.

"Hello, and how is the owner of Betty's Provisions doing today?"

Wistfully, Betty replies, "Oh, I'm okay Julia, just lost in the play on Radio Four. But in truth I was just reflecting on the events last year. You know, the shooting of the vicar and the disappearance of Hairy Bob. I quite miss them both. So does Dolly for that matter. Bob had his own special seat in the pub next to the Koala." In a conspiratorial tone, Betty adds, "Between us, Dolly and me that is, we looked after Bob like a son. Although he was homeless, he was as much a part of the village as any other resident. A gentle and thoughtful man. Even the animals in the woods where he lived would have missed him I suspect. There were those rumours you know. Those about him being in the army and having PTSD. Some gossips even thought he was responsible for the shooting. Blooming ridiculous if you ask me."

"I agree Betty, Bob was a lovely man, as was Peter." says Julia, her eyes moistening. "And I so miss him, he was a wonderful and thoughtful man and much missed in the church."

"No bad looking too for a vicar," replies Betty, with a mischievous wink.

Blushing and smiling at the same time, Julia says, "Absolutely." Avoiding eye contact, she stares down at her arm, her slim fingers fiddle mindlessly with the sleeve of her pink, Bruno Cucinelli cardigan. Rumours about her affair with the vicar left unspoken, hanging aimlessly like strands of broken cobwebs.

"And how is Sebastian? Busy as ever sorting out everybody's financial affairs?" asks Betty.

"Yes, his business is thriving, thank you Betty. I must say that I'm not a big fan of all his clients. There is one horrible man who accosted us when we were having dinner at that new restaurant in Scarborough. A very rude, boorish man called Mr McCarthy. He's one of Sebastian's wealthier clients by all accounts. Lots of money but no manners. Anyway, don't need to bore you with the trials and tribulations of his accounting firm. I popped in to get some items for our dinner. I need mushrooms, garlic, two leeks and some onions please."

Watching Betty as she packs the items in a brown paper bag, Julia takes the opportunity for a subject change. "So, Betty, what do you think of all this mysterious stuff happening around the village? I have to say I have not seen anything unusual myself. No aliens, Bigfoots, lights or flying saucers."

Tutting cynically, Betty replies, "Lots of strange goings on, but I have to say I think the talk of aliens and monsters is all a load of old codswallop. I mean, this is Yorkshire, we don't have nonsense like that here, do we? I have no idea why those two American gentlemen would visit here and waste their time. I can't fathom it."

"I have to say that I agree with you," says Julia as she swipes her credit card, takes the bulging grocery bag from the counter. She says goodbye, her face between the stalks of the two leeks poking out of the top of the bag. Before she reaches the door, it crashes open and the Messruther twins spill inside.

"Careful boys, watch where you are going," chides Julia as she swerves to avoid them.

"Sorry, Miss," apologies Billy, "but we're in a rush, our batteries have run out."

Deciding not to engage further, Julia leaves, giving Betty a final wave. After calling back a 'thankyou' to Julia, Betty turns to the twins and smiles indulgently. She has grown fond of them over the last two years partially out of sympathy for their situation. *A terrible thing having had their mother abandon them leaving the father to cope on his own*, she thought.

"You two get through a lot of batteries. I'm nearly out of stock," she says. Noting the look of disappointment on the twins' faces, she gives them a beaming smile, "But you are in luck, I have four left which I kept back for you as you've been such good customers."

"Aww, cheers Betty," Ben smiles with relief. "You're the best." They pay and whisper to each other about their plans, unaware of the fondness in Betty's eyes as she watches them leave the shop.

·|··|·

Sitting at the table next to Kenneth the Koala, Ashton patiently waits with two pints of Guinness in front of him. He looks over to the front door seeing his friend enter and waves. Shuffling into the seat behind the second pint of Guinness, Steve smiles.

"I can now see you've resorted to mid-afternoon

drinking since you've retired," jokes Steve, as he takes a sip of the stout.

"Thanks for coming, Steve. Did they let you out of Fylingdales early then?"

"Well, it's official business you could say. You asked me to investigate reports of unidentified flying objects, so I did and here I am. We're here to serve and protect you civilians, are we not?"

Ashton grins at the sarcasm of his friend. "And God help us if we have to rely on you lot, especially if we are invaded by aliens."

"Now, now Mr Ashton, that's no way to talk to a senior officer in charge of the nation's security. So how is your alien and monster hunting going? You told me on the phone that a couple of yanks were wandering around the place trying to hunt them down."

"That's true and to be fair to them it was lucky for me that they were. I was out on what they call a night investigation, and I got accosted by a couple of idiots in the woods behind here." Ashton points to the rear of the bar.

"Hang on, hang on mate," says Steve with a chuckle. "What's this about a night investigation? Indeed, what type of night investigation?"

"I knew I should have kept quiet. Yeah, you can take the piss, but a couple of local ladies, my neighbours, asked me to accompany them. They'd seen the lights and wanted to take part in what the yanks call a 'night investigation' where they go looking for more evidence of the lights, aliens, monsters, and whatever else people claim to have seen. These ladies are no spring chickens and I didn't want them wandering around alone. They might have got hurt and, as it turns out, I was right to be concerned."

"Go on mate, I'm intrigued," encourages Steve who takes another swig of his stout.

"Everyone split up for the search and I was with the two old ladies. After about half an hour of wandering around fruitlessly, I heard a noise. So, I held them back and went to investigate and found a couple of idiots scrabbling about in the field dressed as ... guess what?"

Scratching his cheek, Steve gives it brief thought and offers a guess. "Dressed as aliens?"

"In the words of our American cousins, close but no cigar. Get this, they were dressed as Spider-Man," laughs Ashton.

"Spider-Man! Spider-Man?"

"Spider-Man," confirms Ashton, grinning.

"What, both of them?" asks Steve.

"Yep, both. Anyway, one of them starts threatening me and takes a swing with a shovel so I had to take him down. Then the other one takes a pop at me, just here," explains Ashton pointing to the bruise on his temple. Luckily, I ducked and avoided the main brunt of the blow, but the yanks and the rest of the 'hunters' came on the scene and saved the day."

"What about the Spider-Men?" asks Steve.

"They took off into the woods as soon as the others got close. I was too dazed to follow."

"Yer getting on I see. In the old days you'd have got out of the way of the haymaker and sorted them both out," retorts Steve, smiling.

"Maybe, but we all concluded that at least the mystery of the alien sighting was solved. Dressed that way in the dark they could easily have been mistaken for something else, such as aliens. Especially if seen from a distance. Those large dark almond eyes in the masks match the description of the sighting days earlier by a couple of local kids."

"Okay, what does that leave us with then? Mysterious lights and Sasquatches. How are you and your team of intrepid night hunters going on that score?"

"I was hoping you could tell me, given what you said on the phone."

Tapping his nose, Steve says, "I can't offer anything that involves the Sasquatches, but I think I have a theory about the lights."

Surprised to feel a little excited by the revelation, Ashton asks, "Really? Have your experts looked at the recording I sent you and identified what they are?"

"Not with absolute certainty. No, to be honest I cannot say that. But they have come up with a very credible explanation."

"Okay, fire away."

As his friend explains the theory, Ashton sips his beer listening intently to what the military scientists told his friend. He nods but asks no questions coming to the realisation that the mystery may be solved. Steve drains his glass.

"Right mate, I have to get off, but nice to see you and I hope that helps."

"I think it will Steve and I think I now know what to do when the lights next appear."

Shaking hands, Steve rises and calls back as he leaves, "Good luck, let me know if the boffins are right."

Ashton gives his friend the thumbs up.

14

FOUR FINGERS DISAPPEAR, one by one, as the producer's hand transforms into a fist, giving Norman Riders a visual countdown through the studio window. When the producer points at the DJ, the show commences.

"Heellooo listeners, welcome to *Riders Brings a Storm*. It's the evening show that's cooler than a polar bear's fridge, with the host with the most. And do we have a show for you tonight. I'll be bringing you the hottest music mixed with the hottest stories on this steamy summer night on the east coast. We welcome back our American guests tonight after this classic tune which is my personal dedication to them. It's from the Boss himself."

Riders flicks a button, and the music starts.

> *"Born down in a dead man's town*
> *The first kick I took was when I hit the ground*
> *You end up like a dog that's been beat too much*
> *Till you spend half your life just covering up …*
> *Born in the USA…"*

Riders looks over his console at his two guests waiting patiently on their stools and then motions for them to put on the headphones. They oblige and listen to the music. MacArthur runs his hand over his crew cut whilst rolling his eyes upwards to his colleague. Harcourt returns the expression with a knowing wink and massages his goatee. Prompted by the fading final lyrics of the song, Riders sets aside his program schedule and springs into action.

"Can't beat the Boss, listeners. Born in the USA, and so were my two guests, the monster hunters extraordinaire and experts on the other worldly. Welcome Mr Harcourt and Mr MacArthur. For the benefit of those listeners unable to tune in the other night I'll remind you of why our two guests from over the pond are visiting lil 'ol Yorkshire."

Harcourt winces at the DJ's attempt at an American accent and it is his turn to raise his eyes skywards.

"Yes folks, Mr Harcourt is a cryptozoologist. That means he hunts after imaginary beasts such as the Loch Ness Monster and Bigfoot. His partner in crime here is Mr MacArthur who specialises in tracking down aliens. They were my guests the other night to talk about their work in West Ayton amidst the sightings of aliens, Bigfoot, and space craft. For one final time they have very kindly come into the studio to share their findings. We'll have a discussion but feel free to call in if you have any questions and comments. So, gentleman, did you catch Bigfoot?"

"Thank you for having us on your show Mr Riders. It's a pleasure to talk to you and your listeners for one final time before we fly back home." Harcourt smiles and pauses for his partner to give his greeting. "Likewise, Mr Riders, it's been a pleasure," says MacArthur.

Taking a deep breath, Harcourt addresses the question. "Caught Bigfoot? Possibly. We have caught some sounds which merit analysis because we're not clear as to their origin. They could, of course, be local wildlife. Whilst back home we would have no problem distinguishing the calls of coyotes and bears, over here we don't have the same depth of knowledge of the sounds that emanate from indigenous creatures."

With a mischievous glint, Riders strikes to exploit the vulnerability of the answer. "Seems like a long-winded way of saying you didn't catch the creature."

Unruffled by the jibe, Harcourt responds. "Well, as I said, we caught unusual sounds on a recording which merit further investigation and analysis, but we did not capture a visual on camera."

"Is that all?"

"Not entirely, Mr Riders. I believe the police investigating a crime in the area found a hair sample that they have sent for analysis along with an unusual long hairlike strand. But I am afraid they've not shared the results with me at this moment in time. Perhaps you could follow up with them if they're willing to divulge the results of the testing."

Giving a hollow laugh for the benefit of his audience, Riders says, "So, no Bigfoot in Yorkshire then, surprise, surprise. We have a caller on the line who I believe called in last time you were on. It's Duncan Holden. Hi Duncan, what's your question or comment?"

"Seems to me that these two yanks are talking out of their arses."

"Careful, watch your language, Duncan, or we'll have to cut you off," warns Riders.

"Sorry Norman, but you know what I mean. Last time they reckoned that these things appear in public toilets."

"Ha ha. No, seriously Duncan. I think we explained before that they were talking about portals, not port-a-Loos. It's a sort of gateway to another world or dimension. That's the portal, not the portaloo, ha ha."

"If I can interject," says Harcourt before the discussion deteriorates further. "Perhaps I can elucidate. I was merely recounting a theory which explains their uncanny ability to avoid discovery. Neither I nor Mr MacArthur necessarily subscribe to this theory. We like to work on obtaining hard indisputable evidence."

"Of which you have none," responds Holden.

"Hear, hear," adds Riders.

"Wot about them aliens then?" asks Holden.

MacArthur takes the reins. "Yes sir, we do have something to report. We believe we have resolved this claim. During the night investigation we stumbled across two individuals dressed in costumes. Given that the witnesses of the 'alleged' aliens originally saw the figures at night-time as well, we believe that they mistook these individuals for extra-terrestrial beings. With the poor light coupled with what these individuals were wearing, it's an understandable mistake. We believe, sir, that the sightings were genuine and well meaning, but it was a case of mistaken identity."

"Sorry, I don't understand, are you saying two people were in fancy dress? That they were dressed as aliens?" asks Riders.

"No sir, not quite. The description of large black almond shaped eyes, smooth bodies, and no visible hair, plus the fact they saw two figures as well, fits the description of the two individuals we encountered during our night expedition," answers MacArthur.

'Sorry mate, still not with you. If they were not dressed as aliens, what were they dressed as?" responds Riders more confused than ever.

"Spider-Man sir," repeats MacArthur.

"Spider-Man?"

"Yes, Mr Riders, Spider-Man."

"What, both of them?"

"Yessir Mr Riders, both of them," confirms MacArthur.

"Didn't 'appen to see Batman as well?" asks Holden, sarcastically, having remained on the line.

"No sir, just Spider-Man," replies MacArthur, not really grasping Holden's irony.

With a growing sense of dismay at the downward spiralling discussion, Harcourt tries to wrest back control. "If I may, once again, interject, perhaps I can make a crucial point. Sherman and I are professionals, and our interests are grounded in lived experience and hard evidence. It is just as much our role to debunk claims, whether made vexatiously or through genuine error, as to blindly attempt to prove them. We are after the truth. We do believe in what we do and have collected mounds of evidence and it is our life's work to ensure the truth becomes common knowledge and accepted. To achieve this, we must also uncover and make public any instances when the facts have been misrepresented or misleading. I hope that makes sense. In many ways, this is just as much a 'win' as finding genuine evidence of the existence of what we're searching for."

Harcourt leans back, satisfied with his speech and confident he has educated the public. His confidence is ill founded.

"Okay, if not Batman, how about the Phantom?" asks Holden who clearly did not take in a single word uttered by Harcourt.

"No, Mr Holden, no, we did not find the Phantom, nor Batman, nor Robin, nor Superman," responds Harcourt with exasperation. "Just two individuals dressed as Spider-Man."

"Did you catch them, or did they escape using their spider webbing?" asks Riders, sensing blood and determined to get a rise out of the American who he found a little too pompous and smug for his liking. However, Harcourt was not taking the bait.

"As it happens Mr Riders, once challenged, the two individuals fled, but I understand that the police are keen to interview them."

"I thought Spider-Man was on the side of the law," suggests Holden, who doggedly stays on the line.

"Quite," responds Harcourt refusing to be drawn in further and thereby leaving a moment of silence on the airwaves which Riders rushes to fill.

"Okay listeners, stay tuned, we just have a sponsor's commitment to fill then we will be back to wrap up this interesting discussion."

The advertisement plays, the producer cuts off the line to Duncan Holden and Riders leans back in his chair slightly exposing his belly, which hangs over his faded jeans. He gives the thumbs up to the Americans who sit quietly, stony faced.

Over the next two minutes the listeners learn that the best kebabs, burgers, and pizzas can be found at Mustafa's Food Bar. Very few members of the public were aware that Mustafa's real name was Frank Hardcastle. His swarthy complexion and drooping moustache allowed him to pass for someone who may have been born in more exotic climes than his home in Edgehill Housing Estate in Scarborough. Otherwise known as cardboard city.

"Okay listeners, we are back. And with us in the studio are Mr Harcourt and Mr MacArthur. Monster and alien hunters extraordinaire all the way from the U, S of A. To recap we haven't really solved the mystery of the Bigfoot sighting, but we have solved the mystery of the aliens. Pranksters in Spider-Man suits apparently. So well done gentleman for solving that riddle. It just leaves one other thing, the mysterious lights."

Harcourt comes out fighting. "In this regard we do have the visual evidence that you were craving earlier. Would you like to see it?"

"Well, you heard it first listeners, we have visual evidence. I am afraid it will be like those cookery shows on TV where they taste the food and tell you how yummy it is, but you'll never know. What I will do is I'll get the guests to show me, and you'll just have to trust what I say but I promise our illustrious producer will get a copy and put it on our website after the show."

With a few taps and swipes on his mobile phone, MacArthur reaches over the console to hand it to Riders who busily describes what is happening for the listeners. "Right, so I have Mr MacArthur's phone and he has put on a video, and I have to say that there are indeed lights, and I also must admit that they are, indeed, strange. Almost hypnotic and they don't look like any normal aircraft lights to me."

Perplexed by what he is seeing, the airwaves once more fall silent and it is MacArthur, this time, who fills the void. "So, what we have here are four blue lights, hovering above the woods near West Ayton. The video was taken by a group of students who assisted us on the night-time investigation. We will be getting the video analysed by aeronautical experts back in the States to see if they can shed light on the matter. No pun intended," says MacArthur who surprises himself by cracking a rare joke.

Having had time to examine the footage, Riders regains control of the discussion. "All I can say listeners, is that I don't know what these lights are, but they don't look like aircraft to me. At least not like any aircraft as we know it. No plane or helicopter could replicate those movements. Strange indeed. Perhaps viewers have some ideas. Line one, it's Lynn."

"Fireflies, I love them," offers Lynn.

"Nope Lynn, too big, too blue and the way the lights are moving they would have to be kamikaze fireflies."

"Line four, we have Fergus."

"The lighthouse, it's the beam from the lighthouse," suggests Fergus.

"Sorry Fergus, you can't see Scarborough lighthouse from West Ayton. Besides which, there is only one lighthouse, not four as far as I am aware. Also, lighthouses, like pigs, can't fly."

"Line five, we have Duncan. Is that you again Duncan, is that Duncan Holden?"

"Yep I'm back, is it 'The Ray'? Y'know, the light powered superhero in DC Comics. Ha ha."

"Very funny Duncan, did you look that one up? Admire your persistence, but I think we've done the superhero joke to death this evening."

Riders allows a few more calls and ideas eventually fade out. "Well I would like to give a big thank you to our guests, who I understand are heading back home in a couple of days."

"Our pleasure," replies Harcourt.

"Yessir, pleasure," confirms MacArthur.

"As our guests leave let's see them out with an old John Denver classic."

The pair are escorted out of the studio by the producer, as the intro to the song bursts into its opening lyrics.

"Almost heaven, West Virginia
Blue Ridge Mountains, Shenandoah River
Life is old there, older than the trees
Younger than the mountains, growing like a breeze
Country roads, take me home
To a place where I belong …"

14

BREAKING THROUGH THE lush green foliage of the trees, golden orbs of sunlight flicker between the leaves as they rustle in the warm summer wind. Oblivious to the tweets, warbles and shrill songs of the birds bathing in the sun, Ashton pounds the track through Forge Valley with his Beagle trotting behind him. Both man and dog are beginning to breathe heavily as the morning run is coming to an end. With the track exit in sight, which leads on to Forge valley lane, Ashton slows, draws to a halt, and turns off the music throbbing through his earbuds. Barry gives out a grateful bark, thankful that the run has slowed, and then lays on the ground in rebellion. He looks pleadingly at Ashton.

"Okay Barry, we'll walk the rest of the way. It's either too hot for you or you are just getting old. Not sure which." Barry's stare of admonishment seems to convey that he was not the only one getting old. Another shrill bark at his owner is enough for Ashton to get the message and he reaches into the pocket of his shorts to dig out a 'post run' treat. Flicking it in the air, Barry catches it effortlessly and swallows it in one smooth movement.

"You might want to try chewing on occasion mate."

At the end of the lane, Ashton looks over into the car park of the Old Plough and sees the two Americans lifting their luggage into the boot of their hire car. Scooping up Barry in both arms, he gently lowers him over the low stone wall and then vaults it effortlessly. Harcourt's attention is drawn by Barry's cheery bark, and he waves to Ashton who calls over as he approaches.

"Hi there, are you gentlemen leaving?"

Smiling, Harcourt says, "I'm afraid so Mr Ashton. Our work here is done as far as time and money allows and we must make our journey to Heathrow airport, drop off the car and fly to New York."

"Yessir," adds MacArthur, "it has been a pleasure sir and thank you for your help in our investigation."

"Not sure I did a great deal to be honest."

Pointing to the fading bruise on Ashtons temple, Harcourt jokes, "Well I beg to differ, after all, you took one for the team and uncovered the truth behind the mystery aliens. That will be a story I will tell many times to my colleagues back home. The Yorkshire Spider-Man aliens."

"So, you weren't disappointed then?" asks Ashton.

"Not at all sir," replies MacArthur. "It is always satisfying to find an answer to any sighting, even if the answer is not that the witness has seen extra-terrestrials. In this case I think it was an honest mistake rather than a deliberate prank to mislead."

"I guess so."

"What's more," adds Harcourt, "we still have the video evidence of the lights to examine and the samples of hair collected by those detectives. They promised to contact me if the results show anything unusual."

Rubbing the morning black stubble on his chin, Ashton decides not to share the thoughts and theories of the boffins at Fylingdales regarding the mystery lights. Hearing a shout, they all turn to see Dolly doing a waddling half trot towards them, waving an envelope in the air.

"Hold on Mr Harcourt, you forgot a copy of your bill."

"Ahh thank you Mrs Wilkes, we need all the paperwork to claim our expenses from ASS."

"Sorry?" replies Dolly, slightly affronted.

"ASS," repeats Harcourt, "the Appalachian Sasquatch Society. They have given us a modest grant to investigate sightings in the UK, gather evidence and submit a short thesis for their research library."

"Okay then. Well, I hope you enjoyed your stay and, if you are ever in the area, do pop in."

MacArthur shakes her hand. "Thank you, ma'am, for your hospitality, it's been a pleasure."

Through her blushes, Dolly mutters a 'thank you' before heading back to the pub.

"Well then, I will be off and have a safe journey gentleman. Need to get home for a shower and to give Barry a drink. It's hot work running through the valley. Come on Barry, leave those bags alone." Stood on his hind legs with his front paws resting on the bumper, the Beagle is sniffing at the suitcases placed side by side in the open hatchback of the car. Obediently he climbs down and follows his master out of the carpark. Ashton gives a final wave to the Americans as they pass and hoot the car horn on the High Street, leaving the village to start their long journey home.

Funny couple of blokes, thinks Ashton as he unlocks his front door.

"Funny bunch of folks, those villagers," says Harcourt from the passenger seat. Nodding in agreement MacArthur turns onto the A64 to Leeds which eventually connects them to the M1 and on to London.

"Sure are, Septimus. Not always easy to understand what they are all saying either. They speak in a strange accent and have a whole load of unusual expressions."

"Yes, I agree. It is quite perplexing how the English are hard to understand when they speak their mother tongue. If you know what I mean?"

"Yep, they sure like to shoot the breeze in these parts, a lot of chatter for the birds."

"I'll plead the fifth on that one Sherman."

⋅┆⋅⋅┆⋅

Busily preparing the pub for another day's business, Dolly sings along to the songs filtering through the radio speakers. A perfect tool for relieving the tedium of cleaning. A classic from Queen comes through and she joins in with Freddie Mercury singing the title line, 'I want to break free.' Mindlessly wiping the table near the front bay window of the bar, she looks onto the High Street but there is no traffic.

In fact, the road has been very quiet since she saw the two Americans pass by thirty minutes earlier. Sunlight breaks through a cloud shooting an almost ethereal shard of sunlight through the window. It warms her face, washing away the slight blueness of her mood and transforming her dull expression into a beaming smile.

"Well look at you, what are you smiling at? I'd say a penny for your thoughts, but they look a bit naughty, you little minx you."

Her shoulders give a slight jerk in surprise, and she turns to find one of her regulars climbing onto a stool at the bar. He adjusts his blazer to get himself settled, then gives her a mischievous grin. "Well come on old girl, what's tickled your fancy?"

"Morning Donald," replies Dolly, glancing at the clock behind the bar. "Golly, you're early, it is not opening time for another five minutes. Ken must have left the door unlocked after he left."

"I know luvvy, but it is a matter of life and death. It's my half yearly meeting with my accountant and frankly I don't know how I'm going to get through it. I don't know what is more boring, his narrative or his dress sense," replies Donald, straightening his pink bow tie. "So be a love and get me a double gin and tonic before I lose all courage and go back home to bed. I have my meeting in an hour and must toddle off to Scarborough to endure his torture."

"You're the definition of a drama queen," laughs Dolly as she makes her way behind the bar and prepares his drink. When she places it in front of him, Donald asks, "So tell me, what was making you smile?"

"Nothing much really, I was feeling a bit maudlin earlier when I saw the two Americans leave today. They brightened up the place a bit and there was a bit of a buzz around the village with all that talk of aliens and furry monsters in the woods. Some nights it was like Piccadilly Circus in there. Not to mention it was good for business. I was just thinking of those fun times."

Grinning wickedly, Donald jokes, "I have to say I'm sad now you have told me the military one has left. He's a bit of a dish, isn't he? Getting on a bit, but very well preserved. I thought the other one was a tad pretentious and full of his own importance. Having said that, it was fun having them around the place."

"I know what you mean," giggles Dolly, "Mr MacArthur reminded me of Paul Newman later in his career."

"Sure was," agrees Donald, "but the other one was trying too hard to be the English eccentric especially with that slightly affected speech. Anyway, all I can say is, let's have a toast," Donald holds up his glass. "God Bless America."

"I'd drink to that Donald, but it's a bit early for me," laughs Dolly.

"What are you two drinking to?" asks Ken crashing through the front door like a rampaging bear.

"America love," replies Dolly. "We were saying that our guests from overseas livened up the place and it is a bit sad that they have now gone."

"Certainly, helped the numbers on the till receipts," agrees Ken, grabbing his car keys from next to the cash register. "Anyway. I'm going straight off again. I had a call from the brewery manager and he wants to see me about a new line of beer. I've arranged to meet him in Scarborough at half past twelve."

"Any chance you could give me a lift?" asks Donald. "I was going to drive but after my meeting I may pop into Club Bacchus for a couple of snifters and get an Uber home. A chance to connect with my community, so to speak."

"Looks like Paul Newman has got your gander up," jokes Dolly.

Climbing off his stool to follow Ken out of the front door he calls back, "You never know, chance is a fine thing."

·|··|·

Escaping through the open door behind the counter, the deep thudding of a cleaver chopping meat on a large wooden slab reverberates through the premises. Incongruous with the clinical, functional surroundings of the shop, predominantly decorated with white tiles, Julia Henson waits patiently adorned in elegant couture. Eventually, the butcher, with a white cap perched on his bald head and a slightly bloodied blue and white striped apron, emerges with two packages wrapped in plain brown paper.

"There yer go Mrs Henson." Proudfoot holds up the smaller package. "This 'ere is the tenderloin, and t'other is the back strap. It's local venison 'an has been 'anging for plenty of time and ready for cooking. Should be luverly, if it's treated right."

"Thank you, Stan," says Julia, placing the packages in her makeshift shopping bag and passing over her credit card."

Eyeing the bag sceptically, Stan says, "Looks a fancy bag fer carrying meat around. Don't worry though, the venison shouldn't leak but just be careful."

Julia looks down at her bag. "Yes, I know Stan, I wasn't thinking. I just grabbed the first thing that came to hand in the dressing room., It's an old Yves Saint Laurent which I haven't used for years."

"If I may say so, yer also look very nice and very dressed up t'do yer shopping."

Laughing, Julia replies, "I know, I have got the ladies around from the church fundraising committee this afternoon. We are going to brainstorm some ideas."

After a quiet morning, Stan is happy to chat. "Funny old to do with those Americans. I hear they've left. Didn't catch any aliens or Bigfoots, did they?"

"No, a lot of silly nonsense," replies Julia. "It almost got Chris Ashton killed in the end. Apparently, they disturbed two men dressed up in costumes. They think that these two thugs were the ones that the Messruther boys mistook for aliens a few nights before."

"Like I say, a lot of nonsense, 'an judging by the bruise ont 'is head, he was lucky that it only ruined his pretty looks fer a bit. He could have ended up in hospital. Brave bloke though, taking on the two of them. Must be tougher than I thought, these artists," says Stan with a chuckle. "Anyways, my niece got a good couple of stories out of it fer the local paper, so it worked out well as far as she was concerned."

"That's great Stan, but I must be off now, the ladies will be arriving soon. Goodbye."

Mesmerised, the butcher's eyes follow the graceful movements of his customer until she disappears out of sight up the High Street. "Bye 'eck," he mutters to himself.

Closing the front door of her five-bedroom home in Forge Valley Lane, Julia shouts out from the hallway. Her husband, Sebastian, calls back to her from his study confirming that he is home.

His highly successful accountancy firm has provided a privileged lifestyle which includes an elegant home in grounds which are the envy of the women on the church committee, not to mention those at the local golf club. Inevitably, the physical incongruity of the pair generates perpetual gossip and cattiness in local circles. Branded expensive clothes can only do so much to enhance the style and appearance of a short balding man with a middle-aged paunch stretching his Gucci cashmere sweaters. His golf buddies nickname him Danny DeVito, which he takes with strained good humour. Their jealous wives had long concluded that his only attractive feature was his bank balance and if anyone has a label with the words 'Gold-digger' on it, then they all knew where to stick it. Apparently unaware of her husband's sensitivities and insecurity, Julia is oblivious to the parochial bitching. She joins him in his study.

"We're serving venison tonight darling, but God knows it will be wasted on that awful man McCarthy. Why on earth must you have him for dinner? Not to mention the esteemed Councillor Mandelson and his friend Neaves. I really don't know what possessed you."

"I know and I am sorry love, but it is just to discuss business. I am happy for you to leave us to it."

"Well don't worry yourself on that account, I have booked Marcel to prepare the food and I will be out for the evening. He will come at five o'clock and I'll be leaving shortly afterwards to go to my book club. We're reviewing a novel written by a local man who was born in the village. It's a murder mystery based here, very intriguing and a little unsettling given the events of last year."

"That's great love, when I get time, I'll have to read it. Thanks for sorting out the food and good luck with the church committee."

A tentative knock on the front door prompts Julia to leave her husband to his work. "That will be the church ladies. Don't worry darling, we won't disturb you – I'll have the meeting on the patio." Julia kisses him on the forehead and closes the study door behind her. Sebastian becomes immediately engrossed in the columns of figures in front of him. It is not until he hears the loud clattering of pans in the kitchen three hours later, that his attention is wrested from the computer screen. His office door opens and Julia peers through the gap, her exquisite bone structure accentuated by subtle make-up.

"Excuse me darling, just letting you know I'm off. I am out of here, already late. But I've given Marcel all the instructions, he knows where everything is, and I told him to serve dinner at seven p.m. on the dot."

Looking at his Rolex, Sebastian replies, "God, is that the time, thank you love, hopefully they will have gone by the time you get back."

"I sincerely hope so."

The sound of the door closing prompts Sebastian to shut down his computer and get ready for his guests. After checking in with Marcel he rushes to his bedroom to shower and change. He is barely halfway down the stairs when a series of loud knocks signals the arrival of his guests. Opening the door, he welcomes them. His eye contact with Mandelson is relatively easy given their similar height, so he addresses the councillor first. For the other two, he needs to crane his neck.

"Trent, great to see you."

McCarthy grunts in reply. *Doesn't look happy*, thinks Sebastian. Keeping his thoughts to himself, he wonders if his three guests have had a disagreement on the way to his house.

"And Ronald, it's been a while."

"Yeah, I've been away," replies Neaves.

Ushering his guests to the living room, Mandleson and Neaves sit on the cream embossed Edwardian sofa and McCarthy takes one of the two seats which make up the suite. Walking over to his liquor cabinet, Sebastian lines up four whisky glasses and pours a generous shot in each. No ice. As he hands out the drinks he says, "I think you will all appreciate this one, just got it yesterday and I was very pleasantly surprised. It's a Macallan 18-year-old single malt. Matured in European and American sherry casks according to the label."

Mandelson and Neaves take a sip and murmur their appreciation whilst McCarthy sinks the shot in one swift gulp and holds out his glass for another, which Sebastian immediately re-fills and joins them. Taking the spare seat, he makes small talk with an innocuous observation about the weather. Clearly not in a mood for chit chat, McCarthy cuts off the conversation.

"Let's get down to business. What's the story with the hotel? Is it fucking happening or not?"

The three had forged what Sebastian had always considered a fragile partnership. An uneasy alliance. In the early years of his construction business Neaves had severely underestimated McCarthy when a contract to refurbish one of his nightclubs hit several difficulties. Ignorant of who and what he was dealing with, Neaves attempted to strong arm McCarthy for payment only to find his own offices burnt to the ground shortly afterwards. It was a wakeup call for Neaves, who was used to employing his physical size to intimidate people, but McCarthy, he soon learnt, was no ordinary person.

Mandelson and Neaves had been close friends since school. It was an unlikely friendship given the circles in which they moved. Neaves' size automatically placed him in the rugby team whilst Mandelson's physical and academic attributes meant he gravitated to the studious element of the school. The nature of the school they attended inevitably made Mandelson, and others like him, the target of bullying from boys like Neaves. However, Mandelson was fortunate to develop a connection with Neaves. Their friendship blossomed symbiotically, playing to the relative strengths of each. No one would bully the pale, sickly looking Mandelson because they knew they would have to deal with Neaves. At the same time, Neaves's academic credentials rose significantly when the standard of his assignments improved markedly, thanks, in no small part, to the academic prowess of his studious friend.

Psychologically the balance of power developed, as the years passed, in favour of Mandelson who had bailed out Neaves on several occasions when his business wavered. In recent years, Councillor Mandelson, being Chair of the Scarborough Council Planning Committee, had facilitated several approvals in favour of Neaves. This was where the partnership between the three men had been forged. To ingratiate himself, after getting on the wrong side of the gangster, Neaves approached McCarthy, with trepidation, to partner in construction deals. Their latest venture was to develop a hotel on the land next to the church. For his part, McCarthy had little interest in construction and even less in the hospitality and accommodation business. He was, however, constantly on the lookout for convenient channels to launder revenue acquired from less legal activities. On this basis he tolerated Neaves, and provided cash flow funding which, to date, received satisfactory returns keeping all parties happy.

Holding his glass out for a third whisky, McCarthy repeats himself having neither received a response from Neaves nor Mandelson. "Have you all gone deaf? I said, what is happening with the hotel? My money has been tied up in it for over a year now." Pointing to his host, he adds, "As Sebastian here will testify."

He smiles at the accountant who passes the replenished whisky glass over to him. Of the three men, Sebastian is the only one he has any time for. On a good day McCarthy not only has a degree of respect for his accountant but almost likes him, as far as his twisted emotional make-up allows him to like anybody. Sebastian had been very successful in managing McCarthy's financial affairs, minimising tax liability and masking activities that would not bear too much legal scrutiny.

"It's got stuck in planning approval," says Neaves, instantly receiving a steely glare of rebuke from Mandelson. The spotlight falls on Mandelson.

"That's your fucking job, isn't it?"

Trying to appear outwardly calm, Mandelson's insides feel like they are dissolving. He leans forward in his chair to appear earnest and emphasise his point. "I understand your frustration Mr McCarthy, but the planning application process has been subject to audit, and I have to tread carefully or the whole thing will fall apart."

"It's not the only fucking thing that will fall apart if it doesn't get sorted," replies McCarthy, menacingly.

"I understand your concerns Mr McCarthy, but the review was completed with nothing major found by the auditors, just a few minor points. So, I am hopeful that we can now proceed relatively quickly."

McCarthy reaches into the inside pocket of his jacket, opens a flick knife, and uses the wickedly sharp looking blade to clean the underside of the fingernails on his right hand. "I've got a few minor points of my own which I will make if this does not get sorted pronto. Understand?" Both Mandelson and Neaves lean back at the same time, retreating further into the plush sofa.

Looking hopefully at Mandelson for a response that would appease McCarthy, Neaves says "Er, you've got it on the agenda at the next planning meeting, haven't you Jeffrey?"

Aiming a second brief reproachful glare at his friend, Mandelson responds. "Yes Ronald, that's right." Turning directly to McCarthy he adds, "We have a planning meeting tomorrow, Mr McCarthy, and I have it on the agenda. It should go through then and Ronald can get on with the build." His private concerns for the meeting and potential objections from other Councillors are left unsaid given the, already, doubtful expression on the gangster's face.

Breaking the uneasy silence, Sebastian answers a knock on the living room door. The chef announces that dinner is ready and is being served in the dining room. Sebastian leads out the guests, McCarthy directly behind, followed by Mandelson who turns back to his friend and scowls. Neaves responds with a shrug.

No one is disappointed that the dinner goes quickly. Little justice is done to the labours of Marcel, who had prepared the venison two ways, grilled backstrap and a stroganoff using the tenderloins. McCarthy was not a dinner party sort of person and quickly dispatched his food without comment. Neaves demolishes, with equal speed, everything put in front of him including second and third helpings of the Potato Rosti and red cabbage.

Should have just ordered in McDonalds, thinks Sebastian.

At the front door, brief goodbyes are exchanged and McCarthy gestures for Mandelson and Neaves to go to the car whilst he has a private word with Sebastian. When he sees the pair are out of earshot, McCarthy turns to his accountant. He repeats the description, given by Kelly, of the man who disturbed them in the woods and asks Sebastian if he recognises who that might be. After a moment's thought, Sebastian responds.

"I can't be certain who it is, Trent. That description is quite generic. Could be a few people I know, but if it were someone who lives in the village my money would be on Chris Ashton. He's a local artist, lives on the High Street."

No reason for the enquiry is given by McCarthy, and Sebastian knows better than to ask.

"Thanks for dinner Seb." Pointing to the two men waiting in the car he adds, "And keep the pressure up on those two muppets."

"Don't worry, Trent, I will. I think they got the message and we'll be digging foundations for the hotel in no time."

"If we're not, then the only digging we'll be doing is their graves."

Sebastian laughs uncomfortably at the joke, but sees McCarthy is not smiling. The gangster waves goodbye.

The atmosphere in the car could be cut with the proverbial knife. No words are exchanged until the outskirts of Scarborough come into view. Neaves drives with Mandelson in the passenger seat next to him. A glimpse in the rear-view mirror reveals a scowling McCarthy, staring out of his window deep in thought. Pulling into a quiet cul-de-sac, Mandelson climbs out and gives a perfunctory good night.

"Didn't know he was a customer of Daisy the Dominatrix," comments McCarthy, as he watches the red door of number twelve open. Surreptitiously, Mandelson sneaks through the entrance. Neaves offers no comment.

As they drive off McCarthy says, "You can drop me off at my club." It was nearer an order than a request. No offer to join him for a night cap was forthcoming.

When Neaves pulls up in front of the club, the doorman, seeing McCarthy in the back seat, walks over to open the car door and escorts his boss through the entrance and into the main bar. The barman also notes the entrance of the club owner making a bee line for his back office and prepares his usual drink. McCarthy takes off his jacket and, as he settles behind his desk, a generous measure of whisky in a small crystal tumbler is placed before him. He signals for privacy and after the office door is closed, leaving him alone, he makes his call.

Swearing when he sees the caller's name appear on the screen of his mobile phone, Kelly answers immediately, but reluctantly.

"Yes boss, look before you ask, we haven't been to Ayton yet. We're going on Friday because all the locals tend to go out that night. They have music nights and stuff."

"I don't need a rundown of the fucking social calendar of the village."

"Yeah, sorry boss. What I'm saying is that there is a good chance the bloke we are looking for will be in the pub. If he lives there, that is."

"That's why I'm ringing. Just had an exciting evening with two muppets and my accountant who happens to be a local resident," says McCarthy in a sarcastic tone. "I gave him your description and he told me that it may be some ponce called Ashton, Chris Ashton. That said, he cannot be certain because your description could probably fit half the men under fifty in Yorkshire."

"Sorry boss, but it was dark, and I had my hands full with him. He can look after himself."

"I don't need to hear any more of your excuses. Just go ahead with your plan for tomorrow. Have a good look around to check out if this Chris Ashton is the one and the same arsehole who beat the crap out of Doyle."

"If we find him, do you want us to sort him out?"

"No, you idiot. You couldn't sort a three-piece jigsaw. You need to use your fucking brains. First, there is no 'we.' You make sure that you do this on your own without your idiot mate in tow. If you can recognise him, then he will certainly recognise Doyle. He had his bloody Spider-Man mask off, didn't he? Doyle needs to stay well clear."

"Yeah, sorry boss, you're right. Didn't think of that."

"And therein lies the problem. You don't think. If, and I repeat, if, you spot him and you are sure it was Ashton in the woods when you were playing at fucking pirates, I want you to do nothing. Do you understand? Do nothing. Don't approach him. Don't talk to him. Just follow him home and then call me. I will deal with it."

"No problem boss. What if I'm not sure?"

"Just make sure, you're sure."

The line goes dead.

"Shit," says Kelly to himself.

"Morons, I am surrounded by morons," mutters McCarthy as he empties his whisky glass.

16

UNLESS IT INVOLVES matters to his personal advantage, Mandelson finds evenings where he is engaged in the tedium of Council planning meetings, mind-numbing. The gravitas and splendour of the council building's design belies the mundane activity within it. In his opinion, it is wasted on those who are employed within it. All the thoughts occupying his mind are unhappy ones, and negative.

A 1960's prefabricated building would be a more suitable home for the mindless bureaucrats, he thinks as he walks through the grandeur of the baroque eighteenth century council premises. *Bloody council meetings and employees; jobs-worth officials, a bunch of idiots endlessly shuffling papers. This and the clueless bunch of committee members is bad enough but Neaves getting embroiled with the likes of McCarthy is a problem at a whole different level.*

He could cope with the council and its rules that choked the life out of any potentially creative property developments, but McCarthy is an entirely different beast. Tonight's meeting would be removing him from his comfort zone, taking on an unwelcome significance despite the opportunity for financial reward. Failure to get approval for the hotel would be a financial opportunity lost, but no big deal. There would be plenty more down the line. What troubles him is what it means in terms of other consequences. Mandelson had seen enough of McCarthy, and what he had done to Neaves, to know that whatever those consequences are, they will not be pleasant. On his part, he has no intention of finding out firsthand.

Plodding through the bureaucratic treadmill, the mundane meeting agenda items – welcomes, declarations of interest, minutes of the last meeting and so on – are eventually completed. This evening's agenda is mercifully short, and the only important item of the day is the final one which, to his relief, comes up within the hour.

"Mr Prendergast, if you could please summarise the final agenda item and give the committee your thoughts," announces Mandelson. The senior planning officer stands, his ill-fitting brown suit hanging limply off his thin body. After a self-conscious cough, he presents his item.

"Thank you Mr Chairman. As members may recall the proposal to build a hotel on land next to the church in West Ayton was progressing through the application process last year. An independent audit of the Council's procedures was undertaken following a complaint, and all projects, including this one, were suspended, pending the results of the inquiry. Several internal controls were recommended by the auditors, which the Director of Finance has recently confirmed have been implemented. Now all the suspended projects, including this one, have recommenced in the planning process."

Conscious of opposition when the project was last presented, Mandelson expects he will need to manage the discussion carefully. A committee member, who was previously opposed to the scheme, raises her hand prompting an inaudible sigh from Mandelson who reluctantly acknowledges her.

"Yes, Councillor Fosdyke. I recall that, on this particular

project, there was a potential conflict of interest given that you are a member of the church congregation. However, I will allow a question out of good will, but must warn you that, if I perceive a conflict, I may have to disallow any further comment."

Wrestling to contain her anger, Fosdyke pouts with annoyance. "Thank you Mr Chairman, my question is about the audit. You mentioned, Mr Prendergast, that the audit was prompted by a complaint. Who made the complaint and was that complaint related to this project?"

Shuffling uncomfortably, Prendergast tries to formulate an answer remembering the brow beating he took from the Committee Chair when the proposal was tabled originally. Opening his mouth to explain as best he could, he is saved by Mandelson's intervention.

"Thank you, councillor. As you know from our Whistle Blower policy, the identity of complainants is kept confidential at their request. I believe this was the case here. I do think the complaint was generalised about the process rather than specific to this, or any other project for that matter."

Prendergast recognises that the truth was being stretched to some degree but remains silent for fear of the Chair's retribution. Fosdyke persists.

"Well, may I ask if the review found any irregularities relating to this scheme?"

This time Prendergast, feeling on more solid ground, answers before Mandelson has time to comment.

"I can confirm that the findings related to general controls on the process, and none were specific to applications either past or current." Prendergast looks over to Mandelson like a schoolboy seeking approval from the principal. He is rewarded with a strained smile from the Chairman.

"Thank you, Mr Prendergast, for your excellent work. I believe the consultation process has now been completed, and sufficient time has passed for the committee to make a formal determination. As I understand it, nothing material arose from the consultation that should prevent approval of this scheme, which I have to say would very much benefit the local economy of the village. So, without further ado."

"One moment," comes a tentative voice from the far end of the table. It is greeted with an impatient glare from Mandelson, but the speaker is not deterred.

"I think that recent events in the area are pertinent to this approval and perhaps merit delaying the decision."

Outwardly calm, inwardly seething, Mandelson asks for clarification, wondering what has prompted the normally quiet and compliant committee member to speak. "Yes, Councillor Stokes, what is your concern?"

"From reading the newspapers and hearing reports on the radio I understand there has been some unusual activity in the area. Sightings of strange beings, mysterious lights and so on."

"What have mysterious lights got to do with this proposal, Councillor?" replies Mandelson, only just managing to mask his irritation.

Stokes smiles with a benign calmness. "Maybe they are not lights but orbs."

"Orbs?" asks Mandelson, the mask of calm beginning to dissipate allowing his annoyance to rise from its shallow grave. "What are you talking about, Councillor? I am not sure the committee has time to discuss mysterious beings, lights, or orbs. I strongly suggest we move on."

Still smiling, Stokes responds. "I beg to differ. I have studied orbs and have seen them firsthand. People believe these are spirits of dead people."

Having lost his patience, Mandelson raises his voice

louder than he intends. "People believe in Father Christmas, the Bogey Man and world peace but none of these exist. I am not sure I follow, and I really do think that this has nothing to do with building a bloody hotel."

"Parisi," says Stokes.

"Parisi?" replies Mandelson.

"Yes. Parisi. I believe the orbs are the spirits of the Parisi." Leaning forward and placing her elbows on the meeting table to emphasise her point to the committee, she explains. "I believe the activity may be due to the fact that the proposal involves building on sacred ground."

"What the f– " Mandelson manages to strangle the expletive just in time and resets himself. Calm mode. Calm mode. Calm mode. "I mean, Councillor Stokes, I am not following your drift. Who or what are the Parisi?"

"They were an ancient Celtic tribe which lived in the East Riding of Yorkshire. I believe they may be buried in this land, and this is the reason that the orbs are appearing. The ancient spirits are venting their anger at the possible desecration of their holy burial ground. I believe the process should be halted to allow for qualified archaeologists to dig on the site and see if it is, indeed, a Parisi burial ground."

Struggling for an appropriate response, Mandelson suffers a rare loss for words but is saved by another committee member who has, what was fast becoming, an overdue appointment with his mistress. If it got much later, he would have to cancel. He could not afford to arouse his wife's suspicion by staying out too late. She would have more questions than a pub quiz night.

"What a load of bollocks," shouts Councillor Albert Hardcastle, whilst checking his wristwatch.

Relieved at this intervention, Mandelson could have almost kissed his ruddy cheeked, corpulent colleague. Instead, it gave him the perfect opening to take the moral high ground whilst levering the unexpected, but welcome, support of Hardcastle.

"Whilst I must ask Councillor Hardcastle to moderate his language, I have to say, I agree with his sentiments. We cannot refuse planning permission based on a lot of spiritual mumbo jumbo for which there is no evidence to back up the claims. If we told the applicant this was the reason for refusal, we would find ourselves in court being hung, drawn, and quartered. Not to mention we would all be branded superstitious fools for refusing the application on the basis that we don't want to upset the ghosts. We would all be a laughingstock!"

"But ... "

"No 'buts', Councillor Stokes. I will also remind members of the committee that to refuse the application could be seen as negligent. Should this be the case, then members may find themselves personally liable and subject to significant financial penalties. If the court finds in the applicant's favour, then it would be disastrous for all concerned."

"But if the chair will indulge me?" pleads Stokes.

"I think we have indulged this fanciful idea enough, with all due respect Councillor Stokes. Perhaps you could inform the committee as to whether you have found any Parisi artefacts near the site?"

"Well, no, but we have not had the opportunity to dig."

"Have any Parisi artefacts been discovered in the village elsewhere?" asks Mandelson.

"Well, no," responds Stokes, realising she has lost the battle.

"Then I think the matter is settled, unless anyone else has any objection?"

No one has any objection; the fear of financial penalty had been the final nail in the coffin for most of the members. Silence falls upon the room, with no committee member wishing or willing to raise their head above the parapet and challenge Mandelson, or Hardcastle who was already gathering his papers to indicate he deemed the meeting closed. Scanning the table, Mandelson gets the occasional hesitant nod of approval. A barely audible tut from Councillor Stokes was the last vestige of rebellion in the room.

"Well, that settles it then, please record that the decision of the committee is to approve the application for the hotel development in West Ayton. Personally, I think it will prove an asset to draw tourism to the village and the surrounding area. I do not know what all the fuss is about. It's a relatively modest sized development that will fit in sympathetically with the ambience of the locality. If there is no other business, then I call the meeting to a close."

Without waiting for a response, Mandelson scoops up his papers and marches out of the committee room, through the ornate corridors and out of the main entrance. He ignored the concierge at the desk, who was bidding him a good evening.

"Rude bastard," mutters the concierge, after Mandelson disappears through the doors.

Weaving his silver Lexus ES through the streets of Scarborough town centre, Mandelson decides he needs a more serene, scenic route home to decompress. Instead of taking the direct road to the village, he turns off the A170 and drives up Scalby Road taking a left onto Lady Edith's Drive. This leads on to Low Road and into the Forge Valley Woods Nature reserve.

The narrow winding road takes him through farmland, into the green leafy canopy of the valley and eventually to the village via Forge Valley Lane. Once home, settled on his couch, he sips his well-earned whisky soothed by

Act Two of Mozart's opera, the Magic Flute. Its mystical score engulfs the room. His phone, still on silent from the committee meeting, vibrates on the table and he picks it up. It's Neaves.

"Yes Ronald, you didn't waste any time calling, the meeting has barely finished."

"So, what was the outcome, Jeffrey?" asks Neaves, with a slight nervous timbre to his voice.

Being a man who thrives on schadenfreude, Mandelson does not give a direct answer immediately. "The meeting went okay," he offers in a non-committal tone whilst smirking into the phone.

"Come on Jeffrey, did the hotel get approved or not?" begs Neaves, with growing angst.

"There was a couple of objections, mainly from Councillor Stokes."

"Shit!" exclaims Neaves, becoming convinced he is about to receive bad news.

"But I managed to counter them, and you can call your gangster friend and tell him the joyous news."

With an exhalation of relief, Neaves seeks unequivocal confirmation. "So, it is approved, no conditions or anything?"

"Yes, once again I have pulled you out of the mire and you can tell him that it has been approved. You can start construction as soon as the permit has been issued. It normally only takes the Council a couple of weeks to process a building permit, as you know from our previous little projects."

"Thank God."

"Don't know about God, but you certainly need to thank me," quips Mandelson. "And you can start by ensuring that you keep Scarborough's answer to Al Capone as far away from me as possible. No more meetings with him for me, I've done my bit and the rest is now up to you. I'll sit back and wait for my retainer to be paid when you are ready."

·•··•·

In direct contrast to Mandelson, who is drinking alone to celebrate a good day ending with a win, Hardy and Stanley are drinking together but bemoaning a singularly unproductive day. Hardy had agreed to meet Stanley in the Old Plough after work. He had sent Stanley to the village for the afternoon to poke around and see if he could get any leads. The young detective toured the village, chatting with locals, keeping things low key. Nobody had much to offer, and nobody could point to any unfamiliar 'characters' lurking about the place. In fact, Stanley was repeatedly told that all had gone quiet since the Americans left. No further sighting of the Bigfoot. No more aliens to be seen. Even the incidence and frequency of the mysterious lights had died down. He had learnt the last bit of information from the Addinalls, who had taken up half of his afternoon in the village.

Having knocked on their door expecting a short conversation on the doorstep he is greeted by two smiling faces. They both answer the door immediately after his first knock, which Stanley thought was a little spooky, but guesses that they saw him from their front window walking up the path. Before he knows it, he is ensconced in their living room which was a homage to Laura Ashley with flowery throws, curtains, and cushions.

Drinking orange pekoe tea from a Laura Ashley tea set, he sits awkwardly on a small, padded chair covered with Laura Ashley material. Conscious of appearing rude, Stanley trawls his limited 'small talk' databank to dig out something appropriate to say. His first attempt is predictable but, in small talk terms, a solid start.

"What a lovely place you have here. And lovely décor."

"We are a big fan of Laura Ashley," confirms Freda.

This immediately threw Stanley, who did not know that another person lived in the house. Maybe a relative he wondered, as he searched for a follow up.

"Well, that's nice, is she a relative?"

"Oh, you are funny," chuckled Mary. "Quite the wit." He presses on even more confused, not understanding what it was he had said that caused such amusement.

"Nice curtains."

"We got them from Laura Ashley," says Freda.

"Oh, does your relative also make curtains then?"

Freda puts her hand to her mouth and giggles. Mary joins in and through her chuckling manages to say, "Oh my, oh my, detective Stanley, please stop it, you are so funny."

Their breasts jiggle through their cardigans as their laughter grows louder. Stanley waits for them to finish and compose themselves. Once they are settled, Freda takes a plate of cakes from the coffee table and offers one to the detective.

"Please take as many as you like detective Stanley, you look as though you could do with putting on a bit of weight. You're like a piece of string. Here, take one, they are my favourites, French Fancies. But leave the pink one for me."

Stanley takes one, pops it in his mouth and washes it down with a swig of tea. And so, the meeting with the Addinalls goes on. And on. And on. By the end of their chat, all he learnt was, other than he found French fancies far too sweet for his palate, that the mysterious lights were still appearing but less frequently.

If Stanley's latest contribution to solving the jewel heist was low, Hardy had even less to offer. This brings down their mood to a sullen silence as they both sip, unenthusiastically, on their pints. Even the stuffed Koala sat next to them has his head slightly bowed, as if he was sympathetic to their plight. In keeping with the sombre mood, an imposing large shadow looms over them, causing both to look up from their drinks.

"Cheer up lads, can't be that bad. Yer looked so miserable I've bought you over some good cheer," says Ken Wilkes as he places two fresh pints on their table.

"Don't worry, they're on the house. Got to keep on the good side of you boys in blue." The detectives thank the landlord and pass him their empty glasses.

"I hear you've been asking questions around the village. You want to know if there 'ave been any strangers around 'ere. Well, I can't 'elp you out on this, but I can tell you that if strangers do turn up and look a bit suspect I will be straight on the phone to you. Of all the places that visitors are likely to go, you can bet yer life the Old Plough will be one of them. We're 'aving a quiz night Friday, why don't yer come along. If yer don't catch any wrong 'uns yer might at least win the quiz. If we get strangers around the place, it's usually Fridays or Saturdays. And if any are in the pub, I'll point 'em out to you. Is it a deal?"

"It's a deal," replies Hardy, handing Ken his business card. "If you see anything in the meantime, give me a call. Especially if the strangers are in a pair. Two of them were seen in the woods the night Mr Ashton was assaulted."

Laughing, Ken replies, "I've seen Chris in action a couple of times. He can look after 'imself. If anyone got assaulted and came off worse, it will 'ave been those two villains."

17

OPENING THE DOOR after his early evening session in the gym, Ashton is greeted by Barry jumping up and down excitedly and barking with unbridled canine joy. He drops his bag and kneels to cuddle the dog who is licking enthusiastically at his owner's face.

"Jeez Bazza, I've only been gone a couple of hours, you need to calm down. Right mate, I need to get out of this gym kit, shower and then me and you have a little adventure tonight."

Barry follows him, nudging Ashtons bare calf with his wet nose to let him know he is right behind him. Once he is out of the shower, Ashton quickly dresses in black jeans and tee-shirt. Barry is laid on the bed watching his every move and, noticing the dog's intent interest, he explains his wardrobe choice.

"It's all about stealth tonight Bazza. All in black, don't want to be seen and, if you are going to come along, you'll need to be quiet otherwise you'll give us away." Looking directly at his owner, Barry gives a short bark in response. "We're all good then Bazza. Let's get a quick bite and then we'll be off to catch us some aliens."

Barry jumps off the bed and follows his master to the kitchen. The dog looks dolefully at his empty bowl which Ashton had filled before he went to the gym. Microwaving a ready meal, Ashton looks down at Barry.

"The older you get the more of a guts you're becoming. What? You couldn't wait for me to come home and then eat together?"

Microwave pings and Ashton peels off the clear plastic and slides the container onto a plate, grabbing a fork on his way to the living room. He places the meal on a side table, sits in his favourite chair and switches on the television with the remote.

"I'm getting to be a bit of a saddo, Bazza. Sitting here watching the late news with a Marks and Spencer microwave meal for one."

The Nine O'clock News seems to contain very little news. More a rehash of yesterday's events. Absently forking food from the plastic tray, Ashton stares at the screen but barely takes in what he is watching. Occasionally he breaks off a small piece of chicken and pops it into the Barry's mouth. After each morsel, he resorts to intensely watching Ashton's every movement in the hope of hypnotising his owner into giving up more food. The news programme ends with the unedifying update of the scores in the mid-week evening matches. It is almost full time and Ashtons team is one nil down at home.

Switching off the TV, Ashton vents his disappointment at the update. "Bugger." Barry barks in support of his owner's angst and he twists his head, ears pricked, trying to understand what his master is saying.

"Right Bazza, let's get to it." Placing the dinner plate on the draining board of the kitchen sink on his way out of the back door, Ashton walks up the garden with Barry close behind. He looks up to the sky and, with a satisfied smile, tracks four blue lights moving in perfect formation back and forth along the tree-line adjoining Higginbottom's field.

"It's game on, Bazza."

Leaving through the rear garden gate, Ashton jogs across the back lane and skips over the low wall which marks the southern boundary of Higginbottom's farm. Darkness shrouds the field and, as he moves northwards, the ambient light from the High Street is consumed gradually by the night. A cluster of black lumps in the distance mark the place where the resident cows have settled down for the night. When he gets near the herd, he changes direction, eastwards, towards the tree line to avoid interrupting the bovine slumber. Once he reaches the first tree, he crouches down and listens intently, whilst absently stroking Barry who sits beside him. The woods are silent. Satisfied there is no one in the vicinity, he moves northwards hugging the edge of the field towards the lights. Oblivious of Ashton's presence, the lights hover above the trees now barely one hundred metres away. Occasionally, they shift position and perform a series of seemingly random manoeuvres involving vertical ascents followed by sharp turns, left and right, before returning to a relatively static hovering position.

Looks like the Steve and the Fylingdale boys are right, thinks Ashton.

Now less than fifty yards from the lights, he can hear something. At first, he thinks it sounds like a small swarm of bees, but this thought evaporates once he hears voices at ground level. Not constant chatter, just the occasional comment. Creeping towards the noise, two figures, previously hidden by a large oak tree, come into view.

"Aren't you boys out a bit late for a school night?"

The Messruther twins both issue an expletive and swing round towards Ashton. Billy, startled, drops the device he is holding and the lights above plummet to the ground a few metres in front of them. The impact on the ground

211

silences the humming of the rotating blades.

"Jeez Billy, you've trashed it," complains Ben.

"Wasn't my fault, it was him, I almost crapped myself," replies Billy pointing at Ashton.

"Looks like a nice piece of kit boys, expensive too."

Squinting into the darkness, Ben asks, "Is that you Mr Ashton?"

"Certainly is. So where did you get the drone?"

"We didn't nick it or anything, our Auntie bought it for us. Just a present when she last visited us. It's an Ultralite 2000," replies Ben whilst his brother picks up the drone to examine the damage.

"Think it's okay bruv," confirms Billy. "Looks like all the batteries fell out when it hit the ground."

"I don't know if you boys realise it, but you and your drone have caused quite a stir."

"Didn't mean to Mr Ashton, just was 'aving a bit of fun, that's all. Not our fault people thought it was a spacecraft," says Ben in a defensive tone realising, too late, that he had given the game away.

"Don't worry boys, it's not a big deal. But I'll have to let people know. With all the other weird stuff happening around here, people are a bit on edge. I'm sure you understand."

"But our dad'll kill us," moans Billy.

"Why?"

"'Cause we're out real late," says Ben.

"Don't fret, I'll have a word with him, it'll be okay."

"Doubt it," mutters Ben.

"I'll tell you what we'll do. Let's say I saw you with it in the High Street this afternoon, we had a chat, put two and two together and realised that the lights people have been seeing must've been your drone. We can leave the time and place unsaid."

"What if he asks stuff? You know, about when you and those Miss Addinalls saw them before?" asks Billy.

"Knowing your dad, he probably won't put two and two together. But, if he does ask, I'll say that when we saw them it was around seven o'clock. Not late at all. What do you think?"

"Okay Mr Ashton, and thanks."

"No worries boys, best get yourselves home before your old fella notices you are AWOL. I'll catch your dad tomorrow, before I make it public."

The boys walk down the field towards the village deep in conspiratorial chatter, occasionally glancing back. Giving them a final wave, Ashton makes his own way back home with Barry trailing behind him.

"Case solved Bazza, case solved." Barry woofs in agreement.

The next morning Ashton finds himself sitting in the Messruther living room reluctantly sipping a suspiciously flavourless hot brown drink from a tea-stained mug. Settling himself down opposite Ashton, Arthur Messruther takes a sip from his own drink and looks blankly at his guest.

"Nice cup of tea," lies Ashton.

Arthur Messruther offers a grunt of acknowledgement before responding. "So, when we were making the tea in the kitchen, I think what you were saying, Chris, is that the lights everyone 'as been seeing is not bloody flying saucers but the twins wiv that thing that their auntie gave 'em."

"That's right Arthur. But I don't think the boys worked it out like you just did," replies Ashton playing on Arthur's ego. "They didn't seem to have made the connection of the drone with the mysterious lights being reported by villagers. They had no idea until I told them."

"You sure? You sure they weren't up to mischief?

Wouldn't surprise me, I can tell you."

"No Arthur, they seemed genuinely surprised when I put it to them. They were just playing with the toy given to them by your sister, that's all. It's not their fault people got all sorts of silly ideas in their heads. I have to say I didn't realise the lights were from a drone either when I saw them with the Addinalls. It's only when a mate put the theory forward and then I saw the boys with it in the High Street that I put two and two together myself. They're good lads and seem to keep out of trouble."

Mentally kicking himself, Ashton wondered if he had taken the lies too far with his last declaration. *Maybe laid it on too thick*, he wondered.

"Okay Chris, if you are sure that's the case then I'll leave it."

"Excellent, Arthur. Anyway, I thought I would run it by you first, out of respect, before I tell the villagers. A few have been a little concerned and it would be good to lay it to rest and put people's minds at ease. So, I'd better get off as I am sure you're a busy man."

Placing the almost full mug of tea on the table next to him, Ashton hauls himself out of the deep armchair adorned with a faded green pattern and indeterminate brown stains. Shaking hands with Arthur, he says his final 'goodbye'.

Over the next half hour Ashton visits the store, tells Betty what he has found and then lets the Addinalls know of his discovery. Both sisters could not hide their mild disappointment at the mundane answer to the deliciously mysterious events. Nevertheless, having planted the seeds in fertile gossip ground, Ashton was confident that the whole village would know by noon.

All that remained for him to do was to inform the authorities, which he did with a brief call to Detective

Hardy. Expecting to get an answer machine, to Ashton's surprise, Hardy answered the call immediately. After a brief explanation, it was clear from the detective's response that he had grasped what he had been told.

"Just to be perfectly clear Mr Ashton. You can categorically confirm that the lights you saw were just lights from a drone being flown by a couple of kids. And that these same lights are the ones reported by other villagers?" Hardy leans back precariously in his office chair, which occasionally squeaks under the weight it was being asked to bear.

"I believe this to be the case," confirms Ashton.

"And you have seen this drone firsthand?"

"Yes."

"In operation with the lights on?"

"Yes."

"And the lights are definitely the same?"

"Yes."

"Well, thank you Mr Ashton for letting me know. I appreciate it."

"No problem, anytime. Let me know if you need something in writing. Goodbye."

Returning to the list of unread emails on his screen, Hardy does not even have time to open a new one when he receives another call seconds later. This time the voice on the other end has a less welcoming tone. It is DI Parkins.

"Morning Hardy. It's been a while since I had an update. Come to my office please."

"Certainly sir," replies Hardy, with slight trepidation.

Collecting his partner on the way, Hardy knocks on the Inspector's door. Hearing a firm "enter", he finds himself sitting alongside Stanley, facing an unhappy looking boss.

"I've had a bad day Hardy and it is barely lunchtime. Please make it better and tell me you have made progress on your caseload."

Glancing at Stanley for support, Hardy gets a barely perceptible shake of the head confirming that he has nothing to offer. There was to be no safety net from his junior colleague. Inwardly bracing himself, he responds to DI Parkins.

"Well, sir – I can confirm that we have been monitoring the village closely and have asked all the locals if they've seen anyone matching the description of the individual in the Spider-Man uniform. That is, the one that had removed his mask obviously. I am afraid, so far, we've drawn a blank, but we plan to go there on Friday evening when they are holding a quiz night."

Mood darkening further, Parkins snaps irritably. "Really DS Hardy. What do you think question one on the general knowledge round will be? Perhaps it will be … 'Who was the man in the Spider-Man suit?' Are you bloody well losing your mind?"

"No sir."

"So, what will question two be?"

"Sorry sir?"

"Not as sorry as I am. What will question two be? How about this one. Who turned over a well-respected and long-standing jeweller in Scarborough three weeks ago?"

"No, sir."

"Then why, pray tell me, do you think attending some half-arsed pub quiz night is going to crack open the case, Mr Sherlock bloody Holmes? Please enlighten us mere mortals."

"My thinking, sir, is that it may be possible that the suspects turn up. After all, they clearly have some interest in the village and may be trying to contact one of the locals. Failing that, they may even look to exploit the fact that most of the locals will be occupied in the pub."

"So what?"

"Well, possibly they might revisit the area in the woods where they appeared to be searching previously, without fear of interference this time. A long shot I admit but, at the very least, we may find villagers who we have yet to speak to and they may have useful information."

"Well, if they're busying digging up the local field, what bloody use is it having you two displaying your knowledge of history, geography, sport and pop bloody culture in the local hostelry?"

"Division of labour sir. I'll be working in the pub and Stanley here will be outside staking out the area where they were last seen."

This causes Stanley to look over to his boss in surprise because, not only was he unaware of his boss's plan, but it appears that, for his role, he has drawn the short straw.

"Well Stanley," says Parkins, "I suggest you take a raincoat and a warm woolly jumper. It could be a very cold, wet and fruitless night in store for you."

"Yes sir, I will," replies Stanley.

Turning back to Hardy, Parkins raises his hands, open palmed. "So, is that all you have to offer at this stage?"

"Not entirely, sir."

Stanley looks across to his boss with renewed hope, then back to Parkins who rolls his forefinger in a circular motion to encourage Hardy to elucidate.

"Well don't keep me in suspense Hardy."

"I have more news which you may wish to pass on to Councillor Mandelson to put his electorate at further ease. You may remember that we got to the bottom of the alleged alien sighting, hence we are searching for the men in the Spider-Man costumes.

"Yes, go on."

Well, there were also sightings of mysterious lights that local people thought may have been extra-terrestrial. I think we have now got to the bottom of this. It's not alien spacecrafts."

"Highly insightful DS Hardy. So, what are they?"

"Drones sir."

"Drones?"

"Yes sir, owned by local kids. The Messruthers. They were flying a drone which had lights attached to the front."

"You are sure of this?"

"Yes sir, they were caught red handed," answers Hardy, choosing not to reveal that he was not the one who had caught them.

"Well, that is something. I'll pass it on to Councillor Mandelson. At least it shows we have been active in the area. Did you give them a clip 'round the ear."

"Who?"

"The kids with the drone," explains Parkins.

"No sir, you can't do that nowadays," says Stanley keen to get in on the act and claim some reflected glory.

"Yes, I know son, it was a joke," replies Parkins. "It seems we have at least solved the mystery of the lights and the aliens, but there remains the concern over the large hitherto unidentified thing. It may present a danger to the local community."

"You mean the Bigfoot sir," offers Stanley helpfully, which causes Parkins to raise his eye in scepticism.

"I don't know what they're teaching you nowadays down in Harrogate at the College of Policing young Stanley, but I doubt it includes how to apprehend a fictional monster. Of course, it isn't a bloody Yeti, but it is something that is putting the heebee-jeebees up the local populace. Whilst we assume it is a prank, we're going to look bloody stupid if it turns out to be some sort of stalker or sex pest."

"Yes sir … sorry sir," replies Stanley, chastened.

Turning his sceptical glare from Stanley to Hardy, Parkins says, "With that in mind, I suggest that when DS Hardy here deploys you in the local woods to apprehend the jewel thieves you might also keep an eye out for our large hairy friend. If you see him, ask him what the hell he is doing wandering about in the dark frightening innocent people."

"Yes sir, I will."

"Personally, I think there is as much chance of finding a yeti than there is of finding a jewel thief. That chance is somewhere between little and bugger all."

With a cursory wave of his hand, he dismisses the two detectives who reconvene at Hardy's desk.

"Nice work boss, how did you know about the drone? You never mentioned it to me."

Smugly, Hardy leans back into his usual precarious position, with the chair balanced on the two back legs. Once again, the chair squeaks in complaint at the ill distributed weight.

"Years of detective work my son. Just keep looking and learning from the master. Anyway, it's something for Parkins to report back to his best buddy Mandelson, when they're touching each other up in the Lodge. I am getting a bit tired of DI Parkins and his arrogant sarcastic tone. I doubt he has ever done a decent day's detective work in his life."

"What Lodge?" asks Stanley.

"Pardon?"

"You said that DI Parkins was with Mandelson in some Lodge," explains Stanley.

Exasperated, Hardy replies, "For fuck sake, were you conceived in a bloody isolation chamber. The Freemasons Lodge."

"Oh! I didn't know."

"Well, you do now. The bloody Freemasons. You must have heard of them. A bunch of self-serving wankers wearing weird costumes and silly aprons. You know, giving dodgy handshakes whilst beating each other on the arse with a cricket bat, as they sing God save the bloody King."

18

FRIDAY NIGHT ARRIVES. It is Quiz Night at the Old Plough which is bursting at the seams with the total populace of West Ayton who are legally old enough to consume alcohol, bolstered by keen quizzers from surrounding villages. The boisterous bonhomie of the patrons creates a genial and happy atmosphere, which infects everybody with one or two notable exceptions.

Ironically two of the exceptions have, unbeknown to each other, a common purpose and both sit on their own with an untouched pint of beer in front of them. Their common purpose is to recover the diamonds, but their intentions are poles apart.

Hardy, having briefed and dropped off Stanley at the woods, on what was turning out to be an unseasonably chilly night, is sat in the cosy confines of the Old Plough. Despite this, he is riddled with doubts about the chances of success of the plan he had outlined to DI Parkins.

Kelly, sitting on an adjoining table, is wrestling with his own doubts, but hoping to God that the bloke who had got the better of Doyle, turns up. Despite his lack of faith, he is praying that he can report something that improves the odds of leaving McCarthy's office without having his legs broken.

Everyone else is, of course, oblivious to these concerns

and eagerly awaits the announcement of the quiz. As is the norm for all quiz nights around the world, punctuality is a victim and the scheduled start time has long since passed. Most of the contestants are already a bit tipsy.

Ken and Dolly work feverishly trying to keep pace with the orders, whilst Donald watches on from his usual corner seat at the bar. He holds up his empty glass.

"Kenneth … Dolly … My luvvies, when you have a moment can you please replenish me?"

"Sorry Donald, a bit hectic tonight, we're running around like blue-arsed flies. I'll get to you in a minute."

"Interesting expression, that. Never really understood why a blue-arsed fly has the reputation of engaging in frantic behaviour. Nevertheless, message received and understood love, but, when you do, make it a triple because god knows when you'll get back to me again," purrs Donald.

"You'd better think about getting the quiz started Ken," urges Dolly as she pulls a pint. "It should have started twenty minutes ago."

"Will do love," replies Ken, giving change to a customer. "Sharon's just got here to help out, she is getting changed in the back because she has come straight from her shift at the abattoir."

"Thank God," exclaims Dolly, "it's bloody mayhem in 'ere."

"'Ere you go Donald," says Ken placing a very generous serving of gin and tonic in front of his regular, who salutes in acknowledgement.

On the table to the right of Kelly sits Hayes and Hendricks. Having had a reefer prior to coming to the pub, they were both feeling mellow.

"This could be the night," says Hayes.

"Hope so man, the hundred quid first prize would be welcome," replies Hendricks.

"Deffo, my man. Deffo."

Furrowing his brow, Hendricks mulls over their chances. "Probably would have been best not to have had the dope though."

"Yeeaahhh." says Hayes. "Yer could be right. This old noggin is a bit fuzzy."

"Perhaps man, we should seek to even the odds like that bloke on the telly," slurs Hendricks.

"Eh! What you on about?"

"The Equaliser, the private detective who seeks to even the odds."

"Mate, I think you need to lay off the dope, your brain is getting raddled," replies Hayes.

"Nah mate, we should get another team member," says Hendricks, eyeing up Kelly on the next table. He leans over to address him. "Hey man, you here for the quiz? Do yer wanna join us?"

For fuck sake, thinks Kelly, whilst assessing his dilemma. He wants to remain inconspicuous and tell the frizzy haired idiot what to do with his quiz, but equally, he does not want to draw attention to himself. Stealing a glance at Hardy, who is sat to his other side, he already has his suspicions that his other neighbour, engrossed in his mobile phone, is a copper. He could smell them a mile off.

"Sorry mate, not much of a quiz man," replies Kelly.

Not to be deterred, and desensitised to the mood of his neighbour, Hendricks pursues his quarry. "Aww, c'mon man, we need another player."

Conscious of Hardy now looking over at them, Kelly opts for compliance and shuffles over to their table whilst doing his utmost to adopt a congenial manner. "Alright mate, you win. But I warn you now, I doubt if I'll be much use beyond sports questions. Let me get you both another drink. Looks like you're on the lager."

"Bloody legend," says Hendricks as his new team member makes his way to the bar. Kelly glances back and waves to acknowledge his newfound mates whilst surreptitiously checking the customer on the nearby table. Relieved, he sees that the suspected copper is, once more, engrossed in his mobile phone. At the bar he catches Dolly's attention, and soon weaves his way back to the table, artfully holding the three pints between two hands.

"Cheers mate," says Hendricks, "didn't catch your name." Subconsciously glancing over to Hardy who is still glued to his phone, he replies in a tone soft enough to make it inaudible to anyone other than those at the table. "Just call me, Phil."

"Really, I'm Phil as well, but people call me Purple," says Hayes waiting for an enquiry as to why he has this unusual name.

"And I'm Colin," adds Hendricks, when he realises the usual request for an explanation to Hayes' nickname was not forthcoming. Both are oblivious to the fact that their new team member seems a little distracted, as he surveys the pub.

At the next table sits another hopeful quiz team, comprising the Hensons, Mandelson and Neaves. Falling short of being close buddies, Sebastian Henson had formed what could be described as a loose friendship with Mandelson due to their business dealings with McCarthy and the hotel development. Other mutual social and business interests, including membership of the local golf club as well as Mandelson's position in the local authority, made the Councillor a worthwhile associate. In contrast, Henson's attitude to Neaves is lukewarm. Less is more, is Henson's strategy regarding the builder.

Julia sits next to her husband, sipping at her Pimms, vacillating between boredom at the conversation and feeling disgust. The latter reserved for Neaves, who seems to spend an inordinate amount of time staring at her cleavage when he is not gawping at her legs. Regretting that she did not choose to wear a longer skirt, she shifts uncomfortably to alter her position, turning her body away from the leering builder. To take her mind off it she tries to make small talk, directing the discussion away from boring business matters raised by her husband.

"So, Jeffrey, what drags you down here tonight? I wouldn't have thought pub quiz nights was your thing."

"It's not really Julia," replies Mandelson, "but it does no harm to make yourself visible to the electorate on occasion. A man of the people and all that."

Neaves stifles a chuckle at Mandelson's self-description and lack of self-awareness. Henson also disguises a smirk by taking a drink from his gin and tonic. Both actions escape Mandelson's attention, which is focused on their attractive team member with a series of questionable thoughts crossing his mind.

"You look stunning tonight, Julia, as ever. Tell me, what do you think will be your specialist area?" Gazing lecherously into her eyes, his lascivious smile causes her to avert her gaze. She inwardly shivers in mild disgust. It was bad enough with Neaves drooling opposite her.

It is going to be a long night, she thinks to herself, before she replies.

"I suppose history, culture, fashion, and the arts. If I had to choose. And what about you Mr Neaves?" she asks, to redirect the focus of attention away from herself.

Neaves shapes his mouth to reply, but Mandelson jumps with a mean-spirited joke. "Well, it's a good job you've got these covered Julia, because there is not a cultural bone in our Ronald's body."

Sebastian laughs out of deference to Mandelson, but the jibe draws a barely disguised scowl from Neaves who spits out a retort, his ego bruised.

"Jeffrey may have a point Julia, but I suppose I have got the more masculine areas covered which is probably just as well." He looks pointedly at Mandelson by way of revenge. "So, I can do the sports questions. Maybe you can do the rest Jeffrey, such as flower arranging."

This time Sebastian's laughter is less contrived. Not used to being bested by his friend, it is Mandelson's turn to scowl.

"Now, now, team members, let's all be supportive tonight. We need to work as a team," says Julia.

"Indeed," replies Mandelson, still smarting from the insult. "And it would not do to be shown up by the locals, or should I say yokels, would it?"

At a small table near the bar, the Addinalls are huddled together, both getting increasingly nervous as the beginning of the quiz draws near. They are hoping for reinforcements to bolster their team.

"Oh, I do hope Chris can join us. He promised he would, if he gets back in time," says Freda.

"I'm sure he will. Surely whatever business he had in Scarborough must be finished by now," replies Mary.

"Hope so, and on my way back from the toilet I had a quick chat with Donald sat over there in his usual seat at the bar. I asked him if he would join our team."

"Goody," replies Mary, clapping her hands, "do you think he will?"

Leaning into her sister, Freda answers the question conspiratorially. "I think so, but you know what he's like. He promised to join us, if he hasn't drunk too much by the time it starts."

Pointing at a table over the other side of the bar, Mary

tells her sister of her failed plan. "I also asked Betty when I was at the store this morning, but she said she couldn't as she had promised to be in a team with Stan Proudfoot. Apparently, his niece, Lois, is also joining them."

"Well, they will be hard to beat," says Freda. "A butcher, a storekeeper and a budding journalist, they'll have food and drink covered as well as current affairs."

"Not as good as our team, if we get Donald and Chris," replies Mary.

Laden with drinks and packets of crisps, Stan Proudfoot returns from the bar to his own table. It is adjacent to the Addinalls and, realising that they are staring at him, he gives them a nod. The sisters wave back.

"Thanks Uncle Stan," says Lois. She carefully extracts her drink and a packet of crisps from her uncle's grasp, enabling him to pass Betty her glass, whilst placing his own on the table.

"Jeez, it's busier than Piccadilly Circus in 'ere tonight, thought I would never get served. Looks like the whole blooming village is 'ere," says Stan, patting the beads of sweat off his bald head with a handkerchief. "Whilst I was at the bar, I looked back over 'ere and thought our team looked a little light on numbers. Anyway, I saw Arthur sitting at the bar on his lonesome. There he was, stood supping beer with the weight of the world on 'is shoulders. Anyway, I invited him to join us which, after a bit of persuading, he said he would once he got 'imself another pint. Hope that's okay?"

"Okay by me," replies Lois

"And me," adds Betty.

"Good, not sure he'll be much use, mind."

Patting Stan on the hand, Betty says, "it's not the point, it's a lovely thought."

Watching this interaction, Lois wonders if her suspicion

had merit. Had her Uncle Stan and Betty developed a relationship beyond mere friendship? But she keeps this thought to herself with a brief smile, taking a mental note of the fondness for Betty that was evident in her uncle's eyes.

"So, are you courting yet, young Lois?" asks Betty.

"Sorry Betty, what do you mean?"

"Courting, love," explains Stan, "it's a turn of phrase some old 'uns use for dating. Y'know, 'aving a boyfriend."

"Less of the old 'un, Mr Proudfoot," chides Betty, with a smile.

Before Lois can respond, a shadow looms over the table and she looks up to see the dour expression of Arthur Messruther. Her welcoming smile is not reciprocated.

"Ow do Arthur, take a seat and join the A team," says Stan, gesticulating at the spare chair.

"Thanks," responds Arthur, sitting beside Lois.

"Have you met Lois?" asks Stan.

Arthur nods. Lois reminds her uncle that she had interviewed Arthur when researching her piece about the mysterious sightings in the woods around the village. She explains to Stan and Betty that his boys had seen the alleged aliens and it transpires that they had, inadvertently, also been the cause of the furore created by the mysterious lights seen in the woods. This makes them all chuckle and breaks the ice.

At the bar Ken is busily checking that all the necessary preparations are complete before starting proceedings. Taking himself through a mental checklist he decides he is ready. He has the questions; the microphone has been tested, entry fees collected, and all the teams have pre-printed sheets on which to write their answers. Switching on the microphone and testing it with a quick tap, he speaks into it. His voice booms through the speaker, prompting him to adjust the volume before repeating his introduction.

"Ow do all. Welcome to Quiz night at the Old Plough. There will be five categories each with ten questions. The categories are, Music, Food and Drink, West Ayton, Sport, and General Knowledge. Dolly will collect the answers at the end of each round, and we'll read out the scores as we go along."

This was greeted with various murmurings from the crowd, with those teams from outside the village complaining amongst themselves about the unfair advantage that locals will have on the 'West Ayton' category.

"Right, for the first round, 'Music', we'll play the introduction of a song and all you need to do is write down the name of the artist. All quiet now 'cause I'll only play it once."

For the first time in the evening, silence descends on the busy bar and after a short introduction the first lines are played, and the smooth silky voice of a famous crooner slips out of the speaker.

> *"Let there be you, let there be me*
> *Let there be oysters, under the sea*
> *Let there be wind and occasional rain*
> *Chilli con carne and sparkling champagne*
> *Let there be Cuckoos, a Lark and a Dove*
> *But first ... "*

Groans can be heard amongst the audience, when the song is abruptly cut off. Tables with the older patrons give each other the thumbs up. A wag calls out from the back table, comprising of twenty somethings from Snainton, a neighbouring village.

"Hey Mister, are there going to be any songs from after we are born."

Eyeing the heckler, Ken responds, "Sorry son, there ain't no songs from Frozen or any other Disney films for that matter. But maybe yer mum will sing you one at bedtime."

This is greeted by laughter from other tables which get louder when Ken adds, whilst pointedly examining his wristwatch, "yer bedtime is in about an hour, so I'd best get a move on, or you'll be late for your cocoa."

A cheer rises from the table of twenty somethings when the next song plays, which leaves the older patrons scratching their heads.

> *"Mummy don't know daddy's getting hot*
> *At the body shop doing something unholy*
> *He lucky, lucky, yeah (ooh)*
> *He lucky, lucky, (ye-yeah) … "*

Another round of groans as the song ends abruptly. On Stan Proudfoot's table, Lois smiles at the blank looks of her teammates. Struggling to find an answer Betty suggests it might be by Kylie Minogue because she is sure Kylie has a song that had the words "lucky" repeated in it a few times. Without saying a word, Lois, the designated scribe, writes the answer and the others, checking what she has written, all agree that they have never heard of him.

"What! Who the hell is Sam Smith? Sounds more like a bricklayer than a pop star," whispers Stan, in case the neighbouring team hear the answer.

Once the music round ends, the answer sheets are collected and there is a brief interlude enabling the patrons to refresh their drinks whilst Betty marks the sheets and reads out the scores. Stan Proudfoot's team are the early leaders. No one is more surprised than Stan himself, but the mixture of youth and age pays dividends on a round which had recent hits combined with old, very old, classics. Conversation around the bar is animated but quickly silenced when the landlords voice, once more, booms through the speaker.

"Come on now, let's 'av some silence. Right, come on now everyone, settle down, we're starting round two. It's 'Food an' Drink.' Question one. What's the name of the highly prized beef, which is high in fat content, originating from Japan?"

Stan whispers the answer to Lois, who writes it down after checking the spelling with her uncle.

Ken continues. "Question two. What food is also a term for serving a prison sentence?"

Kelly leans over to Hayes, who is their nominated scribe and whispers the answer. Hendricks gives his new friend, and team mate, a thumbs up.

"Question three. "What spirit is traditionally made using the juniper berry?"

When the quiz started, Donald, true to his word, had joined the Addinalls at their table. Three gins later he was a little worse for wear and his attempt at stealthily communicating the answer becomes a stage whisper, audible to the next table. Gratefully, Freda, as well as the scribe at the neighbouring table, unapologetically writes down the answer. All is fair in love and war.

Answers collected and tallied, Dolly announces the positions after two rounds and Stan Proudfoot's team remain firmly in the lead. Ken takes the microphone from Dolly, who returns to help behind the bar, and announces the next round. Groans from the twenty-somethings table, given the subject matter, cheers from elsewhere.

At Henson's table, the conversation has been stilted. Mandelson sits in simmering disappointment that his team is performing below expectations given the intellectual weight and social position of its members. The weak link, Neaves, has failed to answer a single question, but Mandelson hopes that his friend will pull his weight on the sports round.

Ken reads the first question of the 'West Ayton' round.

"What year was the tower, known as Ayton Castle, built?"

More groans from the twenty something table which become vocal complaints after the second question is read.

"What is the name of the ancient Celtic tribe that is believed to have settled in the area?"

Bingo, thinks Mandelson. *So those committee meetings are of some use after all, and that batty old cow, Councillor Stokes, has brought home the bacon with her spirit orbs.*

He leans over to Julia, who has taken charge of recording the answers, causing her to slightly recoil in a mixture of surprise and disgust at the invasion of her personal space.

"The answer is Parisi, my dear," he whispers. She looks at him quizzically, so he explains pompously. "They are called the Parisi, spelt P... A... R... I... S... I. I like to keep abreast of our local history. I believe, as a person holding a position of authority and representing the people for the good of the area, it is incumbent upon me to learn and understand how the parish became what it is today. Wouldn't you agree?"

"I suppose so," replies Julia, relieved that he has retreated and settled back into his chair. When the round of questions ends Mandelson excuses himself for a toilet break and Neaves leaves the table to make a private call outside the pub.

"Really Sebastian, those two are bloody awful, particularly that lech, Mandelson. He gives me the creeps. Next time you want a social get together with them, please count me out. Say I've got a migraine or something."

"Sorry, will do, dear," apologies Sebastian. "Another drink?"

"Yes, same again. And make it a large one. I'm going to need it to make it through the rest of the evening. Quiet now, I can see that Hannibal Lecter is on his way back."

"Hope you didn't miss me too much?" jokes Mandelson, as he settles back into his chair.

At the microphone Dolly gives an update on the scores. Whilst Hayes and Hendricks are disappointed at their lowly ranking, in contrast, Mandelson is pleased that his team have closed the gap on the leaders. Passing the microphone back to her husband, Dolly returns behind the bar.

"Okey dokey people. We are up to round four and its 'Sport'." The first question falls straight into Neaves' hand as a keen amateur rugby player.

"What year did England become the first Northern Hemisphere nation to win the Rugby Union World Cup?"

Around the tables there is a mixed response. Both Stan's table and that of the Addinall's are surrounded by blank faces. Kelly whispers the answer to Hayes. Neaves, at his table, can barely contain himself when giving his first answer of the night to Julia. The next question generates the exact same result.

"Question two – what is the name of the trophy given to England when they won the world cup in 1966?"

By the time the round finishes Stan is only able to answer three of the ten questions with Lois helping with a fourth, which seeks the name of the new manager of Scarborough Athletic FC. This was a fortunate question because she had recently interviewed the first female manager in the club's history.

Despite a zero score at the Addinall's table, the sisters clap excitedly when Ashton joins them.

"Sorry ladies, I only just got back. I guess I missed it," apologises Ashton.

"Don't you worry Chris, there is still one round to go," replies Mary.

Donald mumbles something, but the gin has made him almost incoherent.

"Okay ladies ... Donald ... anyone want another drink? I'll grab one before the last round starts."

Returning with a full complement of drinks for the table, which includes one for Donald who had decided he could manage one more gin and tonic, Ashton settles in his seat just in time to hear the final score update. Nobody seems disappointed at the lowly position of the team with one round to go. It was clear that there were three leaders sufficiently ahead of the pack, making a win by the remaining tables unlikely. Stan Proudfoot's and Mandelson's tables are neck and neck, with the twentysomethings in close pursuit.

For the final time, Dolly hands the microphone to Ken.

"This is it – the final round and it is ... 'General Knowledge'. Question one. Where can you find Cleopatra's Needle?"

"In her sewing kit," shouts out a wag from a table at the back, who gets immediately shushed by the more serious participants.

"Come on lads, don't spoil it for the rest, otherwise I'll have to show you the door," warns Ken. His reputation for dealing with troublemakers ensures that the wag recedes back into anonymity and silence.

Satisfied he has order, Ken continues. "Alright then, question two. What is the world's smallest country?"

A further eight questions follow accompanied by groans and minor complaints from those not in the know. In contrast whispered urgent responses or squeals of triumph arise from those who have the answer. And then the quiz ends, papers are collected and, a few minutes later, Dolly returns to the microphone to confirm the correct answers of the last round before announcing the results. She hits a roadblock immediately when giving the answer to question one.

"Objection,' shouts Donald, with a gin laden slur. The room falls silent, and Dolly looks quizzically at her favourite regular.

"Sorry Donald, what do you mean? I can assure you Cleopatra's Needle is in London. Ken and I saw it when we went down for a long weekend."

"Get you," slurs Donald, "dirty weekends at your age."

Drawing laughter from the crowd, Dolly waits for it to die down. "Very, very funny Donald, but the answer is right."

"So is mine, luvvy," counters Donald. "I can tell you from my years tripping the light fantastic in the big Apple that, it too, has a Cleopatra's Needle."

During the interchange, Ken had googled the answer on his mobile phone and intervenes. "Dolly love, strictly speaking Donald seems to be right. It seems there is a pair, one is in London and the other in New York."

"Told you," slurs Donald, triumphantly.

"Fair enough Donald, I'll adjust your table's score. Anyone else put down New York?" The room stays silent. "However, and I'm sorry Donald, but this does not affect the result I'm afraid. Drum roll please Ken." Her husband slams his meaty hands on the bar rhythmically and finishes with a flurry.

Taking a deep breath, Dolly announces the result. "For the first time in the history of the Old Plough pub quiz, we have a tie for the prize of one hundred pounds. Congratulations to Councillor Mandelson's table and

Stan Proudfoot's team. Do you want to split the hundred pounds?"

It did not escape Mandelson's notice that the cheer for Stan's team was significantly louder than the muted, polite applause for his team. This irked him and, determined to make a point, he calls out to Dolly before Stan has a chance to respond to the suggestion of sharing the money.

"No, no, no Mrs Wilkes, surely, we need to have just one champion. You really must have a tie breaker. There must be a clear winner."

Looking over to Stan to get his approval, Dolly sees the butcher give a shrug, followed by a nod of agreement. Stan congratulates Betty, Lois and Arthur, assuring them that they have all done well to come joint first and tells them not to worry about the tie breaker.

"Okay, silence please," requests Dolly. "What I am going to do is give a gradual series of descriptions of an object. If anyone on your team thinks they know it, they must raise their hand. If they get the answer right, they have won. If not, the other team gets the next clue and only they can answer."

"And what if this is also wrong?" asks Mandelson.

Then another clue is read out and both can answer. We keep going until one team gets it right. Is that clear?"

"Crystal," says Mandelson, brimming with confidence.

"Yes, loud and clear, Betty," responds Stan.

"Here we go. Hand up if you want to answer, but if you get it wrong your team is locked out for the next clue."

"First clue. It flies in the air."

Both teams keep their hands down.

"Second clue. The military uses it as well as civilians."

No one offers an answer.

"It does not have a pilot in it."

Arthur's hand immediately shoots up. Dolly points to

him to give an answer. Mandelson swings round to see who has raised their hand. He sniggers with confidence, seeing the respondent is Arthur Messruther. *That bloody moron can barely tie his shoelaces.*

With his teammates looking on in surprise, Arthur calls out his answer, "A Drone."

"Correct," shouts Dolly, which is drowned by the cacophonous applause around the bar.

Almost apologetically, Arthur explains to his teammates that his boys have one. It was a present from their auntie. Stan pats him on the back and Betty gives him a hug, which he accepts awkwardly.

"Well done, Arthur," says Lois, clapping as Dolly hands the cash to him.

"That's twenty-five quid each," says Arthur, handing out the winnings.

Gradually the pub begins to empty as final orders are called and even Ken is too tired to finish the night singing 'My Way', as he does most nights.

Kelly excuses himself, and quickly exits the pub at the rear. Cigarette in hand, he speaks into his mobile phone whilst constantly scanning his surroundings for any unwanted ears that may be listening in. No other smokers are outside. He had feared a fruitless night until he was greeted by the welcome sign of Ashton, who he instantly recognised, joining the Addinalls at their table late in the quiz proceedings. There was no way Ashton would recognise him despite their encounter at close quarters because, unlike Doyle, he had kept his mask on. Nevertheless, he had kept his head down and shuffled his chair sideways, so he was partially hidden by the body and unruly afro of Hendricks.

"Yes Mr McCarthy, I am one hundred percent certain it is him."

"Is he still in the pub?" snaps McCarthy.

"Yep, but it's closing time. What do you want me to do?"

"Other than follow him and find out where he lives … fuck all."

"You don't want me to sort him out?"

"The only one who did any 'sorting out' was him. If you couldn't handle him with the help of the other moron you hang around with, how do you expect to cope on your own? I'll pay him a visit in the next day or so once you find out where he lives. Just don't let him fucking clock you. Alright!"

"Yeah, okay boss. No worries."

The line had already gone dead, prompting Kelly to stamp out what remained of his cigarette and get to work. Luckily for him, he sees Ashton leave out of the front entrance as he re-enters the bar from the rear. Rushing to the front door, he does not hear both Hayes and Hendricks shout their goodbyes as he passes them.

"Bit rude I reckon. Do you think he was pissed off we didn't win?" asks Hendricks.

"Doubt it mate," replies Hayes, "let's face it, we didn't get close all night."

Once he is outside the pub, Kelly looks around, turning in a 360-degree circle. His heartbeat flutters with concern that he has lost Ashton and the consequences that would follow with McCarthy. Looking first right, then left up the High Street, he finally locates his quarry and trots a few metres to ensure he is close enough to keep him in sight, but not conspicuous. Reaching the butcher's shop, Kelly is taken by surprise when Ashton takes a left up the pathway to his house. He was expecting Ashton to live where most of the houses were located, at the southeastern tip of the village. He pauses at Betty's store, where he can see Ashton unlock his front door and enter the house. Satisfied he has the right man, in the right place he makes another call from the doorway of Betty's Store.

"Hi boss, it's me again. Just letting you know that it is the right bloke and I have his address. He basically lives on the High Street, in the house nearest to the grocer's shop."

"You are absolutely certain?" snaps McCarthy.

"Yes boss. Are you sure you don't want me to do anything tonight?"

"What and risk another fuck up? No. Just make yourself scarce. Crappy little places like Ayton attract gossip and attention when strangers hang about late at night. So just piss off home. I'll deal with it from here."

The line goes dead and Kelly breathes a sigh of relief.

At the same moment that Kelly leaves the borders of the village on his Kawasaki Ninja, Hardy walks out of the pub and makes a call of his own. Cold, miserable, and slightly damp from his evening in the woods, Stanley answers, hopeful that his boss is calling to bring an unpleasant night to an end.

"Yes boss, what's the story?"

"Not a lot, I was hoping you might have something useful to report," replies Hardy.

"Nothing much to be honest. What about you?"

"The place was packed to the rafters with locals who all seem to know each other so most could be written off as suspects. There was one shifty looking geezer sat on his own who joined two equally shifty looking muppets who we both are acquainted with. The time wasting undynamic duo, Hayes and Hendricks, who we first met when investigating the Dibley murder case."

"Yeah, I remember them. The local druggie oxygen thieves. Can't see them involved in an organised jewel heist," replies Stanley.

"Yeah right, they couldn't organise a piss-up in a brewery. However, the person they got to join them in the quiz set off my antennae. Not sure I would bet my house on it, but he has the look and smell of someone who has spent some time in court and, dare I say, prison."

"Did you talk to him boss?"

"No, I didn't. I went to the toilet when the quiz ended but by the time I came out he had buggered off. I asked the two muppets if they knew him but that drew a blank. They couldn't even tell me his name. They reckoned he wasn't local but had no idea where he's from, nor what he was doing in the village. A veritable mine of information … not."

"Shame boss."

"What about you? Anything at all?" asks Hardy.

"Nothing really, I did at one point think I heard some movement in the woods about fifty metres from where I was positioned. Tried to creep around and pinpoint it, but nothing. It sounded quite big and heavy, so it wasn't a fox, or badger or anything like that. I did get the feeling of being watched but nothing other than that." Stanley, with little more to offer, falls silent.

Feeling of being watched for fuck sake, muses Hardy. Disappointed, but not surprised, Stanley's report had nothing, nada, zero, to offer.

"Okay, well no point in flogging a dead horse. Where are you now?"

"Still in position, boss."

"In that case, I suggest you make your way down to the High Street. I'll meet you in the pub carpark and we'll call it a night."

Tracking south along the tree line on the eastern side of Higginbottom's field, Stanley occasionally looks back over his shoulder. Still a little spooked and uneasy, he replays the noises he heard in his mind and feels a tinge of relief when he reaches the comforting haven of the High Street lights.

He is unaware of a big, unkempt figure, stood a few metres inside the tree line of the woods and observing his progress back to civilisation. Once Stanley is out of sight, the figure lifts his large left hand to examine three rabbits held by their hind legs, hanging limp and lifeless. Satisfied with the night's work, the figure treads with heavy footfalls deeper into the woods. An owl hoots, warning other wildlife of the presence of the interloper, but the other creatures stay silent and hidden. Eventually, the owl resumes its own stealthy night hunt for nourishment and the village, like the surrounding woods, falls silent.

19

IT HAD BEEN over a year since Ashton had the pleasure of visiting Scarborough Police station and he could see that nothing had changed. The reception area was still in need of a fresh coat of paint and had the same oppressive uninviting atmosphere as he remembered it. Even the expression on the face of the desk sergeant had not changed, greeting all visitors with his sardonic smile.

Approaching the desk, Ashton explains that he has an appointment with detectives Hardy and Stanley which prompts the sergeant to turn to the constable sat at a table behind him who has his head down, vigorously tapping on a keyboard.

"Oi Pete, if I can tear you away from your spreadsheet? Can you ring through to Mulder and Scully and tell them that their guest is at reception?" Turning back to face Ashton, he gestures for him to take a seat in the waiting area.

Checking his mobile, Ashton sees he has a message from Steve which is simply a 'thumbs up' emoji. Earlier he had sent a text to tell his friend that the theory of the Fylingdale boffins was correct, and the mysterious lights did turn out to be a drone.

The door to the side of the reception desk opens and the more welcoming face and smile of Stanley greets

Ashton. "Come through Mr Ashton." They make their way down the corridor and take a sharp left through a door marked Interview Room 2.

Hardy is sitting at the table in the sparsely decorated room. Stanley takes the seat adjacent to him and Ashton sits opposite.

"Thank you for coming Mr Ashton, I really appreciate it. We could use your help," says Hardy with as much bonhomie as he can muster on a Monday morning.

"Help? Well, that's a relief. Last time I was here I recall you grilled me as a murder suspect."

"Yes, the Dibley case, but I'm sure, with your own background in military intelligence, that you can appreciate we had to pursue all possible channels. Anyway, let's not dwell on that. There are two reasons I asked you in today. Firstly, I notice you were at the quiz in the Old Plough last Friday."

"I was indeed, albeit a late arrival."

"I just wanted to ask you if you noticed the man who was sitting on the table with Mr Hayes and Mr Hendricks?"

"Yes, I know Purple and Colin and I did notice them as well as the other man. Why do you ask?"

Leaning forward Hardy replies. "Because the other man is a stranger to the village according to these two gentlemen and we've been keeping an eye out for newcomers given the odd events in the area. Events including your own altercation with two individuals. I know one was masked but I assume you got a good look at the other one. The one you knocked to the ground."

Wary at where this line of questioning was going, Ashton leans back to gather his own thoughts. *A possible assault charge against me*, he wondered. "I am not sure exactly what you want to know. I did take him out but he was the aggressor. He attacked me. For the record, I was acting in self-defence."

Holding up his hands in conciliation, Hardy seeks to quickly dispel Ashton's fears. "No. No, Mr Ashton. We have no issue with you, nor how you dealt with the situation. In fact, the other witnesses commended your actions at the time. I was wondering if it is possible that the man at the table was one of the attackers?'

"No, afraid not. I did get a good look at the one on the ground, but I am almost certain it wasn't him. The other guy had his mask on, as you say, and all I can tell you is that his overall build may have been quite similar. That is the best I can do. Sorry about that. I couldn't tell you with any certainty that it was the same man."

"Okay, it was a long shot but worth a try," says Hardy, with an air of disappointment.

"And what was the second thing? You said there was a couple of things I could help you with?"

"Yes indeed. I wondered if you would accompany Detective Stanley to his desk. He has dug out a few pictures from our database of local criminals with a record of theft. We wondered if you would look through them to see if any jog your memory and whether any could be the man who assaulted you. Not to mention of course the man in the pub. I've had a look myself, but I must confess I didn't pay him much attention."

Led by Stanley, Ashton is guided further into the bowels of the station and eventually enters an open plan area which proves to be as depressing as the rest of the station. Off white yellowing painted walls and very little natural light, except for a small window at the far end of the room, created a depressing atmosphere. Settled into the chair at Stanley's desk, Ashton leans to one side allowing the detective to reach over his shoulder and tap the keyboard a few times. An image of the head and shoulders of a dark-haired male appears on the screen.

"We have about fifty pictures for you to work through. Just take your time Mr Ashton and scroll right to see the next picture. I'll leave you to it and be back in a few minutes."

Ten minutes later, Ashton was checking through the last three pictures and, hearing voices, turned to see Stanley approaching in the company of two familiar faces.

"Hiya Chris, how ya doing?" says Hayes cheerily.

"Good, Purple. So, what are you two doing here?"

"Helping the police with their inquiries," answers Hendricks, brushing back his afro fringe.

"Is that a good … 'helping with their inquiries,' or a bad … 'helping with their inquiries'?" asks Ashton.

Chuckling good naturedly, Stanley replies. "Nothing sinister Mr Ashton. We want them to look at the same pictures that you've just seen. They had a much closer look at their mystery guest at the quiz. We were hoping that they might recognise him from our rogue's gallery. Talking of which, did you have any luck?"

"Not really. There are a couple that are possibles, but I'm far from certain. Both are possibles from the encounter I had in the woods with the unmasked assailant. If it's one of these, then I'm not sure which one I would pick. As for the Purple's and Colin's quiz mate, I can't say I could recognise him from any of the pictures you gave me. But they spent most of the evening with him, so perhaps they might have more luck."

Whilst Stanley prints out the images and associated file on the two men identified by Ashton, Hayes and Hendricks settle themselves into the seats in front of the screen. Repeating the instructions he gave Ashton, Stanley sets the two friends to their task.

They start to scroll through the images whilst Stanley escorts Ashton out of the building shaking his hand and thanking him before he makes his way through the main entrance. Three repeat visits to his desk and twenty-five minutes later, a relieved Stanley hears Hayes and Hendricks finally announce that they had been through all the images. Given the time they had taken, the detective had high hopes, but these were immediately dashed.

"Sorry officer, we don't think any of these are the bloke in the pub," says Hendricks.

"You both sure? You seemed to take a long time. I thought you might have had a couple of 'possibles' to show me," replies a deflated Stanley, trying to hide his downcast expression.

Realising that any further prompts would be fruitless, Stanley escorts the two men out of the building and, with the printouts in hand, heads straight for Hardy's office. Feet on his desk with a pie in one hand, Hardy greets Stanley through a mouthful of food. An occasional flaky crumb escapes onto his shirt. Brushing off a rogue piece of pastry from his trousers, he sits up straight and throws the remains of his pie towards the bin under his desk. Unaware that his aim is awry, the crust bounces off the edge of the bin and onto the, already heavily stained, carpet under.

"Sorry, got a bit hungry, missed breakfast," he explains taking the documents from Stanley.

"All good boss, I have given you two pictures of persons of interest and a summary of their criminal record. These were picked out by Mr Ashton, who admits he is not committing to a positive identification but believes the man he floored in the woods could be one of them. Obviously, it was quite dark, and it all happened so fast. So he could not in all conscience testify in court. But it could be a start."

Sitting quietly, whilst Hardy reads the paperwork, Stanley checks his mobile for messages. Still no response from his date on Saturday. Across the desk he sees a wide range of expressions cross Hardy's face whilst absorbing the information. Eventually, he puts the papers to one side.

"I must admit, the two he picked do look similar. And you say that Ashton cannot identify either of them with certainty. Does he incline toward one rather than the other?

"No boss, he said that, at best, he can say that the man in the woods looked very much like these two. I agree that they are very similar. Dark hair, brown eyes, late thirties et cetera."

Hardy picks the papers up to re-examine them, before replying to Stanley.

"Not only that, but their records are similar. Both have convictions for low level burglary, so I'm unconvinced that they are in the same league as the Friedman robbery." Waving the photos in his hand he adds, "So, we have a Dennis Martin and Barry Doyle. I've got to admit that looking at these photos they could be twins. I wonder if both are still living local. On the basis that we have bugger all else to go on, perhaps they are worth checking out. See what you can find out. Put a little pressure on and decide whether it's worth pulling them in to make a statement if their alibis are shonky."

"Okay boss." Stanley moves to rise from the chair but is stopped in his tracks.

"Hang on, don't rush off. What about the two muppets?"

"Oh, Hayes and Hendricks. 'Fraid they were a total blank."

"What a surprise," replies Hardy, waving away Stanley.

No sooner had Stanley left the office than Hardy's mobile rings. Examining the screen an unwelcome name appears. Hardy braces himself.

"Yes sir, how are you today?"

"It's been a shit day Hardy and I'm hoping that you may have news to brighten it up a little," replies DI Parkins, not bothering to return the niceties.

"If I'm honest there has been progress of sorts and a couple of leads on the diamond robbery in Scarborough. We have two possible suspects, but it is early days. One witness has potentially identified two ex-cons from our database but, given the circumstances, cannot be certain it was them."

"Why not? What circumstances for God's sake?"

"It was night, therefore the light was poor, not to mention that the witness was being assaulted at the time. Both those identified as potential suspects have 'previous' which involves theft, so it is certainly a possibility. We're going to investigate it with a light touch."

"Meaning?" snaps Parkins irritably.

"We'll see if either can account for their movements on key dates for a starting point."

"Okay, well keep me informed if you get something more substantial."

The line goes silent. Hardy mutters an expletive. His day had just got worse but at least they had some vague lead to follow. Better than nothing. Just.

Later that morning the three villagers who had assisted the detectives are sitting together, drinking coffee in Betty's store. Due to public demand, Betty had set up a high narrow table next to the front window with four bars stools and offers coffee with sandwiches or cake as a sideline to her grocery business. It had proved to be a popular little meeting place amongst the villagers. For once, Councillor Mandelson, seeing the new set up, had held his peace, knowing that Council rules would strictly require a permit to provide catering. He knew only too well that if he raised this and blocked Betty's innovation, that his popularity amongst the villagers would diminish. They are, after all, his electorate.

Ashton had paid for the coffee and ham sandwiches which Hayes and Hendricks were demolishing whilst he sipped his flat white. Having met by chance on the High Street, Ashton had suggested they have a quick chat to compare notes.

Dressed in a Nike tracksuit following his morning run, Ashton looks on at the two friends and waits for a suitable break in their sandwich consumption to ask a question. "So, lads, were you able to be of assistance to Hercule Poirot and his sidekick?"

"Eh! Who's he?" asks Hendricks, wiping a smudge of pickle off his chin whilst also defying the laws of physics by getting a bread crumb lodged in the upper echelons of his afro.

"He's joking mate. Poirot is a TV detective," clarifies Hayes. "To answer your question Chris, we were of no help at all. We didn't recognise our quiz teammate from any of the pictures they showed us. They weren't happy. Sounds to me that they are getting desperate."

Shaking his head whilst scratching his dark stubble, Ashton responds. "Wouldn't worry about it Purple. Although I didn't get as good a look as you two did, I didn't spot him either. Best I could do was to pick out a couple of punters who might have been the bloke in the Spider-Man costume who I had a scrap with."

"So do you think one of the two that you picked is him?"

"Not convinced Purple. Hard to say when you are trying to wrestle him in the pitch dark whilst he's busy swinging a spade at your head. It's less than a fifty percent chance in my opinion, but it is possible."

Polishing off the last sandwich, to the disgust of his friend who had been distracted by responding to Ashton, Hendricks asks. "How would they have the pictures?"

"I suspect they were showing us a rogue's gallery of those with convictions for theft or assault who live in the area."

"Theft?"

"Yep. They seem to think there is some sort of connection between the Spider-Man duo in the woods and the robbery in Scarborough, but don't ask me why, because I have no idea."

"Stupid theory I reckon," says Hendricks dismissively.

"What are you on about mate? How can you say it's a stupid theory? I swear, as each day goes by, I'm convinced you've had too many mushrooms mate. You need to lay off," jokes Hayes.

"Not at all my dear compadre. I doubt if the two blokes in Spider-Man costumes were criminals. Who is Spider-Man, pray tell. He's a superhero not a villain."

"Fair comment," laughs Ashton.

"Yep, fair comment," adds Hayes.

"And what are you three gentlemen finding so amusing?" They all turn around to Mandelson, who addresses them whilst adjusting the buttons on his Armani suit jacket. His presence immediately dampening the mood.

"Not a great deal, Councillor," responds Ashton. "We were just discussing our experience helping the local constabulary with their investigation."

"Into what may I ask?"

"They seem to think the Spider-Men we found in the

woods might also be involved in the Scarborough jewel robbery."

"Oh yes, the Spider-Men. Our very own extra-terrestrials. I also hear you not only solved that mystery but also the alien lights. The Messruther brats, I hear on the grapevine, playing with their toys. A drone I believe."

Frowning, Ashton responds. "I wouldn't call them brats. They are just ordinary teenagers and Arthur is doing his best bringing them up on his own. It was all harmless and unintentional."

"I wouldn't know. But well done, and this only leaves one more mystery to solve."

"What's that?" asks Hayes.

"Finding what those Americans call the Sasquatch. I have to say we have not had any more reports since they left. Perhaps they were responsible for it, to drum up business so to speak. Dressing themselves up in monkey suits or the like."

"No way man," says Hendricks. "We saw it firsthand and that was before the yanks came into town."

"Yep, it's true," confirms Hayes, backing up his friend.

"Perhaps," replies Mandelson huffily. "There again I do wonder how sober you both were at the time."

Without waiting for a reply, Mandelson walks to the counter to give Betty his order. She serves him and he departs with a perfunctory 'goodbye' to the three men as he closes the shop door behind him.

"Never really warmed to him," offers Betty.

"I know what you mean Betty," replies Ashton.

"Bloke's a pompous arsehole," adds Hayes.

20

ABOVE THE FORGE Valley woods the orange glow of the rising moon bathes it's verdant canopy. Between the gaps of the trees the moonshine lights up the forest floor, highlighting a small rabbit transfixed in its radiance.

Heavy footfalls approach causing the rabbit's ears to twitch and the snap of a nearby branch precipitates it's flight to safety. Nearby, two foxes stare in the direction of the sound, give a sharp screech and escape into the haven of their den.

Footfalls get nearer and louder until they stop abruptly. A large figure looms, still as a statue, in the clearing. The woods have gone silent, the figure cocks its head, straining to hear a sound. Gradually, a distant buzzing in the air draws its attention. It turns slowly and strides towards the noise.

Deciding that the village drama has long passed, the Messruther twins agree it is time to venture out on another night excursion, despite the consequences of disobedience which had been laid out by their father. *Not a big deal anyway, the old man's out for the night wrapped in his beer dreams*, they decide. Having discovered a new and unused function on their drone, they couldn't wait to try it out.

"The camera on this thing is mint. I'm glad you worked out how to use it," says Ben, excitedly.

"Yer brother's a bloody genius," replies Billy, smugly.

"We really need to test it during the day though, 'cause it's hard to see anything."

"Yer can see a bit 'cause of the moon," says Billy defensively. "Look, there's the top of the trees and you can see through the gaps to the ground. I even saw a couple of foxes a minute ago."

"Nah yer didn't."

"Yeah I did."

"Okay let me have a go."

"Don't bloody crash it," warns Billy, as he hands over the controls. "See if you can see anything through the gaps in the trees and, if you do, press the record button to see if it works. It's the red button with the word 'Rec' next to it." Billy's instructions fall on deaf ears.

Hopping from foot to foot, Billy nervously watches his brother fly the drone and, to his relief and surprise, Ben controls it expertly. Now relaxed, he encourages his brother to take it further over the woodland and try to find clearings and maybe even record some wildlife. He had visions of doing a job like David Attenborough when he left school. Sweeping eastwards, then westwards, whilst gradually edging the drone north, the boys eyes are transfixed on the console screen. Billy warns Ben to keep checking that there is still plenty of battery power and range. Giving the thumbs up, Ben looks back at the screen and unexpectedly brings the drone to a halt, letting it hover in one spot.

"What's happening, Ben?" enquires Billy, worried that they may be losing power.

"I can see something is down there on the ground, in that gap. It looks big and it's staring up at the drone. It's spooky, it's like it can see us through the camera."

"Don't be daft, yer must be seeing things. Even if

summat is there, it might be able to see the drone, but it can't grab it. It's too high. It can't see us either."

"Yeah dickhead. I know. But it's a bit spooky. I can't tell what it is. Doesn't look like a bloke but the picture is blurry and it's dark. Do they have bears in Yorkshire?"

"Bears? Nah. Give me the controls."

Ben hands the console to Billy, who looks at the screen and presses the record button before examining the picture more closely. As if the figure senses it is being watched, it seeks refuge under the cloak of the trees and away from the clearing.

"Bugger, it's gone!" exclaims Billy.

"Wonder what it was?"

"Dunno, but at least I recorded it for a few seconds, so we can check it out when we get home."

A mixture of excited anticipation at seeing what they caught on camera, coupled with the fear that they might meet it face to face, drives the twins to rush back home. Sitting next to Billy on his bed, Ben waits patiently for his brother to find the recording and leans in closely, so he can see the small screen. Squinting and straining at the images, they both try to interpret what they are seeing, but the footage is blurred and shrouded in darkness.

Billy presses a series of commands which enable the user to enhance the quality of the recording and, when satisfied he has done everything that the equipment will enable, he replays it. It is better, but far from clear. Nevertheless, the figure is visible. It seems to be large and bulky. After a couple of seconds staring straight at the drone, it turns abruptly, causing what looks like long hair on its shoulders to swing as it moves into the trees out of sight.

"Cool," says Ben

"Yeah, cool," replies Billy. "I reckon that it's the Bigfoot. We should send it to Norman Riders, and he might have us back on his show. He told us to call if we saw anything new."

"Excellent idea."

•¦••¦•

"Weeeelllllcome to the show listeners. It's Norman Riders bringing you the award-winning show, *Riders Brings a Storm*. Award winning? I hear you ask. Yeeessss indeed. I had the pleasure of attending the annual NBA ceremony, that is the Northern Broadcasting Awards, which recognise the work of the best of the best. Annnnddd guess what, we won the best night-time variety show. Our unique mix of music, humour and local interest stories won the day. Did I say, 'local interest'? Talking of 'local interest' we have two young people on today who may have captured the elusive Yorkshire Bigfoot on camera. Regulars will recall we did an item on the mysterious happenings in West Ayton. Aliens, spacecraft, lights and Bigfoot. Yep, we even had American guests on the show, who are experts in the field. Now they went back to their mother country, but we will call one of them shortly to get his expert view on the footage. For those listeners interested, I have put the video up on our website. It is barely ten seconds long, but it certainly is hard to explain. So now we have on the line the Messruther twins, Billy, and Ben. Hi boys."

"Hi Mister Riders," say the twins, both shouting down Billy's mobile, which he has on speaker phone.

"Amazing footage boys, take me through what happened."

Taking charge, Billy responds. "We were out flying our drone and testing out the camera because we hadn't used it before. Anyway, we were in the woods where we live … "

"That's West Ayton, listeners," interrupts Riders.

"Yeah, that's right Mr Riders. Anyway, Ben sees something and passes me the controls and as soon as I saw it, I pressed record ... 'cause Ben doesn't know how to do that. But as soon as I did this, it just looked straight at the camera and then walked off into the trees."

"So, listeners, I should explain. The drone was hovering above a clearing when it spotted the err, shall we say for now, Bigfoot. Once it snuck back into the woods, the trees hid it from view. Well boys, do you think it was a Bigfoot?"

"Yep," says Ben.

"Yep," agrees Billy.

"And boys, tell me, did it make any sound?"

"Nope," says Ben.

"Nope," agrees Billy.

"Er, well, did it gesticulate at you or rather at the drone?"

"Nah," says Ben.

"Nah," agrees Billy.

Getting a clear sense that the information the boys can impart had dried up, Riders moves on.

"Well thank you for your time boys and now we have on the other line Mr Septimus Harcourt, who you may recall, is a Cryptozoologist. Welcome and please remind us of what a Cryptozoologist does."

"Thank you for having me on the show again Norman, it's a real pleasure. And 'Hi' to your listeners. Our brand of science searches for and studies animals whose existence or survival is disputed or unsubstantiated. Beasts such as your very own Loch Ness Monster."

"Excellent, well I know you've seen the footage I sent you, so don't keep us on tenterhooks. What is your opinion?" asks Riders.

"It's an interesting one. The images are too unclear to

be definitive and the aerial shot does not enable us to get any detail or perspective regarding its body shape and size. But I have to say that I am leaning to the possibility that it could be a Bigfoot."

"Why so, Mr Harcourt?"

"It is clearly bipedal, which rules out local wildlife such as foxes, badgers, or deer. And there are certainly no bears or gorillas indigenous to England. Also, the way the figure moves when it walks back under the trees is quite interesting. The sheer biomechanics of the beast's movement leads me to say with certainty that it's not a gorilla or bear, even if one had escaped from a local zoo. The body appears very broad, and it is hard to discern a noticeable neck, which is indicative of a Bigfoot."

"Could it just be a man in a suit?" asks Riders.

"It could," replies Harcourt. "I guess the question to ask is what a person would be doing in the woods late at night dressed as a Bigfoot. If it was a joke, the chances of him being seen would be slim, given the time and location. So, you must ask yourself, why would he bother? Unless of course the boys were part of the hoax and expected to catch something on film."

"No way Mister," interrupts Billy on the other line. "It wasn't us. I swear."

"Don't worry Billy," comforts Riders, "we believe you. Mr Harcourt was just exploring the possibilities."

Riders gives the producer the slashing throat gesture, indicating that the line to the twins should be cut off. Once he gets the thumbs up, he continues. "Whilst we cannot rule out a hoax Mr Harcourt, I am reasonably confident that the Messruther boys were not involved. In fact, it was the boys who reported the alleged alien sighting when you were last here and, it transpires, they did see something. Admittedly, it turned out to be two men in Spider-Man suits whose reason for being there, dressed as they were, is unknown. But my point is, the boys were not trying to deceive, and their mistake was entirely understandable. Men in Spider-Man suits in the dark might look like aliens."

"Well, all I can add, Mr Riders, is that if we are ruling out a hoax created by the boys and accept that the scenario of another person alone in the woods late at night is also unlikely, then the Bigfoot theory might be all we have left. To quote Sherlock Holmes … 'When you have eliminated all which is impossible, then whatever remains, however improbable, must be the truth' …"

"An interesting thought. Once again Mr Harcourt I would like to thank you, I won't even ask what time it is over there, but it must be the early hours of the morning. And to our loyal listeners, you have heard it here first. We break the news in our award-winning show and others just report our discovery."

"No problem Norman, it's actually only early afternoon over here, so no problem and goodbye to your listeners, but please let me know if there are any developments in this strange case." Harcourt's line goes dead and Riders introduces a song.

"Once again, we break the news here first. So, what's an appropriate song for a news breaker do you think? A clue, it's Knight time … that's Knight with a K … it's a song first sung by Gladys Knight and the Pips. But my favourite version is this one … the main man, Marvin Gaye." A low rhythmic guitar, supported by the gentle brushing of symbols, followed by restrained trumpets, leads into the song.

"Ooooo I bet you're wondering how I knew
Bout your plans to make me blue
With some other guy that you knew before
Between the two of us guys
You know I loved you more
It took me by surprise I must say
When I found out yesterday
Ooooo I heard it through the grapevine ..."

.·†··†·.

"Bigfoot. Monsters. What a load of fucking bollocks," McCarthy mutters to himself as he switches off the radio in his Mercedes. He issues a few voice commands, and the ringtone of his mobile reverberates around the car. Kelly answers.

"Yes, boss."

"I'm just double checking that you're sure about the address of Ashton, I do not want any more fuck ups."

"Yeah boss, I'd have thought you'd have been round there already, before he gets rid of the diamonds."

"There are many reasons that I don't pay you to think, and this is a prime example of one of them," snaps McCarthy.

"Sorry boss, no disrespect intended. I just thought it was best to strike whilst the iron's hot."

McCarthy lets out an audible breath of frustration. "There are two possible scenarios. One, he took the diamonds to the police which, if that was his intention, he would have done that straight away. If this occurred, it would not be a good idea for me to go steaming in, would it now?"

"I guess not, but how do you know if he did or not?"

"Because, you idiot, the coppers would have been all over the media crowing about the fact that they have recovered the diamonds. Wouldn't they? They don't miss a chance to publicise a result on the few occasions they get one. Particularly on a case as high profile as this."

"I suppose so."

"And nothing has been reported in the media, has it?"

"No boss."

"That being the case, we have the other scenario. Which is, that he decided to keep the diamonds and is looking to offload them. Which means that we can now make our move before he does, safe in the knowledge that he is not going to go running to the cops if we lift them off him. He can't exactly tell them he has been a victim of theft if he can't explain what he was doing with them in the first place. Can he?"

"No boss, but … "

"But what?"

"But, how do you know he has not already sold them?"

"Because he is not going to put them on fucking eBay is he? He would have to go to a Fence."

"How do you know he hasn't?"

"Because, you idiot, there is not a Fence in the north of England that doesn't know me and what I would do if I found out they had been dipping their fingers in my pie. I have put the word out. I will be paying him a visit tomorrow and, for your sake, he had better have them tucked up safely in his cupboard."

"I'm certain about the address boss. Do you want me there as well?" asks Kelly.

"I think not. I'd rather have Coco the fucking clown with me. Just make sure you have your phone switched on in case something unexpected comes up."

Finding himself replying into a line that had already gone dead, Kelly places his mobile back on the bedside table. He immediately picks it back up and texts Doyle.

Just got off the phone with McCarthy. He is going to Ashton's house tomorrow. If Ashton doesn't have the diamonds, we are stuffed.

Doyle's reply is immediate.

Shit, what do we do if he doesn't have them?

Kelly replies then switches off his mobile.

We make ourselves scarce. We'll chat tomorrow.

·ı··ı·

The show has gone smoothly, and Riders is in full flow. "Next listeners we have our *Cooperate With Our Cops* slot with DS Hardy giving us the latest intel. But first we have a sponsor's commitment to honour."

A short jingle plays leading into the advertisement for a local cleaning company. Hardy is already settled into his seat opposite the DJ. The advertisement reaches its conclusion with the announcer finalising his pitch in an annoyingly jocular tone.

"Remember folks, for all your cleaning needs with trusted, well-trained staff, we will tackle any job from a small house to commercial premises. Carsons the Cleaners, we have the best scrubbers in town."

Giving Hardy the thumbs up, Riders announces his guest. "With me in the studio is DS Hardy. Let's get straight into it. Welcome DS Hardy. Thanks for coming in. I don't know if you were listening earlier, but it appears we have video footage of what an expert believes could be a Bigfoot. You've already solved two mysteries in West Ayton. Aliens and spaceships, turning out to be hoaxers in fancy dress and a drone. But what about the Bigfoot?"

After giving a short chuckle, Hardy responds. "Ha, ha. Bigfoot in Yorkshire. I doubt it. My best guess is that it is a hoax. Either the kids have set it up or they've been duped."

"With due respect DS Hardy, our American expert seems to think it is possible."

"Yes, I met Mr Harcourt when he visited Ayton. He also believed in aliens and spacecraft which we have, as you have already pointed out, debunked. I am sure given time we can do the same here."

Undeterred, Riders continues to pursue the point. "But you've seen the video DS Hardy and certainly it doesn't look like a man."

"Well, it's hard to tell, isn't it Norman? It's dark. It's an aerial view from at least fifty feet. I admit, given the size and shape of the figure, it does not look like a man."

"Aaaahhh, so you admit it, DS Hardy?"

"No. Let me finish. The size and shape do not look like a man. But it could look like a man in some sort of monster costume. And, frankly, that is my best guess at this stage."

"Okay then, we will leave it, but our listeners are all on the lookout for the mysterious monster, judging by the emails I've received. Now onto the diamond robbery in Scarborough. Any progress?"

"We have a few leads," replies Hardy, conscious that he does not sound that convincing. "We have two images both of which you now have on your show's website. The photofit sketch is our artist's impression of one of the men who assaulted a villager in the woods. His accomplice was wearing a mask, but we also have another sketch of a person of interest who was spotted in the area. The local pub to be precise, the Old Plough."

"They are clearly two different men. Do you think the man seen in the pub was the accomplice of the other man during the assault?" asks Riders.

"Without lapsing into conjecture, all I would like to say is that if anybody recognises either of these two people then please contact myself or DC Stanley, who is assisting me in the investigation. We need to speak to them to eliminate them from our inquiries. The number to call is on your website."

After reading out the numbers on air Riders moves on to a range of low-level criminal activity including a burglary, shoplifting and an assault outside a Scarborough nightclub. Hardy provides updates, ensuring he devotes the most time to crimes with successful outcomes, where perpetrators have been caught and charges have been laid.

Riders also enquires about a recent case involving a prostitute caught soliciting the local Member of Parliament in a street well known for this type of activity. His guest has sufficient experience to avoid being drawn into the case including a refusal to comment on Riders' query as to what he thought the MP was doing in that particular street, at that time of night.

Leaving the studio with the feeling of a job well done, Hardy rushes to his latest date, hopeful that he is on a roll and, for once, the lady in question would closely resemble the picture on the website. This thought prompted him to think that perhaps he should update his own picture which was now almost six years, and eleven kilos out of date.

21

A TINKLE OF Betty's shop doorbell announces the arrival of Ashton who receives a beaming smile from the shopkeeper.

"Morning, my favourite sculptor."

"Morning, Betty. I've just popped in for a coffee and a sandwich. Can you do beef and tomato?"

"No problem," says Betty disappearing into the back of the shop to make the order. Three minutes later she reappears and takes the coffee and sandwich to Ashton who is sitting at the table by the window.

"There you go love. Enjoy," says Betty as she returns to her seat behind the counter. "Don't suppose you were listening to the radio last night? I was doing the stock taking and had it on to keep me company."

"No, sorry Betty. I didn't. Why do you ask?"

"Well, I was listening to that awful man Riders, God knows why, I just wanted another voice for company. But, as it turns out, it was interesting because he had the Messruther boys. They had sent in a video they made of a mysterious figure in the woods. It was quite amazing really because the recording was taken from the air apparently. He also had that American gentleman who visited here. Mr Harcourt. He seemed to think that the boys had caught a Bigfoot on camera if you can believe it."

"Really, how interesting. I didn't realise they had managed to capture anything on video. I presume they used that drone."

"Yes Chris, I think they did. Do you know I quite miss those Americans – they brought life to the village. We always seem to lose interesting people. Like we did with Hairy Bob last year."

"Yes, I miss him as well."

"Strange, he left just after the police caught the murderer of the Vicar. There's a few, mind you, who don't believe the man they arrested was the killer. Some think it was Bob, you know. As if Bob would do that!"

"Couldn't agree more Betty. Just a bit of prejudice because he didn't live the normal life – he was homeless by choice, although I think he had a few demons to excise. I miss him too. I can picture him now, sat in the corner of the Old Plough with his pint of Guinness."

"My, my, Hairy Bob. Underneath all that hair and beard, he was a good-looking bloke I reckon," says Betty.

"And a man of hidden depths. But good depths."

"Anyway Chris, was meaning to ask you. Did the Police catch those men who assaulted you when you were with the Americans on their expedition?"

"If they have, they haven't told me. Have you heard anything?" asks Ashton.

"No, but I am asking because that detective also appeared on the same show last night. He said they had some leads and pictures of suspects."

"Okay, well I guess we'll have to wait and see what they come up with."

Another tinkle of the shop doorbell.

"Well, hello boys. If it isn't the Spielberg's," announces Betty.

"Eh! What do you mean Miss?" asks Ben.

"You two with your film that has been published. The one with the Bigfoot in it."

"Yeah, but who's Spielberg?" asks Billy.

"He's a famous film director," explains Ashton. "Haven't you seen Close Encounters of the Third Kind or ET? Both very topical given your recent experiences."

"What's ET?" asks Ben.

"Never mind, but well done on capturing the Bigfoot on camera. You could be famous," says Ashton.

"Oh okay. Glad you liked it. We need more batteries for our drone please," says Billy passing a tenner over the counter. They take the batteries and their change and rush out with a quick thanks.

Shaking her head she says, "They're good boys those two. I feel for them a bit with their mother leaving the household. Arthur isn't the brightest light on the Christmas tree, but he does his best for them."

"Yeah, I agree Betty," replies Ashton, dabbing the corner of his mouth with the paper napkin. "Anyway, gotta go. Thanks for the coffee and sandwich. See you later." He waves before turning to leave the shop. At the door, he pauses and holds it open for Hayes, before walking out.

Smiling at her new customer Betty says, "Hello Purple, what can I get for you today?"

"Some ciggie papers please and yer cheapest tobacco."

"Things a little hard love?"

"Bit tight at the moment Betty," replies Hayes as he exchanges a twenty-pound note for the papers and tobacco.

"Hey, I've got some news for you. That thing you saw in the woods has been spotted again."

"What, the Bigfoot?"

"Yes. The Messruther boys captured it on camera using that drone of theirs."

"Wow!" exclaims Hayes. "Have you seen it?"

"No. But they were talking about it on the radio last night. Apparently, the video is uploaded on the website of the radio station, if you want to see it. It was on that awful DJ's programme. Norman Riders."

"Okay, I'll check it out, thanks Betty."

Once Hayes has left the shop, Betty settles down to her knitting, waiting patiently for the next customer.

⋅⋅⋅⋅

"Yooo-hooo Chris," calls Mary Addinall, whilst Ashton searches his pocket for the front door key. Half jogging, half waddling, with a gleeful smile, she bears down on him. "Did you hear the news Chris?" says Mary, struggling to contain herself, "It's so, so exciting. I just can't believe it."

"Hi Mary, what news?"

"The Messruther boys have discovered the Bigfoot. They have it on film. Betty told me this morning when I was buying some milk."

"Yes, I know, I've just been there as well, Mary. She told me the same thing."

"I think we should contact those Americans, Mr Harcourt and his friend, and get them to come back."

"Not sure they will make the trip back to good old Yorkshire again. But you never know."

"Oh, I wish!" exclaims Mary.

Once the door is opened, Barry shoots out immediately circling Ashtons legs, excited to see his owner return. "Calm down boy," he says, patting the dog, who spots Mary and runs to greet her. She reciprocates by crouching down and giving him a hug. Barking loudly, he squeezes free to return to Ashton.

"Have to go Mary, I have an appointment and I've not showered yet after my run," apologises Ashton as he enters the house, unaware that he is being watched by Kelly who passes by on his motorbike. Once beyond the village boundary, Kelly pulls over to the verge, takes his mobile phone from the inside pocket of his leather jacket and taps out a text message. He presses the send button.

Confirming the address boss and that he is not out of town.

Sat in his office at the back of Dukes, McCarthy reads his text and looks up at his bouncer who is sitting in the corner of the office. Struggling to accommodate the bouncer's bulk, the wooden chair creaks as the occupant shuffles to get comfortable.

"I'm going to have to get a bigger chair Sean, if you insist on sitting there," jokes McCarthy.

A yawn escapes from the bouncer, who had finished a late shift at the nightclub the night before. Waving him away, McCarthy says, "I would go and get yourself an afternoon kip so that you are bright eyed, bushy tailed and ready for what could be a long night. We're going to pay Mr Ashton a visit and I don't think he will be putting out tea and cakes for us."

"Yes boss, thanks," says the bouncer, wedging himself through the doorway.

"Come back to the club around eight and we'll then take a trip to the countryside," shouts McCarthy, which the bouncer acknowledges with a wave, before walking out of sight.

⁘

Pursing his lips, Ashton leans backwards on his stool to appraise his current project. He glances at the clock on his workshop wall. Engrossed in his sculpture, three hours had seemed like thirty minutes. Unconvinced at the merit of his creation, he was beginning to doubt whether it was time well spent. A loud bark wrests his attention from his abstract piece, and he looks down at Barry who wags his tail with pleading eyes. Ashton re-checks the time and then pats him on the head.

"Sorry mate, I didn't realise the time. I'll get your dinner, then we'll go off for a run."

Barry barks loudly and spins around in excitement when he sees his master rise from the stool. Looking over his shoulder to ensure he is being followed, Barry rushes excitedly ahead of Ashton through to the kitchen at the back of the house. Scrutinising every move Ashton makes during the preparation of his food bowl, Barry barks encouragement and then buries his nose in the meal as soon as it is placed on the floor. Chomping from his bowl greedily, Barry does not notice Ashton leave the kitchen. In his bedroom, he changes into his running gear. By the time he ties his shoelaces, Ashton finds he is no longer alone. Barry appears at his feet.

"Seriously mate, you must have bloody inhaled that dinner, you need to learn to chew. Come on then, time for a run."

Earphones in, music playing, Ashton jogs down the High Street and, when he reaches the Old Plough, turns right into Forge Valley Lane. With the occasional calf nudge with his wet nose, Barry lets Ashton know he is keeping pace. Along the tree lined Lane, Ashton passes the Henson's residence on his left and then eventually Ayton Castle on his right. He leaves the road to make his way into Forge Valley.

Now waning, the early evening summer sunshine still penetrates the tree canopy but with less vigour than earlier in the day. Musical tweets from the birdlife, the rustle of the leaves on the trees and the distant babble of the River Derwent are all unheard by Ashton. Neither does he really take in the heavy beat and riffs of Led Zeppelin pounding through the earphones because his mind is still wrestling with the direction to take his latest work. He cannot decide whether it is finished or needs more attention.

Almost an hour passes before he arrives back at his front door. He pauses, to catch his breath and dig out his house key from the back pocket of his shorts. Not standing on ceremony, Barry rushes in ahead of Ashton as soon as the gap in the opening door is wide enough. By the time Ashton reaches the kitchen, Barry has lapped up all the water in his bowl, prompting Ashton to refill it before taking a shower. Soon, the two are settled on the couch watching the nine o'clock news with Ashton munching on a salad absent-mindedly, and Barry laid on his belly, head resting on his front paws. Ashton envisages a peaceful, uneventful evening.

It was not to be.

22

AN IRON-GREY MERCEDES A Class saloon pulls into the lane next to Betty's store. The driver switches off the engine whilst McCarthy buttons his coat in the back seat. They both climb out of the vehicle, which presents a bigger challenge for the driver, given his bulk.

In a hoarse whisper, McCarthy gives his bouncer an order. "Okay Sean, let's get this sorted quickly and quietly."

"Yes, boss," replies Sean.

Without any further exchange of words, they walk side by side to the High Street, and take an immediate left towards Ashton's front door.

In the living room Ashton is close to dozing off, due to the heat of Barry's body pressed against him on the couch coupled with the dogs rhythmic snoring. A 1980's comedy is providing background noise from the TV. Ashton had barely paid any attention to it. Man and dog are ripped out of their stupor by a voice from the doorway of the living room. Barry leaps up and barks furiously, stood on his hind legs with his forelegs balanced on the back of the couch. Trying to quieten the Beagle, Ashton sits up to face his intruders.

Menacingly, McCarthy spits out an order." If you don't make that mutt shut the fuck up, Sean here will break its fucking neck."

Cuddling and patting his Beagle, the dog calms down as Ashton stares and tries to take in the incongruous, unwelcome pair he finds in his house. Stood erect with hands crossed wearing a black, slim fit Hugo Boss woollen coat, McCarthy twists his mouth with an expression which is probably intended to be a smile but looks more like a grimace. Running his hand over his shaved head, he gestures to his accomplice, who towers above him and seems almost twice as wide.

"That's better, now sit yourself back down Mr Ashton. We need to have a heart to heart,"

Loosening his coat buttons, McCarthy opens his jacket with one purpose in mind. This action reveals what Ashton recognises as a Glock handgun resting in a shoulder holster. Sean, seems to be unarmed, but his build alone looks like a deadly weapon. No guns necessary.

Settling himself in the armchair opposite Ashton, McCarthy smiles once more but Ashton just holds his silence, having obediently complied with the request to sit on the couch. Behind McCarthy, the bodyguard stands erect, arms crossed in front of his barrel chest and motionless, other than an almost imperceptible ripple of his right bicep which strains the short sleeve of his black polo shirt. Ashton's brief glance to assess the bodyguard, is returned with a menacing stare, emanating from glass grey eyes.

"Let's not piss around," snaps McCarthy, "where are they?"

"Where are what?"

"This does not need to be painful. They are not yours and we can avoid a lot of grief if you just hand them over."

"I am telling you that I do not know what the 'they' you are talking about. So, you can probably guess that their whereabouts is also a mystery to me."

"I can see you think you are smart. Do you think you are clever Mr Ashton?" says McCarthy, his tone threatening.

"Only relative to what's in the room," replies Ashton, eyeballing the bodyguard. Anger flashes across the bodyguard's face and he reacts by shifting forward, only to be halted by his boss's raised hand.

"Take it easy Sean, we have not yet quite reached the stage where we are going to have to beat it out of him. But that time is getting closer, Mr Ashton."

"Well, I would hate to be the cause of any pain to Sean's knuckles, but I am telling you the truth. If you could be slightly more specific, perhaps I could be of help. I am guessing though, that whatever it is, it is valuable. I also assume that you haven't tried the lost property office of the police station to find out if it has been handed in. I also doubt you have a licence for the firearm nor your pet gorilla."

This time McCarthy is unable to restrain Sean, who pushes past him and aims a haymaker at Ashton who avoids any real damage by feinting to his right and putting up his left forearm to divert the blow. Yelping in fear and surprise, the Beagle jumps off the couch and runs into the kitchen to safety. From his sitting position, the most resistance Ashton can offer is a half-hearted kick to Sean's groin, but it has limited power and accuracy. He suddenly feels the considerable weight of Sean on top of him. Ashtons jiu jitsu training enables him to hold Sean and prevent any further punches landing, but he can feel himself weakening under the sheer weight and brute strength of his opponent. His saviour comes from an unexpected quarter. McCarthy's voice barks out a command.

"For fucks sake Sean, stop playing cuddles and handbags and get out of the fucking way."

Breaking free from Ashton's grip, which had loosened,

Sean gives a last defiant push in his opponent's face as he retreats to one side, whilst straightening his shirt. With the bulk of the bodyguard no longer in his eyeline, Ashton can once more see McCarthy, who is sitting calmly on a chair, holding the Glock. It is pointed directly at Ashton's chest.

"My patience has run out. What have you done with the fucking diamonds?" asks McCarthy.

"Diamonds? I don't have any diamonds. Why do you think I have your diamonds, for God's Sake?"

McCarthy frowns. Doubts begin to weave around his thoughts like a spider's web. Reluctantly, he is coming to the realisation that Ashton is probably telling the truth.

Those clueless idiots, Kelly and Doyle had got the wrong end of the stick. Or is Ashton just a convincing liar?

He knew which is the most likely but needs to be sure.

"Let's all take a breather then. Am I right that you had a little wrestling match with a couple of muppets in the local woods a few days ago?"

Screwing his eyes up as he tries to work out where this line of questioning is leading, Ashton responds. "That's true, so is that what this is all about?"

Ignoring the question, McCarthy pursues his point. "These two, er, shall we call them employees of mine, were trying to recover some lost items for me, before you decided to assault them."

"I think you'll find that they were the aggressors, not me. I take it these items were diamonds and I am not even going to ask why the diamonds, if they were yours, were hidden in the woods."

"Not asking questions is a wise course of action. But you can see that I have a little dilemma here. Either you are bullshitting me, and you took the diamonds, or you are telling the truth and therefore they must still be there."

"Unless someone else took them of course, perhaps

your employees. Did you think of that?"

Hiding his annoyance at the suggestion which, despite its merit, had escaped him, McCarthy gives a hollow laugh. "No employee of mine would dare mess with me Ashton. Something you need to keep in mind if you want to get out of this shit-show you've found yourself in. What is going to happen now is that you and me, accompanied by Sean here, are going to go for a little ramble in the woods. You're going to show me where you had your little wrestling match, and we are going to then dig up the diamonds. That is, if they are still there. If not, then we have a problem … or rather you have a problem."

"All sounds peachy, but how do you know exactly where to dig?" replies Ashton sarcastically.

"Let's hope it is easy to spot. I suspect that it will be the only place where the earth has been disturbed, unless there's a pack of fucking moles in the area."

"Labour," responds Ashton.

"What the fuck are you on about?" snaps McCarthy.

"It is not a pack of moles. The collective noun is labour. A labour of moles."

"Well smartarse, you're about to engage in some manual labour yourself. So, brace yourself for some gardening. It would be helpful if you had a spade handy."

"In the garden shed, out the back."

McCarthy gestures to Sean, who goes in search of the spade leaving Ashton alone with his boss, each staring intently at the other in silence. The Glock remains trained on the sculptor's chest. Returning triumphantly, Sean holds up the spade which looks comically small in his enormous hand. Ashton reaches over, indicating for Sean to pass it to him, which the bodyguard almost does, until McCarthy gives a loud tut and shakes his head.

"I don't think we'll hand him a weapon Sean, use your

brain. Give it to him when he needs it, not now. Come on then gentlemen. Hi ho, hi ho, it's off to work we go," jokes McCarthy, caustically. The three leave the house through the rear garden. Ashton walks three paces ahead of his escort. None of the group notice that they have an audience.

•¦••¦•

Running excitedly into the living room Mary cannot wait to tell her sister what she has seen.

"Freda, Freda you'll never – "

Annoyed at the interruption, Freda grabs the remote and presses the pause button. "Really Mary, you can be so annoying, I am at a critical part of my favourite bit and you come running in. It's ruined the mood."

"Oh, don't be such a misery Freda, you've seen Titanic about fifty times. You'll never guess what I saw out of the back window of the kitchen."

"I can't be bothered with guessing games, just tell me," replies Freda, irritably.

"It's Chris. He's walking out of his back garden toward Higginbottom's farm with two other men."

"Who are they?"

"I don't know. Friends, I guess. Though they didn't look like nice men, I have to say. Do you think he is going out again searching for those UFO lights?" asks Mary.

"No silly. They solved that mystery. It was the Messruther boys."

"Oh yes, of course. You're right. Maybe they are Bigfoot hunters. One of them was so big he looked like a Bigfoot himself."

Switching the film back on, Freda gives Mary a pointed stare. "Now leave me alone, I want to finish my film, if you don't mind."

Annoyed at her sister's lack of interest but still intrigued, Mary runs upstairs to her bedroom and peers out of the window. She is just in time to see them leave the back lane and walk into the woods. Torches flicker in the distance, marking their progress.

•┤••┤•

Despite his bulk and powerful demeanour, Sean is not a fan of the countryside and finds it a little unsettling. A bit spooky. A slight breeze causes the leaves to rustle and an owl hoots his night-time chorus. Leading the way, Ashton shines his torch, but it is almost redundant as the full moon bathes the field with an eerie glow, contrasting the impenetrable darkness of the dense woods close by. They make their way along the tree line at the edge of the field. Sean is conscious of the forbidding blackness around the trees to his right, and it makes him uneasy. His comfort zone is the urban environment, despite the danger associated with his job. When he is working on the door of the nightclub, he has a good line of sight in all directions. He can see any threat coming. He is in control. Not so tonight. Ashton has a similar feeling of nervousness, but his psychological discomfort is caused by an acute awareness that McCarthy is close behind, pointing a glock at the centre of his back.

No one speaks.

•┤••┤•

Doyle is sitting in the living room of Kelly's flat. Both hold a can of beer and both are fretting about the outcome of the evening.

"Do you reckon they'll get the diamonds?" asks Doyle.

"I bloody hope so," replies Kelly.

"What'll McCarthy do with Ashton do you reckon?"

Shaking his head, Kelly looks down at his beer. "Haven't a clue mate. Hopefully, McCarthy will get the diamonds, give Ashton a warning and everyone can go about their normal business. Everything hunky dory."

"He won't kill Ashton, will he?"

"Hope not. If Ashton is sensible, does what McCarthy wants, coughs up the diamonds and agrees to keep quiet, it should all be okay," replies Kelly doubtfully.

Taking a sip from his can, Doyle feels a bit better having had the conversation. In contrast, articulating the situation has made Kelly feel worse.

·|··|·

In the Old Plough, there is less action in the bar than in the woods. Hardy and Stanley, having worked the evening shift, decide to pop into the pub for a couple of drinks before closing time. They are sitting at the table next to Kenneth, the stuffed Koala, the only other occupant of the bar.

"What do you think are the chances of recovering the diamonds, boss?" asks Stanley.

"Somewhere between zero and bugger all."

"Do you think they're still in Scarborough?"

With a withering glance at his younger colleague, Hardy shakes his head in despair at the naivete of youth. "They are probably not in the country, let alone the county. Whoever took them will have had buyers lined up."

"Where?" asks Stanley.

"Unlike our dear old government, I suspect they will have remained in the European Union. Possibly Holland."

·|··|·

Continuing along the tree line, the three men remain silent until the crack of a twig filters through the trees. All three stop in their tracks, straining their eyes to find the source of the noise, but there is nothing to be seen. Sean is the first to speak.

Pointing to the trees, the bouncer frowns with concern. "Hey boss, I'm sure we're being tracked. I heard a few noises over there. I think something is walking parallel to us, but out of sight."

"Settle down. It's your imagination. Just concentrate on the task at hand," snaps McCarthy.

"It's probably just a fox, or badger," suggests Ashton.

Waving the glock, McCarthy spits out an instruction to Ashton. "If we wanted your fucking opinion then we'd have asked for it. Just keep moving and be aware that if you are dicking around, I am beginning to get very pissed off. And you do not want me to get pissed off. How much further is the spot?"

"About another fifty yards, I guess," replies Ashton.

"Let's get a move on. And Sean?"

"Yes, boss."

"Stop staring at the trees and keep your eyes to the ground. If we are getting near, you need to keep your eyes peeled so we don't miss where the other two idiots played at pirates burying their fucking treasure."

Sean nods.

They walk on in silence.

·|··|·

Mary is far from silent and once more rushes into the living room, shouting at her sister. Annoyed at another interruption, she histrionically makes an exaggerated pressing movement on her remote to convey her displeasure. However, the gesture is wasted on Mary, who cannot wait to report the latest development.

"Freda, Freda! I've been upstairs in my bedroom

looking out of the window. I can see they are moving along the edge of the field. I can see their torches. They look like they're heading for that place where poor old Chris was attacked by those men in fancy dress."

"For God's sake Mary. I just want to watch my film in peace."

"Forget the film. I think we should join them in the hunt."

"If they wanted you to join them, they would have asked. Why don't you do something useful like make a pot of tea and bring me a slice of that Victoria Sponge you made this afternoon."

Disappointed with her sister's lack of enthusiasm, Mary goes to the kitchen and switches the kettle on. Thinking about what she had seen, she reflects that her sister may be right. Nevertheless, she did not like the look of the two men and began to fret for her neighbour's safety.

23

UNDER COVER OF the woods and the cloak of night, the figure walks parallel to the torchlights, which flicker and die and flicker again as they pass by the trees. It is curious about the intention of the interlopers. It could make out the shadows of three men. It purposely lightens its footfalls to avoid being discovered after inadvertently snapping a twig under its heavy weight.

They had heard the crack and stopped to listen. Their lights tried in vain to penetrate the darkness and discover it, but it darted behind a large oak tree. Mirroring their actions, the figure freezes each time the men stop and does not move until they do.

Concentrating on its quarry, the figure is unaware of the rabbits and foxes which scurry out of its path as it progresses through the trail. Feared by all the wildlife, it has been several weeks since the apex predator has come to their home, bringing destruction and bloodshed to the idyllic woodland.

Eventually the lights come to a halt and, in response it crouches down to observe them, hidden by the dark.

Unseen, it watches the events unfold.

24

THE TWO GANGSTERS stare at the ground, which is illuminated by the beam from Ashton's torch.

"This is the place," announces Ashton. "You can see where the ground has already been partially dug up by your other, er, employees."

"Righty-ho. It looks like we're making some progress and soon we can all go to bed with our little water bottles to keep us warm," sneers McCarthy.

"Right Sean, give him the spade, and he can finish the job. But keep your distance, otherwise he might clock you with it."

After throwing the spade to the feet of Ashton, Sean takes a step back. The glock remains firmly trained on Ashton's chest.

McCarthy barks his orders. "Well get a move on Sneezy, Dopey, Bashful, or whatever fucking dwarf you are. Get digging and no need to whistle while you work. Be quick and be silent."

Musing on the possible outcome, if the diamonds are not where they are supposed to be, Ashton starts to dig with a degree of trepidation. It only takes six full shovels of dirt before Ashton hits something soft. He stops and looks over at McCarthy.

"I think I've hit something. It's not hard, possibly a bag."

Unable to conceal a genuine smile for the first time in the evening, McCarthy motions for Ashton to move out of the way and then points to the hole.

"Put the spade down and get out of the way."

When he is satisfied that Ashton is at a safe distance, McCarthy shouts a further instruction.

"Right Sean, get down there and grab whatever he's found."

Obeying McCarthy's instruction, Sean jumps into the shallow hole and moves some dirt with his spade-like hand. After a brief grunt, he pulls the bag from the ground and holds it aloft in triumph before walking over and passing it to McCarthy.

Placing the Glock in his holster, McCarthy fumbles with the straps before opening the bag and peers inside it. With a widening grin, he looks over to Ashton.

"Well, well, well. It appears you weren't bullshitting me after all. We seem to have what we're looking for."

"Hey, boss," shouts Sean, holding up the second bag, "here's the other one."

"Guess we can all go home then," says Ashton, as he starts to walk away.

"Just hold your fucking horses, I haven't decided what to do with you yet."

Ignoring the gangster, Ashton continues to walk until Sean blocks his path. The bouncer assesses his target and aims a punch. Ashton ducks to avoid the blow but, when he is crouched gets a vicious kick to the chest and falls to the ground. Winded, he looks up to see the menacing bulk of his assailant materialise over him. Although prone on the ground, Ashton wraps his legs around the shins and ankles of his attacker, causing the bouncer to lose his balance and fall over backwards. Ashton springs up to make the most of his advantage, but the bouncer is surprisingly quick and athletic despite his bulk. Catching hold of Ashton's kick, the bouncer locks it in a vice-like grip. He sweeps Ashton's standing leg, sending him back to the ground and, with a victorious grunt, leaps on top of him.

Keeping his distance, McCarthy draws his glock from the holster whilst the other two wrestle in the mud. There is no clear shot, and he gets increasingly frustrated at Ashton, who is manoeuvring his opponent in a series of wrestling moves. Staring in disbelief, he sees that Ashton is getting the upper hand and starts to apply a choke hold.

Pointing the gun into the air, McCarthy fires off a shot.

"For fucks sake, stop pissing around or I'll shoot you both," barks McCarthy.

Releasing his hold on the bouncer, Ashton rolls away. The two men lay side by side, both gasping for breath.

·|··|·

After making Freda's tea, Mary had left her alone to watch the rest of her film, whilst she returned to her bedroom to look out of the window. She sees the torchlights progress slowly along the tree line until they stop in the area where the assault had taken place.

Knew it was where they were going, she thought.

Entranced by the lights, she gives a quiet gasp of surprise and begins to get worried as they move quickly and erratically. Two lights fall to the ground. Straining her eyes, she thinks she can see, in the full light of the moon, shadow figures grappling. She lets out a half-strangled scream when a loud cracking noise pierces the air.

Sounds like a gunshot.

She thinks she recognises the noise from the occasions she has heard Higginbottom, when he culls rabbits.

But Chris was there, and he hates guns. And no one shoots rabbits at this time of night, she thought.

Frightened and fearful for her neighbour, she rushes down the stairs.

"Freda! Freda!" I heard a gunshot.

"What? Don't be ridiculous. Where?" asks Freda, as she turns off the television.

"In the woods. Near where Chris went. I'm really, really, worried. Frightened. I'm going to the Old Plough to get help."

Without a further word to her sister, Mary races to the door and runs down the path and on to the High Street. Through her blind panic she does not see DS Hardy and runs straight into him. She bounces off his belly, but he catches her before she falls to the floor.

The two detectives had called it a night and were on their way to the car and home.

It takes a minute to calm her down and get some sense from her story, which is both panicked and garbled. Once he has everything straight in his mind, he escorts her back to her front door. She takes the two detectives through the house into the back room and then along the path in the rear garden. After leading them to the back gate, she points in the direction of the fields towards the lights in the distance.

Hardy reassures her that they will deal with the matter. "Don't worry Miss Addinall, DC Stanley and I will sort this all out, but you need to keep out of the way and get back into your house."

"Okay but promise you will come back and tell me that Chris is okay," pleads Mary, with Freda looking askance from the back doorway.

"I promise," assures Hardy.

The detectives disappear into the night, moving quickly towards the torchlights in the distance.

•|••|•

"Get up Sean, you idiot. No. Not you Ashton. You just sit yourself there for a moment, whilst we decide what to do with you."

Brushing himself down, Sean scowls at Ashton, feeling a mixture of anger and embarrassment. He gathers his thoughts, trying to reconcile the size of his opponent with the fact that he had struggled, not once, but twice, to beat him in combat.

Every weekend I make short work of idiots twice his size at the club ... but to be beaten by a bloody pottery teacher!

"Just fucking top him boss," he snarls, causing Ashton to look alarmingly at the gun held by McCarthy. The gangster's face is expressionless, pondering his next move.

Whatever decision McCarthy had made, or was about to make, fate took it out of his hands. Amongst the trees, heavy footfalls approach at speed becoming louder and louder until they are drowned out by a primal scream. McCarthy stares frozen in astonishment at the trees, which seem to part, making way for a colossal, bipedal, solidly built figure crashing through an opening. It is hard to make sense of his assailant, which appears as wide as it is tall. It moves like a man but does not look like one. With no discernible neck and no immediately identifiable facial features, McCarthy is unable to process the nature of his attacker.

There are Bigfoots afterall, is the only thought he can muster.

Long strands of grass-like hair ripple with the movement of its arms and body as it charges towards McCarthy. For the first time, since childhood beatings from

286

his abusive stepfather, McCarthy freezes in fear. Unable to process what is coming towards him, he has already psychologically surrendered and stands passively, holding the gun to his side.

Without challenge, the figure swings its arm, hitting McCarthy square on the temple. The gangster is unconscious before he hits the ground.

Sean, who also has the unfamiliar feeling of fear, turns to face his boss's attacker. Beast and bouncer are locked in a staring contest, both holding their ground but Sean feels his knees weaken in fear. Then the world of the bouncer turns black.

The force of the blow causes the spade to slip from Ashton's grasp. First looking at his erstwhile captor lying prone and unconscious, then warily at the figure, Ashton picks up the spade. He is poised to strike for a second time in self-defence, if the beast turns on him.

"Jesus Chris, he's going to have one hell of a headache when he wakes up."

Ogling at the now articulate figure, Ashton is lost for words. Staring in wonderment and confusion, his saviour disappears into the tree line, only to return seconds later with a backpack. Ashton tries to process what is happening.

"C'mon Chris, don't just stand there gawping, give me a hand." The figure pulls out a ball of heavy-duty string and starts to cut off pieces with a penknife.

"Been using this for rabbit snares, but should do the job. We need to tie these two morons up and call the cops. This should hold them for a while, if we wrap it around their wrists and ankles enough times. Don't know what your boy scout skills are like, but I'll deal with the gorilla here and you do the nasty sod with the gun."

"Bob? Bob? Is that you Bob?"

Pulling off the hood of his ghillie suit, Hairy Bob

smiles through a bushy black beard. "One and the same. At your service."

"What the hell are you doing out here in a bloody ghillie suit?"

"I could ask you the same question. On my part, I'm sleeping, eating, and working. Anyway, best we have our chat after we've trussed up these two and called the cops."

The sound of more footsteps causes Ashton and Bob to swing round and peer into the dark at two lights which are fast approaching them. The beams, from the torch app on their mobile phones, morph into the shadowy figures of two men as they draw near. Both Ashton and Bob tense in readiness for another fight. Ashton grabs the spade once more and holds it preparing to strike if needed.

"Call the cops you say? No need, we're here already. It's DS Hardy and DC Stanley. Nice to see you again Mr Ashton. If you'd be so good enough to drop that spade, I won't need to charge you for carrying an offensive weapon and threatening an officer of the law."

Hardy stares at the prone bodies on the ground. "Well, well, well ... what do we have here then?"

25

IT HAD BEEN a long night, made longer by an unwelcome experience for Ashton, finding himself in custody at Scarborough Police Station. The clock on the wall of interview room one displays the unsocial hour of 5:34 a.m. Sat opposite him are the equally as tired looking faces of DS Hardy and DC Stanley. They had just placed an unappetising hot brackish liquid in front of him that purported to be a cup of tea. Ashton had answered all the detective's questions and had given a statement relating his version of the events of the night.

"Unless there is anything else you'd like to add or tell us Mr Ashton, I think we're about done."

"So, is that it then?" asks Ashton.

"It certainly is, at least for now," confirms Hardy.

"Can I ask if you've laid any charges yet?"

"Nothing at this stage, it looks like we're going to have a lot to investigate and unravel."

"But he was armed, and he kidnapped and assaulted me, as well as being clearly involved in the theft of those diamonds that he forced me to dig up," says Ashton in a tone of controlled outrage.

"At this stage, the only obvious offence that could stick would be assault. And it seems, at first sight, that you and Mr Jenkins are the perpetrators, rather than the victims.

When we arrived on the scene, they were unconscious after an altercation with you and your friend. As to your claims and the diamond theft, there is a fair bit of investigation and evidence to collect to make anything stick in a court of law."

"Sorry, what? Who is Mr Jenkins?"

"His name is Robert Jenkins. The homeless gentleman. He disappeared a year ago after the murder of the Vicar in your village. I should warn you that Mr Jenkins was implicated in the murder at one stage. The fact that he left the area at that time still raises some doubts regarding his potential involvement. So, you can see from our point of view, that Robert Jenkins doesn't exactly slip easily into the victim category."

"Robert Jenkins! Oh! Wow! No one knew his full name. You're right, we all know him as Hairy Bob in the village," explains Ashton.

"But you can't be serious about the assault of those two last night. I was the victim and Bob, thank God, popped up from nowhere and saved me. I can't believe he was in any way involved in the Vicar's murder."

"Well, the other two are the one's spending the night in Scarborough Hospital, not you. So circumstantially and medically they are looking more like the victims than the offenders. The larger one, Sean Hughes, could be in for quite a while. From the doctor's initial assessment, it sounds as though you cracked his skull when you hit him over the head. Hit him over the head from behind with a heavy spade, I might add. Neutral observers may struggle to place you two as the victims if you get my drift. The other one, McCarthy, will probably be discharged from hospital today."

"You cannot be bloody serious," says Ashton with a mixture of anger and frustration.

"I am deadly serious. The whole thing is a mess. Look at it objectively from our, and any potential jury's point of view. Apparently, there are four men digging up stolen diamonds in a field in the middle of the night and a brawl has ensued. It raises a hundred and one questions."

"Such as?" says Ashton irritably.

"Try these for size. Were you all involved in the robbery? Did you have a disagreement between you, which caused the fight? How did you know where the diamonds were located if you were not involved in the theft? How come the diamonds were hidden near your house? If you were not involved, why did they come to your house to recover the diamonds?" Hardy pauses to let Ashton consider what he has said, then adds, "You can see a lot of questions need to be answered."

Sarcasm replaces Ashton's frustration. "If Bob and I are the suspects, has McCarthy or his sidekick made a complaint of assault?"

"Look, Mr Ashton, I get where you're going with this. Between you and me, I am not saying this is our view, but the standpoint of a court may differ without further evidence. But let me assure you that McCarthy is well known to us. He's a bloody villain. A nasty one. He's vicious, clever and has influence."

"What about the gorilla?"

"Hughes on the other hand is merely an employee hired for his muscle rather than brains. Ironically, Hughes has more convictions than McCarthy ... mainly for assault. We're reasonably certain who is the guilty party, and we are keen to seize the opportunity to finally nail McCarthy on something substantial. But it will take some unpacking and the statements made by you and Mr Roberts will eventually be of use when we do finally commit to laying charges."

"What about Bob and I?"

"And … to answer your original question … no, McCarthy has not raised any assault complaint against you, because the less involvement he has with the judicial system the better it is for him. It's not like the TV, Mr Ashton. Real criminals do their best to avoid attention, not seek it. As for Mr Hughes, he is currently in no condition to complain about anything. Nor is he likely to do so given that he works for McCarthy."

Sitting back in his seat, Ashton calms himself. "Okay, I suppose I can see your point. He could use the confusion of last night to place doubt on his culpability. So, what do you expect me to do?"

"At the moment nothing. We have your statement, and this is corroborated by Mr Jenkins. Let me qualify that. Mr Jenkins can at least corroborate what happened in the woods. As for the events in your house, it is their word against yours. We're aware of your military background when you assisted in the murder case last year – and this will help, I remember that back then … you've some impressive people high up who attest to your character."

"Okay, but what about McCarthy? Isn't he going to come after me if he is this big evil gangster?"

"I doubt it. He is being edged into a corner and will want to keep a low profile. He knows that, if anything untoward happens to you, he will be first in line for questioning given recent events. McCarthy certainly is not going to want to publicise events and encourage police involvement by pushing us to lay assault charges. Quite the opposite. We're going to take this slowly and low key. If we rush in now, we can only detain him for twenty-four hours without charging him. That's insufficient time to get the evidence we need. I'm hopeful that we can make a few charges stick down the line once we have completed our investigation."

"Such as?"

"Maybe home invasion, threatening behaviour, assault, and possession of an unlicensed firearm. But for now, we want to keep our powder dry and dig much deeper. If we can add the diamond theft to the list then this, when associated with the unlicensed firearm charge, could substantially increase his sentence. Now that we know McCarthy was involved in that little escapade, we can home in on his known associates and the pair that did the dirty work."

Raising his hand to make Hardy pause, Ashton seeks clarification. "Hold on, how did you know it was a pair that did the robbery and for that matter, that it wasn't McCarthy himself?"

"McCarthy doesn't get his hands dirty, that's how he's avoided jail. We know it was two men from the video footage of them after the break in. They were on a motorcycle. If you think about it, you have probably already met them," says Hardy.

Ashton realises immediately. "Of course, that's the two I came across in the woods a couple of weeks ago. The Spider-Men. That's why they were there, to get the diamonds."

"Bingo," says Stanley, speaking for the first time in the interview. "From the known associates of McCarthy, we think we have a good idea of the most likely candidates. We couldn't see the licence plate on the bike, it was probably removed. But we have a good idea of the model and if one of these two owns one, we're halfway there."

Seeing Stanley stifle a yawn, triggers one from Ashton. "Okay officers, I am knackered, am I free to go?"

"Certainly, on police bail," says Hardy.

"Bail? Are you joking, how much?"

"No money is involved – it is police bail. It just means

we can call you in for further questioning. It's routine. Besides, we need to follow protocol otherwise it could bite us in the arse. You do potentially have an assault charge hanging over you, if McCarthy wants to pursue it. We must make things look kosher. It would raise questions of police bias if, given the circumstances in which we found you, we treated you differently from McCarthy and Hughes. I'm sure you understand."

With a fatigued sigh and a moment's thought, Ashton responds. "Yeah, okay, fair enough."

"Your friend is waiting in reception so you can drive him home, wherever a homeless person calls home, that is. I'll show you out. Your car is still in the rear car park," says Stanley.

•∣••∣•

A million questions flood Ashton's mind as he drives home with Bob in the passenger seat.

"So, come on Bob, where have you been and what are you doing back here?'

Scratching his beard, Bob ponders his response. "I've been around and about – doing this and that."

"Way too much detail," jokes Ashton.

Grinning, Bob says, "People here were good to me, so I thought I'd return for a while. Higginbottom found me camping in the woods near his farm. He's a good man. We shared a few meals together in the farmhouse and he paid me cash for some labouring work."

"People are fond of you. You know that. Betty and Dolly missed you badly and always talk about you. Why didn't you at least just pop in to see them?"

"I was thinking about it Chris but got wrapped up in my daily life on the farm and, in recent weeks, I've been working nights a lot."

"Which leads me to the sixty-four-thousand-dollar question. What were you doing wandering around the woods at night in a ghillie suit?"

"Higginbottom has a pest problem. Rabbits ruining his crop. He says it leads to a loss of biodiversity ... whatever that means. So, I have been hunting, shooting, and trapping them for some time now." Bob pauses to gather his thoughts and continues. "I've been setting traps during the night and hunting them in the early hours, It's the best time. I set up camp in the woods."

After giving a little chuckle, Ashton says, "You know that you've been the cause of some excitement and fear in the village."

Screwing his eyes in concern, Bob responds. "Excitement and fear? No way. What are you talking about?"

"People have seen lights and strange beings."

"I saw those lights. It was just the Messruther boys messing around with a drone. They were mucking around in the woods quite a few times, but if I saw them I stayed hidden. Didn't want to frighten them."

"Yeah sure," says Ashton, 'I eventually worked that one out. But the strange alien beings turned out to be McCarthy's men dressed in Spider-Man suits."

"What, why?"

"Don't ask me. I assume they wore them so they couldn't be identified. But the point I am making is that, whilst the lights and aliens are solved, you are probably the source of the Bigfoot theory."

"Me?"

"Yeah— you. Tramping around in your bloody ghillie suit in the early hours of the morning."

"Well, you're one to talk. What about you and your posse of alien hunters wandering around in the woods in the middle of the night? I saw you all and I even thought I heard American accents. I just made myself scarce while you all played your little games."

"Yep, you're right about the Americans. Two came to the village following up the stories in the newspaper and on the radio. They seem to spend their lives hunting aliens and cryptids."

"Cryptids?"

"Yep, imaginary monsters, like Yetis ... Bigfoot ... the Loch Ness Monster. Or, in this case, a hairy bloke in a ghillie suit. They make a good living apparently doing talks, writing books and TV shows. One of them specialises in extra-terrestrials. He said he was ex-military, used to work in Area 51."

Shaking his head, Bobs says, "Takes all sorts, I guess."

Glancing across at Bob, Ashton smiles and ponders the irony of his friend's statement given his own lifestyle. After a few minutes of insistent persuasion, Bob accepts Ashton's invitation to stay at his place for a couple of days to rest and clean up.

Both men are greeted by an excited dog as they enter the house and once Barry has settled down, they decide to go straight to bed for a couple of hours. It is not long before the house falls silent except for the snoring of Bob in the spare room matched by Barry, who lies at the feet of his master in the main bedroom.

26

LIKE WILDFIRE, NEWS spreads quickly, and in Ayton it only has a short distance to travel.

Having woken up just before midday, Bob feels refreshed but finds himself alone in the house. Scratching his head through long unkempt hair and then turning his attention to an itch on his lower back, he ambles down the stairs. In the kitchen, he finds a note:

Morning Bob. Gone out with Barry for a run. There's cereal, milk, bread, tea, and eggs. Help yourself to anything you want. Will be back by 12.30.

Sniffing his armpits, Bob grunts, goes back upstairs, and takes a shower. Once dressed he discovers he has a raging hunger.

Still the reluctant guest, not wishing to impose, Bob surprises himself by taking advantage of the hospitality and is soon sat at the kitchen table with a mug of tea and a healthy portion of scrambled eggs on toast in front of him. It does not remain on his plate for long. Just as he is loading the dishwasher, the back door opens and in rushes Barry, followed by Ashton. With the dog barking and dancing round his feet, Bob crouches down to pat him whilst looking up to greet Ashton.

"Sorry Chris, I was starving so took you up on your offer," says Bob sheepishly.

"Glad you did, Bob. I have an apology of my own. I got accosted by Mary Addinall as I left the house. She saw me with our two friends leaving the house last night. She heard a gunshot and was worried. I gave her some edited highlights, but dropped in the fact that you were back in town, so to speak."

"No worries, Chris, I was planning to say 'hi' to a few people today anyway."

"I wasn't sure what to do, but I said I might buy you a couple of pints in the pub this evening if you are up for it. I suspect there'll be a few people who want to catch up. Why don't you go and grab your stuff, from wherever your campsite is, and bring it back. You can use all the facilities in Hotel Ashton whilst you are here."

"Cheers, I'll do that. Would be good to give all my stuff a wash."

"Good idea, and then just take it easy, it may be a big night at the Old Plough."

And so, it proved.

•┼••┼•

The welcome given by Ken and Dolly feels as warm as a heavy blanket on a cold winter night, and almost overwhelms Bob.

He is guided to the seat at the bar and finds a pint of Guinness nestled invitingly in front of him. Chris had told everyone how Bob had saved his life the night before. Embarrassed at all the attention, Bob endures a parade of villagers taking it in turn to greet and hug him. Front of the queue is Betty who had made him sandwiches almost every day he lived in the village, right up to his departure almost eighteen months ago. She sheds a tear and this, in turn, makes Bob's eyes moisten. Busy behind the bar, Dolly frequently glances affectionately at Bob. She too had taken on the role of mother along with Betty during his previous stay. Ken takes a break from his bar duties and walks over to the jukebox. Shortly, most of the locals are singing along, led by the baritone of the landlord, to the John Denver classic, 'Take Me Home, Country Road.' When the song finishes, the whole bar is drowned in a cacophony of applause.

Inevitably, the conversation turns to the events of the previous night. By mutual agreement, Bob and Ashton filter the information they give and remain circumspect, at the behest of the two detectives. One piece of information is now common knowledge. That is, the final mystery is solved, and this receives a mixed reaction. Some are relieved whilst others, including Hayes and Hendricks, are a little disappointed that there is no Bigfoot in the area. All mysteries accounted for. Aliens, UFO lights and a Bigfoot. Or rather, two men in Spider-Man suits, a drone and a ghillie suited Hairy Bob.

The night ends in a typical Old Plough fashion. Ken puts on 'My Way' and leads the singalong. A very pleasant night ends with a steady parade of happy punters passing by Dolly, she holds open the door and bids each, 'goodnight.'

·••·

Just as the Old Plough empties, Dukes begins to fill up for the night. Top of the bill is Benedict Bunton, and he is going down well with the crowd, trotting out a series of one liners, as old as the comedian himself. As usual, his comic timing and cynical delivery more than compensates for the lack of originality, but as another comedian of his era, Frank Carson, would say if he was still alive – 'It's the way I tell them.'

Despite the presence of his favourite act, McCarthy sits at the back of the room in his booth, sour-faced and inwardly seething. Stood beside the table, a six-foot-seven Māori occupies the space previously filled by Sean Hughes, who is currently staring down the barrel of a long period in hospital and rehabilitation. As far as McCarthy is concerned, it is a like for like replacement. No brighter than his predecessor, the new employee at least looks the part. More so, in some ways. People stare warily at the newcomer, whose neck and face are adorned with the traditional decorative curved shapes and spiral tattoos of his clan, the Ngati-Toi. On the payroll, he declares only one name. McCarthy's accountant, Sebastian Henson, asked him what Kaitoa means. 'It means warrior' came back the reply, typically succinct.

For the moment McCarthy is following the counsel of his lawyer. Keep a low profile and try to avoid the attention of the authorities. Every bone in his body aches for the opposite. He wants retribution, but for the moment he is heeding the advice.

•¦••¦•

Bringing his nightly radio show to a close, Norman Riders updates his listeners. He tells them all the mysteries are solved and that the final piece in the jigsaw is a local man, dressed in a ghillie suit, hunting rabbits. Reaction is unexpectedly vitriolic. Having satisfied the first listener's relatively intelligent question, by explaining that a ghillie suit is camouflage designed to resemble foliage, the calls go rapidly downhill. The villagers are characterised by most listeners as gullible morons and the two Americans are described in what can only be categorised as unflattering racist terms. Others accuse them of being charlatans preying on the fears and naivety of decent country folk. One caller suggests that the Messruther twins should be sent to borstal. At the end of it all Riders is glad to pass the microphone over to the *Roger Rodgers Midnight Show*.

Throwing down his headphones in exasperation, he begins to question and reflect on the intelligence and morality of his listening demographic.

Am I to blame? Am I a magnet for the redneck, racist, ignorant, vacuous, homophobic sections of society? Or is this just the sort of person who has nothing better to do than listen to evening radio? God knows what Roger Rodgers' gets in the early hours of the morning.

Maybe I should consider a new direction?

27

FOR THE FIRST time in a long while, Hardy and Stanley sit in the office of DI Parkins in a happy and confident mood. Nothing is going to bring them down, even when they look across at the facial expression of a man who looks as though he had swallowed five wasps. Sitting quietly, they listen to Parkins in full flow.

"I am looking at you two with dread, doubt, and depression, hoping to God I am wrong and that, against all odds, you have something meaningful to report. The great and the good in the offices above me are climbing all over my back. Not only have we failed to capture those responsible for the Scarborough jewel heist, but the owner, Mr Manny Abrams, has made a formal complaint of racism. Apparently, some clueless green constable has inferred that the owner staged the robbery to claim on insurance and suggested that this is common practice for business owners of the Jewish faith."

"Probably looking for a payout to cover his losses," suggests Stanley.

"Not bloody helpful. Listening to you Stanley, I am beginning to think Abrams may have a point," hisses Parkins.

"Look at this, sir." Hardy hands over his mobile phone and Parkins studies the photograph on the screen.

"It's two small black velvet bags. So bloody what?"

"It is two black velvet bags, which are full of the diamonds that were stolen,'" announces Hardy, with a world beating smug expression on his face.

"I am in no mood for jokes, Hardy."

"No joke sir."

"Really? I hope to God you are not pulling my chain," says Parkins warily. "Why are you just showing me a photo? Where are they now?"

"With forensics sir. Trying to see what genetic material we can harvest. Looking for hairs, that sort of thing."

"Well blow me down. I have to say I'm impressed. Even ecstatic. Anything else?"

"We also have good leads on several suspects who have been questioned. We let them out on bail whilst we gather more evidence."

"Who?"

"None other than McCarthy?"

"What, Trent McCarthy? You're telling me you have something on Trent McCarthy?"

"The very same, sir."

It turns out to be the longest meeting Hardy and Stanley had ever had with Parkins. They go through everything in detail. Their boss who, for once, just listens patiently, sits wondering if he is dreaming. He touches the leather of his chair to make sure he isn't. The version of events presented by the detectives skate close to the truth, but Hardy is determined to put the rosiest glow possible on their involvement. By the time Hardy's briefing has finished, Parkins is left with the clear impression that the relentless pursuit of leads, coupled with dogged determination, has got the right result.

Two days later, after a long evening, McCarthy leaves Dukes. A combination of whisky and medication has eased the throbbing above his left eye but a large plaster and padding, which protects five stitches, does not fully cover the angry looking purple bruise across his forehead. He leaves the club, even though it is still in full swing, having decided that an early night is required. If midnight can be described as early.

It is an unseasonably cold and wet evening, so he walks quickly to his car, hunched up, as if making himself smaller somehow avoids the rainfall. At the back of the club, his car is under cover. Once in the dry, he stands up straight and fumbles for the keys inside his coat pocket. A voice from the darkness startles him, causing him to turn abruptly.

"Evening McCarthy, nasty looking bruise you've got there." Straining to see who is addressing him, his squint turns to a grimace when he recognises the face which appears from the shadow.

"You've got some balls; I'll give you that." Attempting to intimidate him, McCarthy advances towards Ashton, who does not react, but holds his ground. McCarthy balls up his fists in anger as if preparing to strike.

Cold metal at the back of his neck stops the gangster in his tracks. Another voice, this one unfamiliar, barks out an order.

"Just keep still and don't turn around, otherwise my face will be the last thing you fucking see."

"I'd do as he says McCarthy," suggests Ashton, in a contrasting relaxed tone. "My friend here is ex-SAS and his kill rate in Afghanistan is very impressive. Just content yourself with looking at my pretty face for the time being."

Outwardly McCarthy tries to intimidate, but inside his stomach churns. "Go on then, spit it out Ashton, I've had a long day. Say what you've come to say, then, fuck off."

"It's basically quite simple, I need you to drop whatever vendetta you may have against me, and my friends in the village, and leave us alone."

"And why should I do that?"

"Everything that's happened is your own doing or that of the bunch of morons you employ. I don't know what you were told, and by whom, but I had no idea the diamonds existed, let alone that they were buried behind my house. I assume it was your Spider-Man buddies who pointed you in my direction. You must know after seeing what happened the other night that I wasn't involved. Surely, when you broke into my home like a madman and pointed a gun in my face, it didn't take you long to realise that I hadn't a clue what was going on?"

Having already drawn that conclusion himself, McCarthy is reticent to verbalise that he accepts Ashton's account, lest he appears weak. "And if I choose to believe your little sob story, what do you want me to do?"

"As I already said, just leave me alone, and those in the village. Let us go about our business and we will leave you to sort out your own mess. None of it is of our making."

"Or else?"

Pressing the gun harder into his neck, Ashton's accomplice replies with chilling menace. "Say hello to my little friend."

Momentarily perplexed by his friend's comment, Ashton says, "Thanks mate, it's okay, you can go now. Just leave me to sort it out with Mr McCarthy. As for you McCarthy, just keep your eyes on me for a minute."

Seconds later they are alone. All McCarthy sees when finally he looks over his shoulder, is darkness engulfing a back alley devoid of street lighting. He turns back to Ashton and sneers.

"You sure you feel safe without your boyfriend to back you up?"

"Yep. He's probably taking flowers to your poor little bodyguard in hospital," retorts Ashton. "I hear he's not in a good way. But enough of this macho bullshit. I've made my point and I don't want any trouble."

"I could say 'yes' now, but what's to stop me sorting you out later?"

"I suppose because you'll have enough on your hands with the police to waste your time on someone who wasn't even involved. I know that you know my name and where I live, which makes me an easy target. What you don't know is my friend's name or even what he looks like. If anything happens to me, you'll have no idea when he'll come knocking on your door. He could be one of your customers in the club having a quiet drink enjoying the show. He is a trained assassin, ex-SAS, not just one of those muscle-bound gym gorillas you employ. Now don't get me wrong. I know enough about you to realise that threats are pointless. But you asked me the question, and I am just stating the facts. I don't want any trouble and will happily keep out of your business. I am sure you'll have far more pressing matters to attend to than wasting time on me."

"I'll think about it Ashton. Now fuck off."

Confident that they had reached an unspoken understanding, Ashton turns and walks down the alley gradually merging into the darkness and out of sight. He is happy to leave the gangster with the last word, purposely leaving the encounter allowing McCarthy feeling he has some measure of control. Ashton is satisfied his work is done. With a man of McCarthy's psychology, Ashton realises it is all about saving face and hopefully it would prove to be enough.

Windscreen wipers struggling to cope with the now torrential rain, the drive home is slow.

Filling the silence, Ashton turns to his passenger. "Jeez, Bob. What the hell was that line?"

Knowingly, Bob smiles. "What line?"

"Mate, you know what I'm talking about … the 'Say hello to my little friend' line," Ashton laughs.

"It's a quote from one of my favourite gangster films. It just popped in my mind," replies Bob trying to keep a straight face.

"What 'Goodfellas' or 'The Godfather'?"

"No mate, it's Tony Montana from Scarface. Y'know, Al Pacino at the height of his powers. It's his best line."

"I've never seen the film."

"Yeah, well I love it. That film is so over the top, it's hilarious."

"So, what's his little friend, a handgun I presume?"

"Nope. Montana has had about a kilo of cocaine up his nose, and he has hold of a grenade launcher."

"A grenade launcher?" asks Ashton, incredulously.

"Yep."

They both burst into a fit of laughter and, once that subsides, chuckle all the way home.

Despite the best efforts of the investigation team led by Hardy, they fail to pin the diamond heist on McCarthy.

Kelly and Doyle were eventually arrested and convicted, due to a combination of factors. They were identified as the 'Spider-Men' who were caught trying to dig up the diamonds. Their downfall is their failure to dispose of their suits. Forensic evidence matching their DNA, not to mention matching Higginbottom's soil to the mud streaks on the costumes, places them firmly at the site where the diamonds were buried.

Doyle, who had taken off his mask when digging for the diamonds, is positively identified by several of the UFO hunting party. Kelly's motorcycle is impounded and the video evidence of the two on the bike departing the scene was enough to convince the jury that it was one and the same vehicle.

Neither Kelly nor Doyle is foolish enough to implicate McCarthy. Had they done so, then McCarthy could have been looking at the maximum jail sentence of fourteen years for possession of a firearm without a certificate, associated with a more serious crime. Instead, it was only a possession conviction that stuck to McCarthy which, on its own, only yielded the minimum mandatory five-year sentence.

Whether the jury believed the story, presented by the defence counsel, that McCarthy had the gun because he intended to join the Pickering Rifle and Pistol club, is uncertain. Certainly, a visit to the house of the club president by parties associated with McCarthy did, unbeknown to the jury, occur. So, when the president gave evidence, which supported this claim and attested to the character of McCarthy, the Judge saw fit to use his discretion to ensure the minimum mandatory sentence was mitigated further. Considering McCarthy's clean record, his actual time under lock and key is likely to barely reach three years.

Outraged, the police considered an appeal to the Attorney-General's office, but this was rejected given the workload and backlog of what were deemed to be far more serious cases.

Retrospectively, the prosecution team regretted its decision not to call Ashton or Hairy Bob to the stand. Their reason for not doing so was a concern that this could weaken, not strengthen the case. It might be hard to convince a jury that McCarthy and Hughes are hardened armed criminals who kidnapped Ashton, when the outcome of their interaction left the alleged serious criminals in hospital with Ashton relatively unscathed. It left too many questions, such as how a sculptor and a homeless man overcame supposedly armed criminals? Indeed, what was a homeless man doing on the scene in the first place and how could he have the mental and physical wherewithal to overpower men who are supposedly career criminals with a violent past?

The Prosecutor felt this would stretch the credulity of his case, if presented, and play into the hands of the defence. All other matters aside, the Prosecutor concluded that without the testimony of Doyle and Kelly, a conviction of conspiring to commit a robbery also had little chance of success. By pleading guilty, coupled with the absence of any violence in the crime, the two men received sentences of seven years. At the end of the process, the authorities and victims are happy with the outcome. The perpetrators are in jail, the diamonds are recovered and Mr Abrams, ecstatic with the outcome, dropped his racism claim.

·|··|·

Council approval for the hotel was rescinded when it was leaked, by sources unknown, that a convicted criminal was involved in the development. This left Mandelson and Neaves with mixed feelings but, overall, the scales fell in their favour.

Less cash in the bank but a small price to pay for McCarthy's incarceration.

Mandelson was re-elected in the subsequent election and remains as a councillor for the Scarborough and District area.

Neaves Construction continues to flourish following the recent planning approvals for additional housing on Council owned land at the south-east edge of the village.

·|··|·

News of the heroics spread, like softened butter on toast, around the village. Versions of the events morphed into an ever increasing drama, but the heroics of the two men, particularly Bob, blossomed from the proverbial acorn into an oak tree.

Worn down by days of nagging, led by Betty and Dolly who were always his prime advocates, Hairy Bob decides to stay for a while, feeling the love around the village. At Betty's insistence he takes up residence in a small room at the back of her property, which an optimistic estate agent would describe as a granny flat. No rent was ever asked.

Higginbottom, whose advancing years were beginning to catch up on him, is more than happy to have his offsider for an extended stay. Gradually, other duties were added to the rabbit culling project.

Bob is now a fully paid-up member of the village and, out of respect, the descriptor "Hairy" is dropped and he is now simply known and referred to as Bob.

Omer Cohen had changed his name to Septimus

Harcourt in his early twenties. Being an obsessive anglophile who dreamt of living in Victorian England, he believed this new name more truly reflected his character. Entranced by the life of the fictional adventurer from the Jules Verne novel, he saw himself as a modern-day Phileas Fogg. His main problem being that getting around the modern world in eighty days is pretty much a doddle. Not discouraged, he sought alternative exotic and esoteric challenges that Jules Verne would be proud of. Thus, he found cryptozoology, where he could travel widely seeking out strange outlandish discoveries in the shape of legendary life forms. Following the less than successful West Ayton expedition, he travelled to Ontario with his trusty partner, Sherman MacArthur. They had been sponsored by a local TV channel to investigate recent sightings of Bigfoot coupled with the presence of lights in the night sky and claims of alien abductions.

Accompanied by a cameraman to record the events for the program, the team of three set off into the Orillia area, which seemed to be the epicentre of the reports of supernatural activity. Two days later, Harcourt lay in hospital claiming he had been attacked by a Bigfoot. The cameraman could confirm that some sort of beast rushed into the campsite whilst they slept in their tents, but he was knocked unconscious almost immediately, waking only to find Harcourt groaning and bleeding with his tent ripped to shreds.

Their other team member, MacArthur, had left camp earlier to go on a solo investigation at a location where the mysterious lights had been reported. Given the activity in the area that day, including tree knocking, Harcourt and the cameraman had chosen to stay put, so they had set up camp. MacArthur returned after a period of four days in a state of confusion unable to remember and account for his whereabouts during that time. His only clear memory was approaching a bright light in a clearing and then a floating sensation when the light engulfed him. Inevitably the local medical community had a different interpretation of cause for both Harcourt and MacArthur. Official medical and police records attributed the Harcourt's injuries to an assault by person or persons unknown, or possibly a bear. As for MacArthur, the doctors concluded that he had probably experienced a rare type of seizure. Medical tests revealed some damage to the occipital lobe at the rear of the brain, which possibly occurred during his active military service.

·|··|·

Phil Hayes and Colin Hendricks, in collaboration with Betty's store and Higginbottom's farm, established a local tourist attraction. For the price of ten pounds per person, visitors are given a night-time tour of the locations where the Bigfoot, aliens and mysterious lights were seen. With permission by the farmer to walk on his land, the events are recounted during the 'Strange Goings On' tour which lasts for ninety minutes. For good measure, a visit to Ayton castle and the story of the local ghost, Sir Ralph Eure, is also included.

Tickets can be purchased at Betty's store where she has set aside a corner of the shop to publicise the attraction. The table has leaflets, furry toys of the Yorkshire Yeti and plastic figurines of the Ayton aliens.

A five-year-old boy, whose parents are passing through the village, is in Betty's store. He snatches one of the alien figurines from the table and shouts, "Hey Mum, they've got Spider-Man here, can you buy me one please?"

THE END